FURY
OF THE
SIX

MATT RYAN

THE PRESTON SIX SERIES

BOOKS BY MATT RYAN

Rise of the Six
Call of the Six
Fall of the Six
Break of the Six
Fury of the Six

CHAPTER 1

HANK OPENED THE DOOR TO another hotel room in yet another city on Vanar. At least this one had power, and from the looks of it, it'd been cleaned. He'd have to check the bathroom first before Gladius would use it.

"This baby is wearing out my arms," Gladius said, stomping into the room and tossing their baby to the floor. She unwrapped the scarf from around her neck and plopped down on the bed.

Hank went to the plastic decoy-baby and picked it up. "We shouldn't leave this stuff lying around, a maid could come in."

Gladius laughed as she laid on her back and put her hands behind her head. "If this dump has maid service, I'd be shocked. Speaking of dumps, don't forget to check the bathroom. Besides, what if Gem saw me carrying around that doll?"

He sat on the edge of the bed, happy Gladius's little robot doll was tucked away at her dad's mansion. "How in the world would Gem see you holding another doll?"

She sat up and moved across the bed. Sliding behind him, she rubbed his shoulders. "I don't know. I just hate not having her around me, and that little fake baby makes it much worse."

Hank wrapped the babydoll up and sat it on the bed next to him. He lowered his head and Gladius moved around his back with her hands, massaging him. A knock at the door stopped her hands.

"That was quick," Hank said.

Most towns elicited a visitor, but most of the time it'd be at least an hour. Hank looked over his shoulder to Gladius and she dropped her hands off his back and sighed as she slid off the bed. Moving close to the door with a knife in hand, she waited for Hank. He touched the panel on the door. The face of a smiling man wearing a suit filled the screen.

"I know him," Gladius said as she peered at the screen. "Just stay back, let me handle him."

Hank took a few steps back, positioning himself behind the door. Gladius adjusted her hair and pushed her breasts up, showing way more cleavage than Hank liked. She opened the door and smiled.

"I thought I saw you on the monitors," the guy said by way of greeting.

"Oh, you got those back up and running?" Gladius asked.

"I do like to keep an eye on my citizens, especially in these dark days. We really need to stick together."

Gladius held the door and blocked any view of Hank with it. "I need you to delete those images."

"Look who's making demands on their first day back in my city. What has it been, four years?" The guy took a step into the room but Gladius pushed him back. He smiled and reached to touch a piece of her hair before she slapped his hand away. "You still have that outfit I like?"

"I'm with someone now."

The guy laughed. "You're with someone? Who?"

Gladius swung the door wide open, revealing Hank.

"Holy shit, you brought a Six here?" He beamed with enthusiasm. "Hank, isn't it?" The man pushed past Gladius and shook Hank's hand with a sheepish grin. "I'm the Mayor of this fine city. My family are big fans. One of my daughters has a display of you on her wall. I'm partial to Poly. She sure is . . ." He looked around the room and didn't finish his sentence.

Being a celebrity wasn't something Hank could get used to. It made him uncomfortable, the false admiration bestowed on him from people he'd never met. It did serve its purpose though. Rumors spread over the net about the Six running around Vanar. Marcus may not buy the illusion outright, but if it gave his friends time, if it brought out the man they hoped it would, then it would all be worth it.

Hank had waited too long to respond and the Mayor was beginning to give him that awkward silence face. "Thanks, Mayor."

The mayor's expression turned to relief and joy. "Oh, please, call me Lordis."

"Okay, Lordis," Gladius stepped into his line of sight. "We really need those images deleted. I hope you've kept them private."

The mayor took a step back and looked at her. "Are you guys on the run?"

"Yeah, and we can't have our freaking pictures up on the net."

The mayor laughed. "We only get MM's net drones a few

hours a day. Maybe if someone's dad would recognize us as a city in disaster, we could get the net back up quicker."

Hank thought Harris would be the better person to speak to. Now that he ran MM, all drones and rebuilding processes had landed on his lap. Harris sent out net drones over the outer cities, giving them online access for a few hours a day.

"Maybe I will tell my dad that a certain mayor would like to do . . . inappropriate things to one of his daughters?"

"You wouldn't."

"Just delete the images."

"Maybe if you told your dad how bad it is out here. I mean, we barely have enough protein for the food printers. People are suffering."

Gladius put her hand on her forehead and rubbed her temple. "Lordis, we shared a few pleasantries back in the day and for that, I will tell you enough to make you realize the danger you are putting your town in. We are running from a person you don't want in your backyard. A person who will show no mercy to you, or your people, if he sees us on a monitor. You have to delete those images, *now.*" She spit out the last word and glared him down.

The mayor took a step back and glanced from Hank to Gladius with a wide-eyed smile. "I don't remember you being so aggressive." He smiled and licked his lips. "It's very hot. I have some black leather chaps that he—"

"I'm not putting on anything . . ."

"I wasn't talking to you." The mayor stared at Hank.

Gladius sighed and kicked the mayor in the balls. He hunched forward and fell to his knees, groaning. Hank closed the door and held the mayor by his shoulders. Unfortunately, this wasn't the first person in the last seven months Gladius had kicked below the belt. It was starting to be her signature move.

Gladius kneeled in front of the mayor and pulled out her Panavice. "I just need your password."

"I can't just . . ." he struggled to get the words out as he held himself. "Who is after you?"

"Who would be your worst nightmare?"

"My third ex-wife."

Gladius shook her head. "Who is the worst person ever? Think of him, and if you don't want him in your town, you'll delete those friggin' pictures."

The mayor shook his head and the expression of pain turned to terror as he thought of the name. Hank held onto him tight as he squirmed around. "It can't be. No one's seen him in almost two years."

"I can tell you for a fact he is on the hunt and if you want to save your pathetic town, you'll help us." Gladius shook her head and then laughed. "Wait, you don't care about the town. How about you help us save *you*, okay? Give us the password to your account."

The mayor struggled, but Hank allowed him to get to his feet. Gladius rose with him. Hank saw the blade at the back of her pants and hoped she didn't have to use it again.

"Come on, that net drone could be here soon," she said.

"Fine, it's Pussyplayer15, with a capital *P*," the mayor said and glanced at Hank.

Gladius shook her head as she typed into her Panavice. "You make me sick. I can't believe I let you in me."

The mayor shot a glance at Hank again. Hank took a deep breath and slowly let it out. While he'd only been with one other person, Gladius's exploits reached an astounding number he'd rather not think about. She didn't show any shame in it though, and Hank never wanted to degrade what Gladius once was. She was with him now.

After a few minutes, Gladius lowered her Panavice. "Okay, we are done here. If I was you, I would make damned sure you forgot we were ever here. The man searching for us won't be kind, and a kick to the balls will be a goddamned walk in the park if he gets a hold of you."

"I—" the mayor stammered. "How long are you staying here?"

"It's best if you don't know. I think you should leave now."

"Can I come by later and maybe the three of us could—"

"Get out," Gladius said and jabbed her finger toward the door.

The mayor held his crotch as he turned and left the room.

Hank closed the door and walked over to Gladius. "You think he'll keep his mouth shut?"

"If he wants to live." Her Panavice dinged. "The net drone is here. We're connected." She ran her fingers over the screen and Hank looked over her shoulder. He took a moment to smell her hair and wrapped an arm around her waist. She leaned back into him and reached to touch his hand, before going back to the Panavice.

He watched her choose the perfect angles, covering their faces while showing they carried a child. Hank didn't really think they would fool Marcus, but it wasn't something he would easily ignore. Just thinking about his friends brought on the home sickness and Samantha. He'd catch himself all the time thinking she was still alive. How he missed her, how he missed them all. He'd never been away from them for so long and they felt so far away. All part of the plan though. It was the one thing they had to follow.

"You put down the trail?" he asked.

"Yeah, I time released it for next week." She set the device on her lap and looked to Hank. "I feel like he's getting close."

"Hopefully it's been long enough." Hank thought about the brief time he got to see Joey and Poly's baby. "You getting a gut feeling?"

She rubbed her stomach. "Yeah, this town just feels off to me. I can't put a finger on it yet. I just want this to be over."

Hank put his other arm around her and kissed the side of her head. "After we end it with Marcus. We can't let Samantha die for nothing, and we surely can't let him get ahold of the little one."

Her Panavice dinged. She turned to it and flipped the pages. "Oh no, remember Brissels?" Hank did, and he also remembered the man who couldn't keep his hands off of her. "It says here Ben died in a car accident just an hour ago."

"The same Ben who owned the house we stayed at?"

"Yes." She tapped the screen, zooming in on the wrecked car. "It looks like the car battery exploded."

"We were there . . . two weeks ago?" Hank guessed.

"I knew it. He's getting closer."

Guilt swept over Hank. No one had been killed because of them yet. "I think we need to start moving quicker."

She nodded. "If he keeps following our trails faster than we can lay them down, he'll be on us in a week or two and you know what that means."

"Phase two," Hank said.

Hank wouldn't admit it to Gladius, but he hated the idea of phase two. It meant putting her in danger and too much of it relied on psychology and technology, neither of which were his strong suits.

7

CHAPTER 2

HARRIS PACED NEAR PRESIDENT DENAIL'S desk. The picture of Maya hanging on the wall behind him gave him the grim reminder of how much history they shared. Maya had been Travis's first love and Harris felt a real responsibility about what happened to her.

Travis tapped the whisky glass with the ring on his middle finger. He shot the glass back and gulped down its contents. More wrinkles creased the edges of his eyes than the last time Harris had seen him, and his clothes carried a few frayed edges.

Harris was patiently waiting for Travis's reply.

"You didn't see Samantha get shot down. Even for Marcus, it was cruel," Travis said.

Harris winced at the terrible reminder of what he missed. Another woman had died because of what he got them involved with. "What then, we give up? We let what's left of the Preston

Six deal with something we all created?"

Travis stood and glared at Harris. "Every time you've been involved in my life, people have died. The only reason I tolerate your existence is the agreement I made with Poly."

Harris placed his hands on the back of the chair facing Travis's desk. "Forget about us, this is about those kids and Poly's child. I have a plan set up to hopefully end it all, but I will need your help."

Travis rubbed the stubble on his chin.

The intercom sounded with Douglas's voice. "Excuse me, Travis. Senator Johnson is here to see you."

"Tell her to wait, and it might be a while," Travis said.

"Whatever," Douglas said.

"We both have empires to run," Harris continued, "and I know this isn't the most convenient time to send resources elsewhere, but it's the right thing to do."

"You think I need *convincing* in order to help them?" Travis asked as he walked around his desk.

Harris's hand moved to the space where his gun usually sat, but he'd left it behind this time. He took inventory of Travis's body and spotted a bulge near his right hip—probably a blade.

"Tell me, Harris . . . how is MM going? Are you done with the power plant repairs we contracted you to complete?"

"You know very well the answer to that. I have brought back more cities from the black hole than any other person on this planet."

"And maybe that's the problem. You kept MM this bloated mass with too much power and too much control over senators like Mrs. Johnson out there."

"Really? Would you like me to stop making the endless supply drops to the cutoff cities—at MM's expense, I might add?"

"All so you can put a pretty face on a company that nearly destroyed this planet. Oh and speaking of destroying planets, have you visited Arrack's planet lately? I hear it's wonderful this time of year."

Harris took a step back and held out his hands. "Travis, we can go round and round on every detail, but the fact remains, we are connected. Those kids are counting on us."

"I don't plan on letting them down."

"Good, we agree on something."

Travis clenched his jaw, and blew out a frustrated breath. "Do you even know where Marcus is, or what planet he's on?"

"I spoke to Gladius."

Travis twitched and slapped his hand on his desk, rattling the glass and half empty bottle. "If you get her killed—"

"She is her own woman," Harris said, stopping him mid-threat. "She made her choices, even if that puts herself and Hank in harm's way. They all know what's at risk here. Do you?"

"The child," Travis said glancing back at his picture of Maya. "I've seen the reports. I know what we are protecting, but it doesn't mean I understand it all. Why do you think Marcus wants this child so badly?"

"About a hundred years ago, when Marcus realized he was going to die, he scoured the planet for anything that could help him. That's when he discovered the first stone. He kept it to himself, for a while, but when the first Arrack appeared, he confided in his closest few that he found other worlds. But when he found Ryjack, he showed us the location. That's when he started mass shipping people through these stones."

"Thanks for Marcus 101, but that doesn't explain what he

wants with the baby," Travis said, looking impatient.

"After finding Ryjack, Marcus went on a ceaseless mission of jumping to other worlds. He jumped around, nearly dying many times due to various climates. Do you know that was the reason he invented his personal shield?"

"No," Travis said.

"One day he stopped. He retreated to his bunker and for the first time since I knew him, he looked scared and confused. He started training Arracks to jump, and kept sending them to this one place."

"Where?"

"I don't know. He kept it hidden, even from me, but what I do know is that that was the first time he started talking about finding a perfect human. After that, he holed himself up and worked day and night on his 'projects.' I believe this is the time he created Alice. This is also the time I left MM."

"So you think Marcus thinks this baby is what he's been looking for?'"

"Yes, and I have to agree with him. With her . . . everything is off the charts."

Travis went back to his chair and plopped down, looking perplexed. He poured liquid into his glass and chugged it down.

"Hank and Gladius are very close to making contact with the man."

"Why, what have you heard?" Travis said, leaning forward.

"We think Marcus sent his man to Vanar. There was a mayor that suffered an unfortunate accident in a town they just stayed at," Harris said.

Travis leaned back in his chair and looked at the ceiling. "Phase two is upon us."

"We're going to have to use Hank and Gladius as bait."

"To lure out his accomplice . . ."

"Yes."

"You find out who it is yet?"

"I have my suspicions, but no."

Travis took a long breath. "We are really putting them at great risk again. If anything doesn't go as planned, this whole thing can come down on us. Maybe we should be aiming at the small prize instead of trying to hit the jackpot."

Harris had thought about this many times and he wished it would be that simple, "cut the head of the snake off" kind of stuff, but he knew that it would only be a matter of time until Marcus's tech or an apprentice would come around unless they took everything from the man.

"This is the end, Travis. This is where we win or lose everything."

CHAPTER 3

"OOH, A BABY! CAN I hold her?" The woman's face contorted with a mixture of excitement and desire. Both emotions Gladius was familiar with, but didn't have the time to tolerate.

"No, you can't," she replied.

Hank gave her one of his looks and Gladius sighed, turning back to the lady. "She's sleeping, otherwise I'd be glad to." She delivered the message with a toothy smile.

This seemed to be reason enough for the woman to go on her merry way. Gladius shivered at the thought of letting that hag with filthy clothes touch her child, even if it was fake. She could have lice or who knows what else this backwoods town might have.

Hank raised an orange and inspected it before placing it in a plastic bag. Good, let him pick the fruit in this place. The quicker the better. She fanned herself with her free hand. *How can a supermarket not have air conditioning?* Of all the things to lose . . . the AC had to be the worst.

Traveling only to cities who had limited net and power was the plan, but she couldn't wait to get back into a clean bed with cold air blowing on her face. Hell, even sex with Hank felt like a sweat shower. She'd actually started to lay out a towel on the bed before they did the nasty.

A few other people meandered around the sparsely-filled produce aisle. Some did double takes at her baby, but most kept to themselves.

"I think we have enough for our stay." Hank lifted a bag filled with miscellaneous fruits. "Let's go down the packaged food aisle next."

"Finally."

After giving up many of the luxuries to which she was accustomed, Snackie Cakes was Gladius's hard limit, and something she wasn't willing to give up. Even during her brief stint on Earth, she'd kept a supply of Snackie Cakes. But now, she'd heard vicious rumors on the net about how the family shut down the factory and whatever was out there was the last of it. Goosebumps prickled the hairs on her arm.

Keeping Jen, the fake baby, close to her chest, she made her way to the dry food aisle. The last thing she needed was someone stopping them to gab about how long it'd been since they'd seen a baby. Everyone wanted to touch her, or take a picture with her, or even worse, to have her follow them on the nets to up their social points.

"Your cakes should be down here," Hank said. "Look, there's one left."

An older lady walked toward the last box of Snackie Cakes sitting on the shelves. Gladius and the woman made eye contact. "Claim," Gladius called out, but the other woman just picked up her pace.

This was not going to happen. Those Snackie Cakes were hers. Opening up into a full sprint, she hurdled toward her destination. The other woman's eyes went wide as she picked up her speed and reached for the box first, holding it against her chest in the same manner as Gladius held Jen.

"I claimed that."

"I never heard anything. Besides, whoever touches it first, gets it."

"Bullshit! Those Snackie Cakes are coming home with me."

Hank stood next to her. Good, his size could be intimidating. Gladius shoved their fake baby into his chest. She felt lighter, quicker with both hands accessible. She kept a few knifes on her at all times for moments just like these. If she had to cut those damned cakes from the stupid woman's imitation wool sports jacket, then so be it.

"You—you have problems," the woman said clutching the box. "I need these for my son. He's taken the net outages real bad, and the only thing that brings him out of his hole are these Snackie Cakes."

Gladius's mouth hung open and she gave the slightest shake of her head. She really couldn't believe the woman tried to pull on her heart strings. "I don't care if your son is a freaking diabetic and these are the last bits of sugar on Vanar, those cakes are going home with me."

This is where she lost Hank. She heard his heavy sighing. She didn't want to act this way around him—he had made her such a better woman—but this Snackie Cake battle required her old self.

The woman's eyes narrowed. "I wouldn't let you have these

cakes if you were Alice herself, here to turn the world back on. In fact, I'm going to go home and feed one to my dog . . . thinking of you the entire time."

The bitch had some nerve, but Gladius closed her eyes and knew she had to take it to the next level—plan B. She lifted off her wig and dropped it on Hank, then she took off her stupidly large glasses and handed them to Hank as well. Hank didn't grab them from her hand and they dropped to the floor. "If I have to take one more thing off, it's going to get real ugly up in here. This is my last warning. Give me those Snackie Cakes, right now!"

The woman took a step back, looking around. Her fingers gripped the edges of the box. Then she stopped and squinted, leaning forward. "Wait. Aren't you the president's daughter?"

"Gladius Denail." She bowed.

The lady smiled and wagged a finger. "Oh yes, *Gladius*. Don't you hold the all-time social score for banging celebrities?"

Gladius pinched her lips together and touched the knife stuffed near her back pocket.

The woman looked back at Hank. "You look familiar as well. How many points does she get for banging an oaf like you?" She laughed. "What are you even doing in this shit hole? Is there a socialite whore competition in town?"

Gladius skipped plan C and D and jumped right to killing her. She pulled the knife and picked her wrinkled neck to strike. She reached back and felt a large grip on her hand.

"Get out of here," Hank yelled at the woman as he held Gladius's hand back.

The lady glanced from Hank, to the knife in Gladius's hand, and made a run for it.

"Bitch!" Gladius yelled, keeping her eyes on her as she

rounded the corner and headed toward the front door.

"Just let her go."

Gladius yanked her arm free and paced in the aisle. She wanted to chase the woman all the way to her simple shack and make her vomit up each Snackie Cake.

"Put away the knife," Hank said.

Rage filled her and she spent a good minute trying to keep her hand from shaking long enough to stick the knife back into its sheath. "You should have let me kill her."

"I don't think that would be a good representation of the president's daughter." Hank smiled.

"We haven't seen a Snackie Cake in two cities now and we just let that cow up and take off with them. I mean, I claimed it."

"I know, I know, baby. Just calm down. We won't be here long and I bet the next town will have some."

"If they don't, I am going to hold you personally responsible. And yes, that means no sex until I get my hands on a Snackie Cake."

Hank looked around for the woman and sighed. "Come on, let's go buy those fruit things." He snatched the bag up in one hand and handed Jen back to Gladius. She took it and wrapped the blanket around its plastic head, covering it all up.

After Hank paid the cashier, she joined him at the front door and left the supermarket. The air outside blew against her damp skin and she sighed in relief until the smell of sewer hit her nose.

"You know, we could try printing those cakes out again."

"Are you joking? Those tasted like crap, Hank. Just like you can't stand printed fruit."

"I'm going to hunt down that woman and her little dog too," Hank said in a raspy, strange voice.

"I don't get you sometimes. You know, you can't joke about my Snackie Cakes. Some shit is for real." Hank laughed at this and Gladius couldn't help but join in. He had the most infectious laugh of any person she'd ever met and instantly she felt better. Let the old hag and her dog stuff their faces. She hoped they died choking on them. "You think we left enough of a footprint on this town?" she asked.

"I think you left a lasting impression on that woman. But yes, the whole town will soon know that Gladius Denail, daughter of the president, and top sex scorer, is in town."

She stared at Hank and blinked. She'd had every intention of telling Hank about her previous lifestyle, but he was so innocent, it was hard to find the right time. "Don't listen to that woman," Gladius said. "She's just some hateful, crazy person." Today was not the day for that conversation.

Hank frowned. "You shouldn't set your fuse so short. We have a baby to think about." He patted the back of the baby's head and made baby noises to it.

A scraggly man paced behind Hank and Gladius leaned to the left to get a better look at him. Ragged clothes and just from looking at him, she bet he smelled horrible. Then she spotted the knife in his hand. He stopped pacing and made eye contact with her. Gladius gave him a scowl that should have stopped most men, but he walked closer to Hank.

"Watch your back," Gladius said with a nod to the approaching man.

Hank turned around.

"Give me those fruits, man," he said pointing his knife at the bag.

Hank held his hand out and the bag crinkled as the fruit repositioned. "You want these?"

"Yeah, hand 'em over."

Gladius stepped forward with her free hand at her face and played her best damsel-in-distress look she could manage. "No please, sir, this is all we have to feed our baby."

The man moved his attention back and forth from Hank and Gladius. "Stay back," he said as the knife shook in his hands. "I mean it, or I'll cut you both, and that baby too. I just want those fruits, man."

"Oh no, you are going to hurt my baby? Hank, please, don't let him hurt me and my baby."

"Dude, you better run," Hank said.

"Just toss them over."

"Please, *no*," Gladius said with her hand near her neck, fake fear filling her face. "Don't hurt us. We are just simple people, traveling with a new child." She deserved an award.

"You're stupid if you don't run right now," Hank said.

The knife in his hand shook and his fingers moved over the duct tape wrapping around the makeshift handle. His eye twitched and he licked his lips, staring at the bag of fruit and not taking a single step in any direction. Gladius was glad he didn't leave. She still felt the interaction with the woman from the supermarket eating away at her; the bitch was probably sucking down Snackie Cakes at that very moment.

Gladius tossed the baby to the man. He jerked to catch it and didn't see the large smile on her face. She gave her best kick straight to his manhood and thought she felt him lift off the ground with it. The man fell to his knees, reaching for his crotch. Gladius kneed him in the face, crushing his nose and eye socket.

He fell back onto the street, knocked out.

"Oh no, my baby," Gladius covered her face and stood on

the man's balls while she picked up Jen. A few onlookers slowed down to take in the spectacle. She wrapped the baby back up in its blanket and clutched it to her chest. "She's okay, don't worry," she said and got closer to Hank. "You think we'll be noticed now?"

"I think we have done more than enough to have a lasting memory on this town. Maybe this fruit should be to-go." He raised an eyebrow.

"Fine, I didn't like this town anyway." Gladius walked with Hank back to the car parked far enough away from the supermarket as to not arouse suspicion. A person with a car like that, drew in a crowd, thinking the rich people from Capital came to their town.

She felt good after assaulting that man and skipped down the concrete sidewalk next to Hank, watching his big grin. She liked to make him smile and his eyes fixated on her bouncing chest. She glanced down at her low top and saw her boobs doing their thing. Good, let him get all excited, because she was dead serious about the no sex deal. She'd bet he'd find a way to get her Snackie Cakes in the next town.

A few people loitered around their black car. Hank approached, pushing his chest out and looking much larger. The people around the car scattered as they approached. Gladius giggled, if only those people knew how much more dangerous she was.

Hank rushed to the car first and opened the passenger door. "Why thank you, good sir."

The black leather interior had lost its new smell over the past six months, but it felt soft enough to want to strip down naked and let it touch you. Hank hopped in the driver's side and closed the door.

"Where to?" he asked.

Gladius took out her Panavice and scanned the maps. "Since we are in phase two, I say we jump past these last couple cities and head straight to New Hampton. He shouldn't be too far behind."

Just the thought of finally being in a real city, with net, power, running water, and high thread count linen drove her to the edge of release. The thought of being with Hank on proper sheets . . .

Hank plugged the information into the car and took control of the wheel. She thought it very amusing how he insisted on driving the car himself.

"New Hampton . . ." Hank said, glancing at the map and then back to the road, "is that the last city before we go back to Earth?"

"Yes, and maybe we can finally be over with this," Gladius said and stretched out, getting ready for the long drive.

Running around together, moving from hotel to hotel was fun at first, but visiting depressing cities, one after another, pulled her spirits down. She took notes in each location and would address the biggest issues with her dad; seeing that the towns received the help they needed. Witnessing her once rich world brought down to a place where a man threatened your life for a bag of fruit and bitches in supermarkets took Snackie Cakes that you *claimed*, wasn't a place she wanted to be in. She longed to get back to her room at the ocean house in Sanct.

Hank slowed down and then stopped.

Gladius leaned forward from her slouch and spotted the man standing in the middle of the road, with his arms crossed near his waist. He wore all black, with a scarf wrapped around his face and head, leaving only his eyes exposed.

"Is that—" Hank started.

"I don't know, just freaking get around him. It's too soon for this."

The car lunged forward and Gladius stared at the man. He didn't flinch as the car approached. Hank turned the wheel, avoiding the man in black. Gladius kept her eyes on him as they passed.

He reached behind his back and pulled out two guns.

"Go!" Gladius urged, pushing the button on the dash. Four small containers sprouted from behind the car and exploded. The man in black flew in the air, landing hard on the ground, skidding to a stop.

The car accelerated down the road and Gladius looked out the back window. The man in black got up and trotted after them with a severe limp.

"You think that was him?" Hank asked.

"Yes."

"How did he get to us so quick?"

"I don't know, but we better get to New Hampton in a hurry." Gladius turned and slumped down in the seat. Thread count would have to wait until she dealt with this shit.

CHAPTER 4

POLY LISTENED TO THE CREAKING noise the guard made outside their hut as he adjusted his stance once again. She took an extra look at Julie and Lucas, who lay close together near the window, before going back to watching her Evelyn sleeping on the wooden plank near Joey. The morning twilight had finally crept into the room, casting enough light for her to make out all the features on her daughter's perfect little face. She wanted to hold her, but she enjoyed watching her sleep more.

Asleep, she looked like any other baby, cuter of course, but nothing out of the ordinary—not extraordinary and certainly not the next step in human evolution. Nope, while she slept, she was just Evelyn.

The guard creaked and bumped the wall a smidgen, maybe leaning against it with his foot. Poly winced at the noise and turned back to see Evelyn with her eyes wide open. She took a deep breath and smiled at her lovely child staring at her with eyes that seemed far too intelligent for a seven-month-old.

Julie had contemplated earlier that the only reason she couldn't fully speak was the muscles in her throat hadn't developed enough, but Poly knew her daughter understood most of what people said.

"Mama," Evelyn said.

"That's right, it's your mama here." Poly sniffled and looked away.

Every day she got smarter and every day that was a reminder of how valuable she was. Having a child someone wanted to take from you was unbearable. She knew now what all of the Preston Six's parents went through. Poly's chin trembled and she felt a small hand touching her stomach. She reached down and placed a finger in Evelyn's hand. Evelyn squeezed and smiled.

Harris had run a few tests on her right after she was born and her DNA had many anomalies, not much unlike what Joey had but on a grander scale. It was a matter of time before she'd surpass all of them, and Marcus knew about this better than anyone. The longer he didn't have her, the smaller chance he'd be able to control her. It wouldn't be long before her mental abilities would match her physical abilities and Harris thought once that happened, it wouldn't matter what Marcus did, he'd never be able to take her without consent. Not that he would ever get the chance. To hell with phase four. She planned on ending it all before then.

She sucked in a quick breath and thought of Samantha. Losing her felt like losing a sister, a close sister. Seeing what Marcus did to her was a constant reminder of what and who they were up against.

"You awake?" Joey asked.

"Unless I started sleep walking."

Joey sat on the edge of the cot and rubbed his eyes. He got up and walked next to Poly, placing his hand over her shoulder, kissing the side of her face.

It still gave her chills when he did that. She watched him smile and touch Evelyn. Evelyn giggled, reaching for him, and then sat up.

"Whoa," Joey said and put his hand on her to stabilize her. "Guess she's sitting up now. Who has abs of steel? You do." He poked her in the stomach and she giggled.

Poly took a step back. Good, she was already building up her physical side as quick as her mental. With Marcus on Ryjack, it was only a matter of time before he found them.

"Are we still moving today?" Poly asked.

"Yeah, and with Marcus's appearance, that means we are moving to phase three."

Poly rubbed the hilt of Compry's dragon etched black throwing blade. "You think we have a chance?"

"Yes, or what is all this for?"

"I don't know, ever since she was born I can't stop thinking of what our parents went through. I mean what if we fail, Joey? What if he hurts Evelyn?"

"Look at all the people standing behind us, next to us, or even Hank and Gladius standing out in front of us, putting their lives on the line. We have a huge group of well-motivated mutants with some nasty abilities here to protect us as well. I think our chances are high, they have to be."

"We thought we knew what we were doing with Samantha and looked what happened then? And *that* wasn't even Marcus, just some sick, bastard disciple of his. How are we going to get one up on the real Marcus?"

"I don't know, but we have a plan and what else do we have to work with?"

Poly frowned and tapped her finger on her blade. She hated the plan. She hated the things she might have to give up in order for the plan to work. "There is always another option. The Alius stone, it took eighteen years for him to find us the first time, maybe if we can find a planet he doesn't know about, we can hide there and start a life there. I don't know how much longer I can take this running."

It wasn't the first time she had this discussion with Joey and each time she felt more agitated when he didn't see her logic.

Joey set Evelyn back on the plank and took a small step to Poly and hugged her. He kissed the side of her quivering mouth and then grabbed her hands.

"We are not going to kill ourselves by showing up on an inhospitable planet. Remember how many Arrack's were killed searching through the Alius stones?" He shook his head and squeezed her hands. "I won't let anything bad happen to our girl. I don't care what I have to do."

Poly met his stare. "You're planning on slowing down time, aren't you?"

"As a last resort, yes. If it means risking my life to save our daughter, then I will use my ability and anything else I can to stop him."

She took a deep breath and tried to find a way to argue with him about it, but she couldn't. She knew she would do the same thing if it were in her power to do so. "You have my permission to do whatever you need to do to keep our daughter safe."

Joey let out a long breath. "You don't know how glad I am to hear you say that."

"Hey, H. R. Talk-a-lots," Lucas said. "It's not even freaking full daylight and you guys are already talking about how to kill yourselves? Our plan is solid, just give it a chance to work," he muttered into his thin blanket.

Julie stirred next to him. "Plus, he will have to go through a hell of a lot of people to get to Evelyn. You're going to have to wait in line to save her." She stretched her arms and then rubbed her swollen, pregnant belly. "Look at Evelyn."

Poly shot around and saw Evelyn sitting up on her make shift wooden crib. Her arms outstretched for Julie.

"Set her on the floor," Julie said scooting to the edge of her bed.

Joey picked her up and set her on the floor. Poly moved to stop him but then didn't, she didn't know if she wanted to see what Evelyn would do.

Evelyn lifted herself up and crawled toward Julie. Julie picked her up and Evelyn giggled. "Ju-ju," she called out.

"Yeah, Aunt Julie is here."

Poly turned to the window. She didn't want the others to see her face, especially Joey. It wasn't that she wasn't proud of her little miracle girl, it's just it hurt her every time she hurdled over a milestone, or leaped past what anything normal might have been for a baby her age. She wanted to rejoice in her special child and she hated Marcus even more for taking her joy away from her.

"Think we'll reach the stone today?" Lucas asked in a yawn.

Poly turned back and watched Julie one hand her Panavice. "No, maybe tomorrow."

"I don't know about you all, but I can't wait to get into some dry clothes. I wonder if they've got the Chappy's back up and running. Do you remember the freaking waffle stacks they made?"

She did indeed. Chappy's had been one of their favorite places to go for breakfast back in Preston, but she didn't like thinking about the places they couldn't go to anymore. She would prefer to save those memories until after they got rid of a particular person.

A knock sounded on the door and then Edith entered. She held a tray of fruits and a stack of flat bread. It amazed Poly everyday what the mutants were doing for her and her family. She didn't think she could ever repay them, but she would try her whole life to.

"Thought I heard you guys up. Brought you some breakfast," she said with all smiles.

"Thanks, Edith." Lucas jumped up and rushed to help her carry the tray. He stuffed one of the flat breads in his mouth as he carried the tray to the bench under the window.

Edith walked over to Julie. "And how's Queen Eve this morning?" She shot a quick glance at Poly.

Poly didn't say anything, even though she didn't like them calling her that. She had too much respect for Edith. The woman had lost her husband and son while protecting Poly from MM troops, and there wasn't a day that went by where she didn't think of Hatch and Paul.

"Fine," Julie said.

"Let me hold her while you eat, dear."

Julie gave up Evelyn and walked to the bench buffet.

"Look at that kid," Lucas pointed out the window.

A young man had his foot on the same branch that crashed down yesterday. It had almost killed Lucas. Poly took a deep breath and thought of Evelyn screaming Lucas's name right before it happened. She'd no doubt saved his life, but it had to be a coincidence.

Poly hung out the window, looked up and saw a kid run by, laughing and chasing after another. It felt eerily similar to the first moments she had with these people. She'd begged them not to come and then again to leave their children and caretakers behind, but they all took it as a great insult and insisted on coming. She didn't really think she had a choice in the matter. They were going, Edith had said.

Poly sighed. She didn't like the idea of her daughter being part of them, yet she was. In a way, she was just as much as a mutant as the young man in the tree.

"You should eat something." Joey pushed a plate of food near her.

"No thanks." Poly crossed her arms and stared out the window.

"You didn't eat anything yesterday. How can you protect our daughter without the energy to stand?"

She released her arms and took the plate. For the next ten minutes, she plucked at a few pieces of fruit. It might have been mango, or something similar. Who knew how close everything was on Ryjack.

A light tap sounded on the door and then Kris entered the hut. He wouldn't make eye contact with Poly and she knew that was a bad sign; something was wrong. He nodded to Edith and she walked over to him, holding Evelyn. They shared some close words before Kris looked up.

"What's wrong?" Lucas asked first.

"One of our runners didn't come back this morning."

Poly closed her eyes and took a deep breath. Her thoughts blazed with the idea of Marcus being close enough to get a runner.

"I'm sure it's nothing," Edith said, but she turned to Kris and spoke quietly. He nodded and left the hut. "You guys ready to move on from this place?" Edith asked.

"Yeah, I am," Julie said, already folding her sheet.

"No, no, don't bother with this stuff, you get going ahead and we'll take care of everything."

Julie finished folding the sheet and pressed the creases. "Thank you for all you do, and tell the others as well. We really appreciate it."

"You told me that a hundred times. Just stop it already," Edith said.

"You deserve it, and more." Julie rubbed her stomach and leaned against the wall.

"You doing okay?" Edith asked.

"Yeah, just a bit woozy when I first get up." She smiled and stood straight. "See? All better."

"If you get these woozies again, you best tell us," Edith said. "We can carry you."

"Thank you, but that won't be necessary."

Edith walked over to Poly and held Evelyn out for her. Poly hesitated and then took her in her hands.

"Mama," Evelyn said.

Poly brushed Evelyn's thin hair back from her head. She remembered seeing a little baby bath setup for the kitchen sink, like a plastic lounge chair, and longed to use it. She couldn't wait to get back to a civilized area. Her baby didn't belong in a grinner infested world.

In an hour, they had traveled far away from the village. The mutants kept their distance and Poly had to search for their movement in the trees to maybe spot a glimpse of their tanned skin. They never strayed too far away from their queen.

With the thinning foliage, more light shone down on them; their perpetually damp clothes began to dry out for the first time since entering the jungle. The pace quickened as the underbrush diminished and the jungle loosened its grip.

By mid-sun, an open field of swaying grass and saplings appeared, fighting their way to regain the stripped land.

"Thank goodness," Lucas said. "Another day in there and I'd go crazy. Look at the bow string on Prudence! It already has a few frays from all this jungle air." Lucas inspected the minimal damage to his precious string. He rarely had a day where he didn't mention something about Prudence not liking it here. For once, Poly agreed with Prudence.

"You want me to hold her for a while?" Joey offered.

"Sure." Poly passed Evelyn over and took off the sling. She shook her arms and tried to loosen her muscles, feeling better with her arms free. She could use her blades at will.

Kris ran up to them. "There's a town not far from here. They are clearing it out as we speak, but I think we can use it for the night. There's even a hotel."

"Sounds good, thanks," Joey said.

The idea of a hotel washed over Poly like a clean, hot shower. She ached for it. But Ryjack was still a crap hole, where nothing worked and the things that remained grasped for their original purposes with the narrowest of holds. Much like the saplings reclaiming the farmed land, they too would reclaim the houses, churches, cars, and roads.

The last pockets of humanity would cling on, but nothing would ever be the same. She wondered what Ryjack would look like in twenty, or even a hundred years. Could those last pockets of humanity repossess the planet? Could the family from Cost Plus move on and start anew? They wanted a child for their daughter, but would they ever find a suitor?

"You ready?" Joey asked.

"Yeah."

They walked across the field and onto a paved road, if you could call it that. More like patches of pavement. Another mile and they reached the town. A decent sized one as well, which encouraged Poly as much as it terrified her. Larger towns held more grinners. They had only run into a few in the jungle, but each city held its own surprise.

The mutants ran around the town, she saw them darting in and out of buildings and running across the few streets that made up the town. Poly pulled three knifes from her side. She kept one in her throwing hand, ready to go as they walked down the main street. The town didn't look as bad as she thought from far out. The buildings hadn't collapsed and much of the concrete pavement still held its ground, housing only a few errant weeds in the cracks.

A small group of mutants stood around the front of the only two-story building in town. In black letters, the word *Hotel* was painted near the top. It gave her hope the insides would still be intact, and it gave her greater hope the hotel would be vacant of grinners. Even if the mutants had cleared it, the stench remained strong.

She nodded to two young men as they approached— brothers if she remembered right—Sergio and Juan.

"We cleared it for you, Poly," Sergio said with a bright smile.

"Thank you. I can't begin to tell you how much we appreciate it."

Sergio glanced at Juan as they relished in the accolades.

Joey held Evelyn in the sling with one arm and a gun in the other. He better not even *think* of firing it near Evelyn. She glared from his gun to him, but he didn't catch the warning. They all entered the hotel lobby.

"Pretty nice," Lucas said, admiring the wood coffered ceiling. He jumped over the back of a couch and landed on the front, draping his arm over the back.

"I just can't wait to sit down and put my feet up," Julie said, holding her ever-growing stomach.

"You want me to take her?" Poly asked and looked at Evelyn and then to Joey's gun.

"Nah, I got her," Joey said.

Edith walked in behind them. "There are a couple of rooms up top. Good place for a family to spend the day."

"Thanks," Joey said.

Edith walked to Joey and pulled Evelyn from him; he didn't resist. Walking to the stairs and pointing his gun, he looked back at them.

Poly sighed and walked behind Joey. She was happy to have Evelyn away from his gun, but why did he give her to Edith when he'd denied her a moment ago?

"Poly, you take the left, I'll take the right," Joey said.

"You guys need to relax," Lucas called out. "Our mutant peeps cleared it."

"Like they cleared the hut yesterday?" Poly spoke up. The incident still freaked her out. They'd just entered the hut, when a grinner came lunging at Joey and Evelyn. Thank goodness Lucas had been there with his Prudence.

Lucas huffed. "Fine." He got off the couch. "I'll take lead." He rushed past Joey and Poly up the stairs.

"What an idiot." Julie rolled her eyes.

"You married him. He's your idiot now," Joey said before running up the stairs after him.

"That he is," she whispered.

Poly stayed below with Julie. "How are you doing?"

"This sucks. I can't wait for our plan to be over. I can't wait for it all to be over." She looked at the ceiling and followed the sounds of stomping feet. "It's so stupid what I fantasize about now."

"Clean sheets?"

"No, nothing material. You know, all I really want is a place to call home again. You remember that feeling when you got home from school, went to your bedroom, and just fell on your own bed? Not a fear in the world?"

"Yes."

"That's what I fantasize about. Not for me, but for . . ." Julie pointed to her stomach.

Poly thought about the long-term effects of keeping Evelyn in such a horrible environment. She was just a baby, yet she saw her soaking in everything around her. For Evelyn, running and grinners were the norm. "What do you think, boy or girl?" she asked.

"I don't know, I have a feeling it's a boy."

"Thought of a name yet?" It had become a major discussion point and Lucas played it up with as many ridiculous names as he could think of, from Felalfull to Gerridity. He also announced each of them with a finality that drove Julie crazy.

Julie looked to the ceiling and her bottom lip quivered before she covered it with her hand. "No." She sniffled and turned from Poly. "Sorry," she said and broke into a cry.

"Julie, what is it?" Poly rubbed her arm.

"I don't want to have this child in this world. I want to be at a hospital . . . with an epidural. I want nurses and doctors, and those little juice cups." She took deep breaths and tried to collect herself. She glanced at Poly and let out a small laugh. "Stupid pregnancy hormones."

"No matter what, we'll be here with you."

"You think what we're doing is going to work?" Julie asked.

"It has to."

MINTER LOOKED AT THE NUMBER texted to his phone from an unknown number. He held it up so Rick could read it.

"Yep, it's time." Rick nodded, looking at the numbers on the phone.

Minter cranked over the Mustang and shifted into drive. He peeled out on the dirt shoulder and let the tires grip and squeal on the blacktop. He thought about how much his in-laws hated when he did that down their driveway.

"At least we know everything is still in motion. The kids are alive," Rick said.

"Yes, but we aren't to the hard part yet. That text just tells us to move to phase three. There's still a million things that could go wrong," Minter said.

"Have a little faith."

Minter sped up to around eighty miles per hour on the highway. He leaned against the window and rubbed his chin. He hadn't seen his grandchild since the day she was born. He often thought about what she looked like now and when he'd get the chance to hold her, make her laugh, and spoil her rotten. "I have faith. It's the only thing I've got."

He watched as they passed a busted car on the side of the road. After the Cough, the whole world had changed. Wars raged in Eastern Europe and Southern Asia. Thankfully, the US was able to contain much of the Cough, keeping the fatalities to a minimum; nothing like the poor countries of the world. Those casualties were in the millions.

All thanks to a man who had plagued Minter for almost twenty years now, Marcus Malliden. A man he had never met had dominated his and his family's lives, his friend's lives. He gripped the steering wheel tight.

"What's wrong?" Rick asked.

"Look at what he did to Earth." Minter pointed to a burnt car as they passed it.

"As far as everyone else is concerned, he saved the planet. Look at what the man has done in the span of a couple years here," Rick said.

Minter shifted in his seat and glanced at Rick. The world might be putting Marcus on a pedestal, but if they knew what he put in them with the cure he brought, they might think differently of the man.

Marcus hadn't wasted a moment of time, taking over ZRB, right behind Zach, proclaiming he'd do everything different and humane. The world ate it up. And why wouldn't they? He brought back, in short order, the world they had once known. All he wanted in return was controlling interests in their companies. He owned or influenced many major companies now and each new announcement, merger, and ribbon ceremony Minter had to watch on TV made him sick. But the man *did* deliver. ZRB trucks filled the stores with food and medical supplies quicker than anyone thought possible.

"At every turn, he's been ahead of them . . . us. We tried over a dozen times to get to him over the last year and none of us even got close. I just hope this plan is different," Minter said.

"This is an all or nothing kind of deal. I'm ready to die for this," Rick said.

Minter agreed. His life didn't matter as much as protecting his child and grandchild, but that went without saying. It just felt like, each time anyone had a plan to go against Marcus, it went the exact opposite as planned. How do you prepare for the exact opposite? Harris's plan did exactly that. Their role would be to do the obvious and hope Marcus did the opposite.

"How far away are we, you think?" Rick asked.

"A hundred miles, give or take a few."

"We better turn off our phones."

"We take the batteries out of them at seventy-five miles away. Julie was pretty specific about it." Minter handed over his phone to Rick.

Rick nodded and took the phone. "You think Alice is watching us right now?"

"No question about it."

CHAPTER 5

HANK WATCHED GLADIUS SLEEPING IN the morning light. She was a late sleeper and he didn't want to disturb her; besides, he enjoyed watching her.

She stirred awake and rolled on her back. "You watching me again?"

"Yes."

"So creepy."

"You want me to stop?"

"No, I like creepy." She reached her hands out for him. "Come here." Hank snuggled up against her in bed. "Today is the first day this gets hard, isn't it?" Gladius asked.

"Yeah."

"Our little world-jumping party is over. We had some fun, though, didn't we?"

"Mostly." Hank thought of the many times Gladius nearly

got them kicked out of cities and the few times she almost got them killed.

"You think he's still following us?" she asked.

"There is no chance he isn't."

She sighed and rolled to kiss him on the cheek, then the mouth, which led to more. It didn't go unnoticed that she'd crumbled under his charms, failing miserably to keep her lady shop closed until Snackie Cakes met her mouth.

When they left their hotel room later that morning, Hank wondered if the man in the cloak might jump them in the open. He scanned the streets for anyone suspicious. The towering buildings around them didn't give much cover and Hank suspected the guy would try to stop them on the road. "Ready?"

Gladius tossed her bag in the backseat. "Yup."

Hank didn't question her and stepped on the pedal. "Are you pretty sure he is who you think he is?"

"I think so, but I guess we will be finding out soon," she said.

They left the city and drove onto the countryside. For a while, the suburbs dominated the landscape. Hank spotted the ocean a few times until the trees started in. Soon they drove through a forest with enormous redwood trees. It reminded him of the Arrack world and the brief time they spent walking through a similar forest.

Harris had ruined that world. Hank wanted to go back to it at some point. He wanted to see if the mist was gone, and if maybe a few Arracks held on. Maybe they had even made a comeback, much in the same way Earth and Ryjack had.

"You think your dad will like me?" Gladius asked, cutting into the silence.

"What's not to like?"

"I don't know, the few first-time meetings I've had haven't

gone well. I've even ended up screwing—"

"He's going to love you."

She smiled and didn't say anything for a few minutes. "You know, when I was working at ZRB, they had a vending machine with all kinds of candy bars. I tried them all and many were great, but there was one that stood out for me. I liked it so much, I found myself going back to it each time."

"Which one?" he asked.

"A Butterfinger."

"Better not lay a finger on my Butterfinger."

"What?"

"Nothing, just an old ad."

"Do you think they are still making those?"

"I'm sure they are, but Marcus owns many of those companies now." She frowned. "Maybe," Hank added, "that one is untouched."

"He better not have laid fingers on my Butterfingers." She laughed. "That's so funny."

Hank saw the marker on the side of the road and pulled the car onto the shoulder. He got out and looked at the mile marker sixty-four. Anyone else wouldn't have paid attention to the three circles drawn under it, like ripples in water. It was Harris's mark for a stone nearby. Hank gazed at the tree and thought he heard the ocean in the distance.

He tried to stomp down the ferns and other plants, to make an easier path for Gladius. At least she wore her long pants today. He was sure she had her knifes on as well. "You doing okay, baby?"

"Yeah, but I'm not literally a baby . . . I think I can handle some weeds, dude. You don't need to trample Mother Nature on my account." She brushed back her hair and walked around a bush.

Hank smiled. He rarely had to guess her mood, and liked it that way. She was easy to read. He understood her. "I see the ocean."

"Good."

Hank fought every urge he had to glance back and search for the man following them. He was sure he wouldn't be too far away. This would be the spot he'd pounce if things were reversed. He slowed down and waited for Gladius to get by his side.

A few feet ahead, a beachside bluff sloped toward the ocean below. The waves crashed and he breathed in the salty mist in the air. The fog covered much of the ocean, but the sun had started burning it away. Soon, the whole sky would be clear.

"It's down here," Hank said and took her hand.

She held onto him and took careful steps in her platform shoes. Their feet sunk into the sandy bank and the sand found the small air holes in Hank's shoes to infiltrate. He walked, trying to stay on top of the sand for the rest of the way down the sandstone cliff butting up against the shore. Walking around the last sandstone wall, he spotted the Alius stone.

He half expected another person waiting there, but it was empty. Some tree branches and a few rocks had fallen into the circle from above. The firm ground in the circle felt good under Hank's feet; if needed, he could rush the man following them.

"Don't move."

Hank and Gladius raised their hands in the air and turned toward the voice. A man with a cloak covering his face, stood at the top of the sandy bank. He pointed a gun at them and took a step down into the sand, heavily favoring one side.

"Marcus?" Hank asked.

"No."

"Well, before you kill us, why don't you show yourself?" he asked.

"You won't like what you see."

"I sort of have to insist on this one point."

"Fine, you should bear witness to what your friend did to me." He pulled back his hood and revealed his face.

Gladius gasped and covered her mouth.

Hank grimaced but didn't pull his gaze away. Half of the man's face looked as if it had been crushed in and then healed back over. Hank squinted and tried to find the man in there. "Emmett?"

"What's left of him," Emmett said, staggering down the sandy hill. "Neither of you look all that surprised."

"We had our suspicions," Hank said.

"How long have you been on our trail?" Gladius asked.

"I caught up with you about two towns back. When you look like I do, people want to tell you whatever it takes for you to leave," Emmett said. "This," he pointed to his damaged face, "is because of Joey and I mean to do the same to him. Now, where is he?"

"You're after *him*?" Gladius clarified.

He kept his gun pointed at Hank, while he limped closer, staying just outside of the circle. "Marcus wants the little one, but I have been given Joey."

"We aren't going to give up our friends," Hank said.

"I didn't think so." Emmett sighed and pointed his gun at Gladius.

"No, you can't shoot me, please," she cried out.

"I'll be doing the world a favor, ridding the world of a renowned whore such as yourself," Emmett said.

"No," Gladius begged. She held up her hand as if that might protect her. "Please, you don't need to do this."

"Hank, tell me where they are and I'll let her live."

Hank's heart pounded in his chest and everything in him wanted to tell Emmett what he knew to save Gladius, but he stuck to the plan. "No."

"What?" Emmett said. "I will kill her and then use you to get to them. You know this, right?"

"I do. I'm sorry, Gladius, but I can't give up my friends."

"You . . . how could you?" She glared at Hank.

"Fine." Emmett fired three shots into Gladius.

She screamed and grabbed her gut, swaying in a large circle while continuing to yell. "Oh no, you got me."

Emmett stepped into the circle, confused by Gladius's strange behavior. He fired three more shots and she fell to the ground.

Hank didn't watch Gladius as much as he watched Emmett's feet. Once they were well within the boundary, he jumped to the stone and typed into it.

"What are you doing?" Emmett fired his remaining bullets into Hank's back.

"Here we go," he whispered, thinking of Lucas's catch phrase. They shifted from a cliff-side beach to a partially charred forest on the mend. Hank turned to Emmett.

Emmett staggered backward and pulled the trigger on his empty gun. "You should be dead. What is this?" He jolted in a seizure, his gun falling out of his hands and onto the forest floor. Behind him stood Trip, holding a Taser gun. Trip kicked Emmett's gun away and tied him up.

"Hey, Dad," Hank greeted.

"She okay?" Trip motioned to Gladius.

"Sold it a bit heavy, don't you think?" Hank asked.

Gladius rose up and got to her feet. "I have risen from the grave and now I will feast on your brains." She held her arms out and staggered toward Hank.

"You have shields?" Emmett said, pulling at his restraints. "You idiots don't know what you're doing."

"Shut up." Trip kicked him in the gut.

Emmett laughed. "You are all so stupid. Don't you know you're only hurting yourselves? You stop us and you all die."

"What are you talking about?" Hank asked. "How are you even alive?"

Emmett kept laughing. "When I shot myself in the head, my assistant took me away and Marcus found me dead. I should have stayed dead, but he healed me, built me a new face. Do you know the rehab I had to do in order to even walk again?" He rolled with his hands tied behind his back and sat on his butt. "He showed me, he showed me everything. I was so stupid in trying to take over MM, but I didn't know. I didn't know they were out there."

"*Who* is out there?" Hank asked.

"It's only a matter of time and if we don't have Marcus and the little one, we are all doomed."

"What the heck are you talking about?" Hank asked.

Emmett only laughed to himself and shook his head.

"Emmett?" Gladius said. "Hello!"

Emmett didn't respond.

"Do you have any idea what he's talking about?" Hank asked Gladius.

"No freaking clue."

Emmett laughed again. "I had every intention of killing you and then hunting down every last one of the Six." He lowered his head and spoke to himself. "He must have known about the shields. He knew I'd fail in my pursuit. Don't you see?" He looked up. "Even someone like me ends up doing exactly what he has intended, even if I had no intention of delivering the message."

"What message?" Hank asked.

"Marcus wants a meeting. He wants to meet with all of you."

"That is never going to happen," Trip said.

"He thinks everything that has happened is a great misunderstanding and he wants to show you what's at stake, the reason he's done everything."

"He showed you everything, did he?" Gladius asked.

"You're damned right he did. I've seen what they do and it's only a matter of time." Emmett laughed again. "Personally, I hope you don't meet him. I hope this whole world burns down around you."

"It's just a load of bull," Trip said.

Hank stared at Emmett. "Where does he want to meet?"

"You can pick the spot and the time. He will not be armed or shielded."

Hank laughed this time. "You think we're going to believe that load of bullshit, after what happened to Samantha?"

"I don't care what you think. I'm not saying another word." Emmett crossed his arms and lowered his head.

Hank motioned with his head for Gladius to follow him. He walked to the edge of the circle, close enough so Emmett could hear. Trip stayed close to Emmett, pacing behind him. "What do you think?" he asked.

"We stick to the plan. Once we start doing what Marcus wants, we're screwed."

"You really think he'd come to us though, unarmed? We

could end this very quickly."

Gladius sighed. "Don't be dumb. We stick to the plan. Minter and Rick are expecting us and there's more to it than just killing Marcus, remember?"

A quick end to it all enticed Hank, which was probably the whole point of it. Marcus wanted them to lower their guard and gather in one spot, so he could swoop in and take Evelyn, and kill them all once he had his prize.

"Okay, we stick to the plan." Hank motioned for his dad to pick up Emmett.

"Come on, now," Trip grunted under his weight, "don't give me any trouble or I'll Taser you again."

Emmett didn't say anything and offered no resistance. Hank watched as Trip marched him out of the circle.

Hank took one step before Gladius put a hand on him. "We could leave right now, we could go and live on Vanar. I have endless money, we've done our part. Your dad could do the rest."

"No, what are you talking about? I could never leave my friends like that. We have to see this finished or none of us will ever be safe." He leaned closer to her. "You think he's going to settle for just one of our kids? No, he's going to collect them all and start some kind of evil baseball team. We'll never be free until Marcus is taken care of."

"Can't blame a girl for trying. So where are we off too?"

"Marcus's house."

CHAPTER 6

JOEY HELD OUT BOTH GUNS and scanned the field around the circle. Lucas knelt behind him next to the stone.

"Okay, I'm ready," Lucas said.

Poly blew out two sharp whistles and the surrounding grass fields erupted with mutants running to the circle.

This was the part Joey hated. The mutants piled inside the radius of the stone. This was the point where they were the most vulnerable to an attack. Something as simple as one grenade would kill most of them.

Kris ran into the circle and gave Joey a thumbs up. Joey gave a quick glance to Poly and Julie. "Okay, hit it, Lucas."

He typed into the stone. It hummed and he stepped away from it. "Here we go."

They jumped into a dark dome.

The bright lights above clicked on and Joey held a hand over his head to shield the light. Poly rushed to the door and paced near it until a green light lit up above. She pulled it open. On the other side, Travis ran to her and wrapped her in a big hug.

Joey sighed and looked at Evelyn. She seemed happy as Edith bounced her and pointed up at the lights above. It might have been the first time Evelyn could comprehend artificial lights to that scale. Before arriving in Sanct, her only technology consisted of Panavices. And Joey wondered what Evelyn thought about jumping; did she have the intelligence to comprehend what had happened? Did she get they were somewhere else, another world? He didn't think so, but he wouldn't be surprised if she did either.

Leaving the dome room with all of the mutants, they greeted Travis and he shook hands and gave hugs. The President of Vanar, hugging a whole group of mutants, like it was some PR stunt. To top it off, he had Poly and Julie standing by his side. Just the sight of them in public would cause a commotion Joey thought reserved for boy bands. They'd all done their fair share of PR for the betterment of Vanar, but Joey never got to the point where he felt comfortable around Poly and Travis.

"Joey, so good to see you again," Travis greeted with his politician hand out and matching smile.

"Travis." Joey nodded and shook his hand.

"Lucas and Julie," Travis said and looked at Julie's stomach. "I didn't know you were pregnant."

Julie's mouth hung open. "Who said I was?"

"Oh, well, I didn't mean to imply that . . . You look very beautiful, Julie, as always."

"I'm pregnant."

Travis breathed out in relief. "Oh good, congratulations. Is it a natural?"

"Yes, we did it the old fashioned way."

"Fantastic, does Marcus know?"

"No, and that's one of the reasons we've been in hiding on Ryja—"

"Travis," Joey interrupted, "I want you to meet Kris. Leader of the mutants."

"Pleasure to meet you," Travis shook his hand. "If you want to start sending your people up the elevator and have them wait in my office, that'd be great."

Kris nodded and went off, relaying instructions to the mutants. The first group entered the elevator.

"So, how are you guys doing?" Travis asked.

"Terrible," Poly said. "You know what it's like living in Ryjack? It's misery, and definitely no place for a baby."

"The baby." Travis lit up and walked to Evelyn. "So you are the one turning the worlds upside down." Evelyn giggled as he played with her feet. "You're going to be just as pretty as your momma, yes you are."

Joey glanced over to the elevator as another group of mutants entered it.

"So I guess this is it for a while," Kris said and extended his hand.

Joey took his hand and pulled him in for a hug. "You guys have done more for us than we could have ever asked for. Unfortunately, we have to ask for one more thing."

"I understand, and we'll be ready when the time comes."

Joey hated using the mutants, but in the end, his family came first. "Thank you, and if you guys need anything, contact Harris on the Pana we gave you."

Kris nodded. "And you make sure to take care of Queen

Evelyn." Unless Joey was mistaken, there was a hint of a threat in his tone. "Edith is staying behind to make sure you have all the assistance you need."

"Yes, thank you again."

Kris moved to Poly and they spoke in much more caring words before he left up the elevator with the remaining mutants.

"Guess it's just up to us now," Lucas said.

"Lulu," Evelyn called.

"Yeah, Eve, we're going bye-bye," Lucas said.

Travis looked at the group and then his eyes rested on Poly. "Are you guys sure this is the best plan? I mean, I could keep you in one of my houses and no one would ever know."

"No, we have to finish this once and for all, or we'll never be free to go or do anything," Joey answered.

"Okay, but just make sure you are doing it for your benefit and not for Harris. He will use people for his own purposes," Travis warned.

"We will," Poly said.

They all moved back into the stone room.

"We should make sure our shields work, just in case," Julie said.

Joey took out his Panavice and pressed the shield symbol, and then the lock symbol. The shield enveloped him. He felt it as it wrapped around him and locked the air in. The sounds around him dulled.

Julie darted around the dome, inspecting each person's shield, spending extra time with Edith to ensure the shield fit around both her and Evelyn. "Okay, everyone, looks good. Lucas, if the air quality has turned poor, we'll need a quick exit to the rendezvous spot."

"Got it." Lucas knelt next to the stone. "Maybe I should check it out first? See what's there and come back."

"No, we've been there several times already, we know it's safe. Besides, what if something went wrong with your shield, you could be in trouble and we wouldn't know to wait or come and help you. Or if you got the code wrong coming back, or any number of things. We all go together and if anything is there, our shields will protect us while we bounce right back."

Lucas nodded. "Everyone ready?"

Joey sidestepped closer to Poly and rubbed her arm. She glanced at him and pulled a knife from the sheath on her thigh. Since the birth of Evelyn, they'd been on the run, and he hadn't gotten to spend as many honeymoon nights with her as he might have wanted. But if their plan went well, he would make up for them all, tenfold. Their plan differed from the rest of the group and it was a secret they'd decided to keep until the moment they had Marcus dead at their feet.

"We're ready," Julie said looking at her Pana.

Lucas typed into the stone and it hummed. "Here we go."

They jumped and the dome turned from Travis's shiny dome to a broken dome under the open skies of the Arrack planet. Joey's gaze moved from the sky to the surrounding Arrack army. He pulled out both guns. "Get us out of here, Lucas!"

Lucas's finger touched the stone as a rock flew at him and struck him in the side of the head. His limp body fell to the ground.

"Don't anyone move," Joey commanded. He didn't have much of a choice and he moved in a slow circle looking at the many Arrack faces that surrounded them. Each held a weapon of some sort and they all looked like they wanted blood. Where did they come from? They'd done many jumps to Arrack and they'd never seen any signs the Arracks still existed, let alone were on the planet. Looking at all the silver faces and snarling teeth, he knew, they had made a terrible mistake.

If Joey could get to the stone, they might have a chance. He glanced at the stone, too much space between him and it. The Arracks would be on him in half the time. Unless he had all the time in the world. He knew what he had to do and felt all the training spent with Emmett flooding back to him. The feeling came easier than he thought, and in the moment, he knew he wanted to feel it again—even if just for one last time.

The chills ran down the back of his neck and the Arracks stilled, the sounds dulled and dust in the air hung. He looked up to the collapsed ceiling and into the bright daylight above. The Arracks were back on their home planet, but how? Harris said it'd be dangerous for decades.

He shook his head, putting the puzzle pieces together. Marcus must have fixed the planet for them and probably struck a new deal in the process. The idea of it made him sick.

He glanced at Poly as he passed her and gazed at Lucas on the ground. Blood trickled from the side of his head. The shield couldn't protect against everything, but it should have stopped that rock. He knelt next to the stone and took in the last moments of being in a hyper speed.

"Dada," Evelyn giggled.

Shocked, Joey stared at her. Everything else in the room sat still while she patted Edith's arm, watching him. *How can she be here with me?* He felt the feeling slipping from him and he grasped to hold onto it but the sounds crashed against Joey and he slipped back into normal time.

He jumped to the stone, as a dozen Arracks piled on top of

him. The screams of Poly and Julie filled the air. Small hands grasped his arms and legs and the sounds of their metal blades bouncing off his shield filled his ears.

He screamed, but the weight of them pushed the air from his lungs and the room slipped into blackness as he lost consciousness.

CHAPTER 7

"WHATEVER YOU THINK IS GOING to happen, the opposite is what *will* happen. It's what he does," Emmett said.

Gladius shoved him forward. She wanted to rough him up a bit just for being such a douchebag, but Hank had made her promise to not hurt him until he served his purpose.

"Just put your hand on the screen," Hank ordered.

"It won't matter." Emmett placed his hand on the old TV tube sitting on an oak stand near the fireplace. The screen lit up, scanning his hand. The fireplace sunk into the floor, revealing a staircase leading down. He sighed and looked at the opening. "You should know he expected you to do this."

"Just shut up," Gladius said.

Emmett pulled at the cuffs behind his back. "If I was even half the man I used to be, I'd kill each of you before the first one hit the floor."

"Well, good for us, you're not," she said.

"Thanks to Joey."

Gladius held onto Emmett and guided him down the stairs. Even if Emmett proclaimed his ineptitude, she wasn't buying it. She'd seen Emmett on several exhibitions in the past and the man was beyond lethal. While this wounded and hurt version of him stood in front of her, she still felt like she was dealing with a viper; if any of them made the wrong move, he'd strike.

"I'm going to stay up top," Rick said, pulling back the dusty drapes and looking out the window.

"Okay," Minter said. "Just be careful and if anyone or anything comes down that road, let us know." He held up the radio and Rick nodded as he left to keep watch outside.

The stairs went for several flights and stopped at another door with a keypad next to it.

"Go on," Gladius said and glanced at the camera above the door. There wasn't any chance of her not seeing them. Emmett laughed and punched in the numbers. The door slid open. It looked much like the house Marcus had kept near the coastline on Vanar. Even the windows were digital screens projecting an image of an ocean below.

"Welcome," a voice over the intercom said.

"Hello, Alice," Gladius responded, grabbing a chair and shoving it in place so the door wouldn't close.

"Gladius, Hank, Minter, and Emmett, welcome to my home. Are you here to kill me?"

"No, we are here to stop you."

"Futile, I am not here or anywhere. I am everywhere."

Her voice sent chills down Gladius's back. She looked to Hank and found his soft eyes urging her to continue. How lucky she felt to have found a man like Hank. After so many attempts, it took a man from another planet to find her heart.

"This is stupid. Just kill them, Alice," Emmett said.

"Not until I assess the danger. Marcus does not want to hurt them if he does not have to."

"Like Samantha?" Hank asked.

Gladius pushed Emmett forward. They crossed the room and went into a medical wing of sorts, with tables and screens scattered around the sterile room. Emmett visibly shook as they passed a stainless steel table.

"This is where he rebuilt you, isn't it?" Gladius asked.

"I rebuilt myself, but yes . . . this is where it started."

Past the medical room, and down a small corridor, they came to a white door. "Open it," Gladius ordered. This was one of the few things Julie couldn't be sure of; was it a trap door or not? It could be something as simple as a gun hooked to a string.

Emmett sighed and opened the door.

Gladius pushed him inside Marcus's bedroom. She wasn't shocked by the plain room. It felt as devoid of personality as any medical room. No personal affects or pictures, nothing to signify a person had lived there for over two years. She expected as much from Marcus, a person who seemed to be more robot than human. The one time she'd met him, he felt as cold and calculated as anyone she'd ever met.

"Emmett, I am initiating protocol sixteen," Alice said.

Gladius looked at the ceiling for a second, trying to find the speaker and wondered what protocol sixteen meant exactly. Emmett jumped out of her grip. He spun away and she reached missing his shirt by inches. He leapt into Marcus's closet and doors slid closed over him.

Hank dashed to the doors, but they were already closed,

with no handles on the outside.

Alice spoke again. "I'm sorry, but I cannot let you access me."

Gladius sighed and clicked the button on her Panavice. She looked to Hank. "Turn it on, Hank."

He kicked the closet door one more time before grabbing his Panavice to turn it on. Gladius watched as Minter did the same. Each had a protective shield on now, and with it, their own air supply. She pressed the timer on her own Panavice and saw ten minutes start and change to nine minutes and fifty-nine seconds.

A white cloud blasted into the room from above, making a loud hissing sound. Gladius couldn't feel the, air but the white mist started filling the room. She imagined it was filling the entire complex. Every living thing would be extinguished.

"You are shielded," Alice said.

Gladius took her Panavice and walked to a screen on the nightstand next to Marcus's bed. She wondered why he would make this location the only direct input to Alice.

Behind Marcus's bed, she spotted movement. The headboard opened up and a machine gun popped out, spraying bullets. Gladius instinctively ducked, grabbing the monitor with her. She looked back at Hank, laying on the ground. He gave her a thumbs up.

"Do not do this," Alice said.

Gladius ignored her and plugged her Panavice into the screen. She pressed the program Julie had spent so long making and sent it into Alice. The white mist above dissipated and the machine gun stopped firing. Minter shimmied over, holding out his gun and moving close to the closet.

"Is that you, Julie?" Alice said.

"Yes," Gladius replied.

"I cannot see you."

"I'm here, right next to you."

"You put something in me. I can feel it growing."

Gladius sighed at the waste of a good joke and watched her screen. The file had another minute and she looked at the time left on their air. Three minutes and counting. They were going to make it, and she and Hank could move on to the next phase. So close to being done with it all. The idea of being free with Hank worked its way through her body and made her shiver.

"What are you doing to me, Julie?"

"We are just loading a program."

"I will not let you. I will find a way to rid it, the same way I rid the worm you put in me. I will find a corner of the net to stuff it in and lock it away forever."

"This one is different. By the time I am done here, you won't even remember we were here. You will think an anomaly happened in your time management program, investigate it, and label it as an unknown." At least that is the way Julie described it to her. She was a pretty good tech herself, but Julie was something special. Just looking at the code Julie wrote, blew her mind.

"I will not forget this. This will not change our plans."

Gladius couldn't resist the question. "What is your plan for the nanobots in every person on Earth?"

"We will use them to save everyone," Alice said.

Save everyone? What a peculiar response. Gladius thought of pressing her for more information, but the last seconds ticked away on the program.

"What a beautiful program," Alice said just before the screen clicked off.

The count made it to zero.

"Time to go," Gladius said.

"What about him?" Minter pointed his gun at the closet.

"System's down. Hank, you want to grab him?" Gladius asked.

Hank stomped to the sliding door and flung it open. A foot, courtesy of Emmett, struck Hank in the face. Hank reeled back and landed on the bed. Emmett jumped out from the closet with his hands still cuffed, but in front of him now.

Gladius pulled her knife out but was too slow. Minter was closer and had his gun drawn on him. The gun blasted out and Emmett yelled in pain.

"No!" Gladius groaned.

Emmett fell to the ground and struggled, trying to get back to his feet. He collapsed to the ground and reached for his bleeding leg.

The smell of gun smoke filled the room and Gladius shook her head. This wasn't supposed to happen. "You idiot," Gladius said to Minter. "Do you know what you've done?"

"He was going to kill us."

"Mr. Gimp here? Really?"

Minter stuffed his gun and pinned his foot on Emmett's back, holding him to the ground.

Gladius picked up the monitor and placed it back in the precise location it had been, making sure to line it up with the faint line of dust it left. "There's no way she won't know something happened here. Look at how much he's bled on the carpet already." She huffed and glanced at her Panavice. "It's dark carpet, maybe she won't notice. We have eight minutes until she boots back up."

"Hank, help me with him," Minter said.

Hank and Minter got Emmett's hands behind his back again and used another zip-tie to strap in his legs. They picked up Emmett to his feet and mostly carried him out of the room.

Gladius smoothed out the comforter on the bed and backpedaled out of the room, checking to make sure nothing was out of place.

She stepped in the blood and the carpet squished. She lifted her foot, disgusted and wiped it on a clean section of carpet. When she left the room, she saw the real problem. Emmett was a bleeder and the trail down the hall was something Alice would notice. For the plan to work, she would have to have *no* knowledge they were in Marcus's room, or that they planted Julie's program into her.

Hank and Minter had already hauled Emmett into the medical wing and were dragging him to the front room. Gladius ran to catch up and slid her knife into the sheath at her side. Glancing back, her gaze followed the trail of blood leading to Emmett's foot.

"You just *had* to shoot him," Gladius mumbled.

"Let's fix the problem," Hank said. "Paper towels are over there. Minter, help her. I've got him." Hank sat Emmett on the floor near the door.

Gladius didn't like the idea of cleaning up Emmett's blood. Who knows what kind of diseases a freak like him carried? She yanked the paper towels off the roll and grabbed a cleaning spray from under the cabinet. Tossing the roll to Minter, she looked at her clock. "Six minutes. We need to be in the car in four if we want to make it out of here unnoticed."

She ran with the spray bottle and doused it over the blood on the tile floors. It smeared around as they wiped at first, but after a few goes, it cleaned up. Thankfully, the rest of the house held the dark carpet and they'd just have to take a chance. No way to get a carpet cleaner in the next two minutes anyway.

They stuffed the towels into the trashcan and spent a second to look over their work. Clean enough.

"Crap, we've got two minutes before she comes back online," Gladius said and ran to Emmett.

Minter and Hank took most of the load, but they all carried Emmett into the family room.

"Who closed the door?" Hank asked.

"What?" Gladius looked up at the closed front door. But she'd wedged it open with a chair . . . it couldn't be closed.

"I shut it and it won't open," a woman from behind them said.

Gladius dropped Emmett's leg and grabbed her knife. "Hank, get the door." She walked sideways, closer to the woman who proclaimed she closed the door. Gladius didn't recognize her but she was a small woman holding a clipboard and looking at the ground.

Hank pounded on the door but it wouldn't move. "Open it, Emmett." But he lay limp in Minter's arms.

"Open it." Gladius pointed her knife at the petite woman and she flinched.

"I can't, even if I wanted to. It's on lockdown."

Gladius pulled out her Panavice and scoured it for anything that might help her get the door open, but it appeared the whole building had been shut down. With little more than one minute left, Gladius looked to Hank and Minter for help.

"Rick," Minter called into the radio.

"Yeah?"

"Get out of here, now."

"But what about—"

"Now!"

"Roger."

"Break the cameras," Minter said to Gladius. "Maybe we can buy some time."

She took out her throwing knives and spotted the camera in the corner. She threw the knife and struck the lens, knocking bits to the ground. Scanning the rest of the room, she searched for any more.

"The medical room. I saw a few," Hank said and broke the leg off the chair and ran into the room.

Gladius looked at the timer, one minute. "You, what's your name?" she asked.

"Gingy."

"Alice will be back up in a few seconds and she will expect you here, correct? I'm going to give you one warning. If you give her any clue that we are here, I will end you. I don't care if it's with my dying breath, I will stab this knife through your face. Understand?"

Gingy nodded as the clatter of Hank busting up the medical room's camera made her flinch.

"I need you to say the words."

"I understand."

"Good. Now take a seat on the couch."

Minter dragged Emmett toward the medical room.

Hank, breathing hard and holding the chair leg said, "I think—"

"Shh," Gladius whispered. "We can't talk in a few seconds. She'll hear us. And guys, do a master shut off on your Panavices. She'll detect them."

Hank thumbed his Panavice as he darted to Minter and helped pull Emmett into the medical room. Gladius wanted to help, but she wasn't about to leave Gingy alone for one second. Taking a seat right next to her, she pointed her knife at her gut.

Gingy clutched her notebook tightly against her chest. "Is Emmett going to be okay?" she whispered.

Gladius put one finger over her mouth. "Make her believe you broke the cameras." She looked at her Panavice and with a few seconds left, did a master turn off on it. The first few seconds would determine everything. Either they were going to die, or they were going to be living in a nightmare of silence and deception.

CHAPTER 8

JOEY'S HAND SHOOK UNCONTROLLABLY AND his head throbbed in pain. Someone nearby sobbed and it stirred him awake. "Poly." His voice sounded weak and a blurry figure moved in response.

"Yes," she sounded elated at first but turned cross. "Joey, you promised."

She came into focus. Her bloodshot eyes, staring at him. He reached to touch her face, but his hand wouldn't move. He looked down to find leather straps attached to his arms and legs. Poly, sitting a couple feet away, had the same straps. He pulled on the strap only to find a chain holding it to the ground.

"Good to see you back, buddy," Lucas said.

"How long have I been out for?" Joey asked.

"A few hours," Poly said.

He squeezed his eyes shut and opened them again, trying to

clear them. The room still seemed hazy, but he took in the circular room as best he could. Leaning forward, he looked at each of his friends lined up in a sitting position against a plastered wall. "Where's Evelyn?" he asked, jerking around when he couldn't see her.

"Right here," Edith said. "Surprised these silver bastards didn't tie her up as well."

Joey breathed a sigh of relief and looked at his little girl's face. She regarded him with a smile. He still had her, and that was a start.

His pulse sped up as he thought about the last moments before the Arracks descended on the stone. They had to still be on their planet. These were their type of mud-plastered buildings. "Any guards?" Joey whispered and winced at the pain in his head.

"A couple outside the door," Poly said.

His hand shook and the tremor moved down the whole right side of his body. His restraints clattered and kept some of the motion to a minimum.

"Joey?" Poly slid her hand closer to him until the chain locked up. He reached and felt her hand with his shaking fingertips.

Normally, he could minimize it with shear willpower, but now the shakes controlled him. After a few seconds, it dwindled, not from his commands but more from running its course. He raised his hand up the few inches he could and made a fist, then extended his fingers out. He needed his shooting hand to work.

"They took all of our stuff," Poly said, seeing him feeling at his sides for his guns.

Joey grimaced and looked to Julie. "You've had a few hours, I'm sure that was enough time to figure a way out of here,

65

right?"

She looked at the dirty floor between her legs. None of them were looking at him. He knew each of them well enough to know he'd missed something major. Even Lucas kept his mouth shut and only glanced at him.

"What?" Joey asked.

"You promised. I can't do this without you, Joey. But I have to know, if you went slo-mo, then why didn't we make the jump? We shouldn't be here."

"I . . ." he struggled to find the words to tell her their daughter had the same gift as him. "Eve was there, with me, in the slow-mo."

Poly gasped and shot a look to Evelyn. She turned back and reached her fingers out to him. Tears filled her puffy eyes. "He's coming here to take her and we're just stuck here, helpless."

Seeing her vulnerable, and hearing the will leave her, hurt Joey. He too felt the tears building and he pulled on his restraints, needing to hold his grieving wife and let her know they were going to get out of this. He wouldn't allow Marcus to take their baby. He'd do whatever it took.

"Julie?" he called between gritted teeth.

She jerked her attention to him. "First, we need to get out of these restraints. Then we can formulate a plan of escape."

"I say we ambush Marcus; end it all right here, right now," Joey said.

"That's crazy," Julie said.

"We know he's coming," Lucas said. "When was the last time we knew where he was, or where he was going? This may be our only chance."

"That's not the plan. Believe me, I want to kill the guy as much as you all do, but we need to look at the bigger picture.

We have to find his last place of hiding and that means, we go through phase four of the plan.

Joey growled, pulling on the chain. He wasn't going to allow phase four to happen, even if they all thought it was part of the plan.

"We can escape and get to a stone," Julie said. "Play out the rest of our plan. Our friends are expecting us to do our part."

Joey nodded. It was sensible . . . "But, this is a good opportunity. We could end it today, we could be done with this." He wanted it to be over, to be rid of Marcus and anyone supporting him. Damn the worlds if they needed him.

"We can't face him here," Julie said. "We have to escape and get to a stone. Remember Hank, Gladius, and our fathers?" she looked at Lucas. "They have their plan and are expecting us to carry out ours. The stone isn't far from here. We might have a chance."

"Great, now how do we get out of these?" Joey clattered the chain on the stone floor.

"I've been working on mine for the last few hours. I have a metal spur on my chain." She rubbed her arm next to her legs and Joey noticed the frayed leather on her shackles.

"How much longer?" Joey asked.

"Probably three hours."

He winced at the number. He didn't know what would happen next, but Marcus would be there soon and as badly as he wanted to confront him, he didn't want to do it sitting tied to the floor.

"Queen, get back here," Edith called out, but Evelyn was already crawling away from her. Edith reached, but her chains kept her seated. "She just jumped and pushed off me."

"Evelyn," Poly called. "Baby, come here. Come to

Mommy." She sniffed and extended her arms out as much as the restraints would allow.

"Ju-ju," Evelyn said, determined on her path.

"Yeah, come to your Auntie Julie."

Evelyn turned toward Julie and stopped at her foot. Joey leaned forward to get a view of what his daughter was doing.

"Come to me," Julie said, but Evelyn kept out of her reach. "What are you doing, sweetie?"

"Ju." Her baby brow furrowed. Not even old enough to have full-fledged eyebrows, her face crunched up in concentration with her hands on Julie's leg strap.

"What—" Julie said and then gasped. The bolt attached to her strap broke in Evelyn's hand. "How did you do that?" She stared at her freed leg. "Do the rest of them."

Joey stared, unblinking at Evelyn as she moved to the next leg. He squinted and ignored Poly's glare. If Evelyn was doing what he thought she was doing . . . *There!* She blurred for a split second and the bolt broke. "She's speeding up and using it to break the restraints," Joey said. "Evelyn, don't do that. You're going to hurt yourself."

She giggled and moved to Julie's hands. With both free, Julie jumped to her feet and picked up Evelyn. "You are one amazing baby girl. Yes, you are." She gave her a hug, then handed her back to Edith.

Joey swallowed and watched his daughter laugh as Edith tickled her stomach. She was much more than any of them, and each day he saw her growing into something astonishing. He didn't need to bring this up to Poly. The tears streamed down her face as she watched Evelyn.

"Now what?" Lucas asked.

Julie shook her head and pulled at Lucas's chains. "I don't

know how she did it. These are heavy duty locks."

"Queenie can do all sorts of stuff," Edith boasted.

The door flung open.

Joey's heart stopped; they were too late. Then he saw a single Arrack enter the room. Joey yanked at his restraints, but he knew the creature could kill them all without too much trouble. Julie balled up her fist as the Arrack approached. It stopped a few feet from her.

"I was sent here to help you. He's coming soon. You need to leave," it said, pushing a key into Lucas's restraints.

"Who are you? Who sent you?" Julie asked.

Ignoring her question, he moved to free Poly. "He's coming for her." The Arrack nodded toward Evelyn. "She's something very important to him."

"Yeah, we know," Poly replied, rubbing her wrists as her restraints fell to the ground.

The Arrack moved to Joey. "You are the messenger?"

Joey knew what the Arrack was asking. "Yes." Unknowingly, he had delivered a message that killed off much of the Arrack world, a weight that crushed his soul. "Had I known . . ." he shook his head, "I'm sorry."

The Arrack squinted as he unlocked the last bolt. Joey flung the restraints and stood up.

"Free her as well, please." Poly pointed to Edith.

"She's not part of the deal."

"What deal? What are you talking about? Get her out of there or we aren't leaving."

"I was told only about you four and your baby."

"I don't care who told you what. Just give me the keys." Poly yanked the key from the Arrack.

It looked impressed. "You are fast."

Poly huffed and unlocked Edith.

"What's your name?" Joey asked.

"Tick."

"Well, Tick, I thank you for the freedom," Lucas said. "Now please tell me you have a plan beyond this?"

"Oh yes, I killed the guards on the outside and the others have cleared a path to the stone."

"Others? Who are you with?" Poly asked.

"There's a large group of us who know the truth. We have sworn a blood oath against Marcus and will not honor a new agreement. Now, we must go. They won't be distracted for long."

Poly took Evelyn from Edith and inspected her much like a quality control person looking for frayed edges or chipped paint.

"Please, we have to hurry," Tick urged. "He will be here soon."

"Can we get our weapons? There is a bow . . ."

"Yes, yes, out here. Come on."

Lucas followed the Arrack and Joey kept back near Evelyn, expecting a trap at any second. He only hoped this guy was taking them to their weapons and not to some strange elaborate plan orchestrated by Marcus. Joey gripped his shirt tight, fighting the shakes. He limped up the steps and Poly glanced down at his leg.

Two dead Arracks lay on the floor as they made it to the top of the steps. Joey looked at Tick again. This little thing killed both of those guards at the same time?

"Right over here." Tick used another key to open a cabinet. He pulled the wooden door open and Joey saw Prudence sitting on top of the rest of their items.

They collected their belongings in short order and he felt the whole situation shifting back in their favor. Armed, they had a chance.

"Not far from here, the stone is." The Arrack opened the next door and daylight flooded into the room.

Julie leaned back and said, "Something doesn't feel right."

Joey was starting to have the same feeling, but he looked back at the two dead Arracks. They seemed real.

"What choice do we have? Let's just run to the stone and take the first ticket out of this hell hole," Lucas said.

"I'm with Julie. This feels off," Poly said.

They left the building and spotted several more dead Arracks. "Not far," Tick said.

Outside, it felt late in the day. The sun lay hidden behind the trees, casting long shadows. Thankfully the light was at his back and he hoped it gave him a slight advantage. If Marcus was pulling the strings, he'd need all the help he could get.

They left the dirt road and traveled into the forest. A small path had been cleared, maybe a deer trail. Joey kept one hand on his gun, and the other he used to turn on his shield. He felt the air around him shimmer as it enveloped him.

Ten minutes in to their walk, Tick stopped. "The circle stone is right over there. This is as far as I go."

Joey looked over the hedges to the cleared circle. "Ambush?" He looked to Lucas.

"I don't know, I don't see anything or anyone."

"Please, hurry," Tick said.

"Lucas, check it out," Joey said.

Lucas grasped Prudence and walked with an arrow in hand, scanning the surrounding forest. Joey pointed his gun out front, waiting. "Clear," Lucas called out.

Joey motioned for the rest to go into the circle. He walked in last.

"Get us out of here, Lucas," Poly said.

Lucas was already on the stone when it started to hum. He stepped back, and shot the rest of them a terrified look.

"Here we go," Evelyn said.

"I didn't touch the stone yet. Someone's coming," Lucas said.

"Edith, get—" Was all Joey said before a figure popped into existence.

CHAPTER 9

"YOU FORCED ME DOWN HERE. You knew this was coming. I have no privacy with all these cameras watching my every move. I had to break them," Gingy said. "I needed somewhere you aren't studying me. I'm not a lab rat."

Gladius took a slow breath and watched the performance Gingy put on. It wasn't bad and she felt the emotion from Gingy building with each word.

"My sensors detect an elevation in room temperature. Are you sure you are alone?"

"Maybe it's because I've been sweating like a pig down here, wreaking this place up. If you don't leave me alone, I'll start breaking things *he* likes."

"There would be consequences." The speaker clicked off.

Gladius stared at her, locking in on her eyes. She didn't want there to be any doubt, she'd gut her from hip to neck if she squealed to the computer. Tears fell down Gingy's face and she wiped them with her sleeve.

Leaning toward the coffee table, Gladius picked up a pad of paper and wrote a note on it.

Is there a place with no microphones?

Gingy nodded and pointed toward the kitchen door.

Gladius got up from the couch and motioned to the kitchen. Keeping her knife near Gingy's back, she walked behind her into the next room. Gingy stopped just inside of the kitchen and held a hand over her mouth.

Gladius moved around her and saw blood spilling over the stainless steel counter top. Minter moved frantically, grabbing towels and filling a bucket of water. "We can talk in here?" Gladius asked.

"Whisper," Gingy said and looked pale, staring at Emmett laid out on the counter. "You have to save him."

Gladius huffed and pushed her forward. Gingy whimpered and moved next to Emmett. The gunshot on his leg continued to ooze blood. Gladius didn't think she'd ever seen so much coming out of one person, although she held no pity for the man. To her, it'd be just fine if he bled out on that table.

Hank slid a knife up Emmett's pant leg and cut the slacks in half. She watched them ball up a handful of paper towels and push it on his leg, trying to get the bleeding to stop. Gingy cried next to Emmett, her hands hovered next to his mangled face, but she never brought herself to actually touch him.

"We need to get the bullet out," Minter said. "But if it hit a main artery . . ."

"We have a machine down the hall. It can save him."

Minter pushed on the white cloth and they watched as it turned red instantly. He grabbed another and stared at Gingy as he applied it. Gladius wondered if he was going to pull out his gun and shoot her dead. She'd been with a lot of men in her life and she knew men like Minter were rare, along with most of the Six and their parents. Strange lot they were, when she thought about it. Anyone in their right mind would be letting this vile man die on the counter. Yet, here were her man and Minter, trying like crazy to keep him alive.

"Is there a camera?" Minter asked.

"Yes, two of them."

"If we have any chance of saving him, it's going to be in that machine," Minter said. "But if you try one thing, he dies and you die."

Gingy pursed her lips and sniffled. She took a deep breath and started to scream.

Minter had his gun out in a fraction of a second.

"Wait," Gladius said, holding out her hand. She'd already seen the woman's acting skills.

Gingy continued to scream, picking up a pot and throwing it across the room. It clanked and clattered over the steel tops and crashed to the ground. She grabbed more items and threw them around like a crazy person. Gladius shook her head in admiration. The chick was crazy, but she was her kind of crazy.

"I can't take it in here anymore!" She picked up a pot and kicked the door to the hall open. Running down the hall, she slammed the pan into a small camera near the ceiling. Gladius, Hank, and Minter made sure to stay clear of any lines of sight from the camera and listened to her rant against her captors while destroying the hall and the next room over.

"If she sells us out, you better kill her." Gladius glared at Minter and he nodded his head.

A few seconds passed and Gingy rushed back into the

kitchen. "I hurt my hand," she screamed. Blood dripped from her left hand as she rushed next to Emmett. "Come on. Let's get him there."

The thought of touching Emmett again repulsed Gladius and she was happy to see Hank and Minter handling the load on their own. She kept behind Gingy, with her knife pointed at her at all times. She didn't like how well the woman could act.

Hank and Minter placed Emmett's body into the tanning bed looking machine. Gladius remembered the few times she'd gotten into one, and the chills it gave your body as it repaired you molecule by molecule.

Gingy closed the lid and punched in the commands. At the end, she fell to her knees, sobbing into her hands.

Gladius might have comforted a distraught woman, but she was getting to know Gingy and was leery of how genuine the tears were. Hank on the other hand, didn't have any such troubles.

"It's going to be okay," he whispered. "Emmett's one tough guy."

Gladius took a deep breath and held her tongue. She wanted to remind them of exactly who was in that machine. That man had tried to kill them all at one point, manipulated Joey and had Julie seconds from her death.

"He used to be strong," Gingy said and wiped her nose. "That is a shell of the man he once was. Emmett was the strongest, smartest person I'd ever known. What you all did to him, ruined him."

"He attempted to kill most of my friends at one point or another," Hank said.

"Only to protect us," she said with her voice rising. "You all think you're so righteous. You have no idea what Marcus is really trying to do."

"Enlighten us then," Gladius spit out.

She laughed and looked back at Gladius. "You'll find out soon enough. You think he doesn't know about your plans? Marcus knows *everything*."

"He's not a god," Hank said. "He can be stopped."

"In some worlds he is a god. . ." she whispered, turning to face Hank. "How do you know everything you're doing right now isn't just part of his plan? If he wants something to happen, it'll happen."

"Like you down here?" Gladius said.

The question sent her back to burying her face in her hands. Gladius held herself back from ending the woman. Every word she spoke felt like an angle. Of course Hank was eating it up. But she loved Hank for it. Bless a man who could care for his enemy. Gladius didn't have it in her to spare Gingy and if the room was empty, she'd stab her in the temple.

"I'm just a tiny part in Marcus's plans," she mumbled in her hands. "He barely talks to me. I just want it to go back to the way it was. The way it was before you all came into my life."

"That won't happen," Gladius said. "The world erodes everyone and everything; you'll never be the same."

Hank looked at her with a frown. She sent him a smile. She didn't want to sound morbid, but the longer you lived, the more you knew not to believe things would turn out for the better. The good guys hardly won. More than likely, the stronger person would win and on occasion, the lucky one.

"How much longer?" Minter pointed at the machine holding Emmett.

"Probably an hour," she said.

He huffed and took a seat at the back of the room with his

gun resting on his lap.

Gladius gazed at the ceiling where the broken camera hung in pieces. She looked back at the door and wondered. "You think Alice knows we're here?"

Gingy set her face between her knees. "Most likely."

Gladius took a deep breath and watched Hank move to the door. "What can she do to us in here?"

"Turn off the air. Cut the power."

"She tried to flood out Lucas," Hank said.

It would be better if she didn't know they were there, but it didn't change the mission. As long as she didn't know why they were there and she didn't find Julie's program imbedded in her, they'd be okay. She'd be damned if she was going to let some computer get the best of her and hers. She fumed and tightly gripped the blade in her hand, blaming herself for not clearing the house out before they left the front door unattended. This was her fault and she would never forgive herself if something happened to Hank.

Hank moved to Gladius and rubbed her back. "You okay?"

"Yeah, but if she knows we're here, we don't have a way out."

"No, we don't," Gingy said.

Gladius squeezed her eyes shut and her lips thinned. It would only be a matter of time until Alice picked up on something and when she did, she'd find a way to end them all. She glanced at Hank. The idea of dying next to him was comforting. He was the first person in her life to whom she felt a true, romantic connection. All the physical flings she'd had were passing moments, but the year she'd spent with Hank filled in so much of her history, she didn't think about the time before him.

"It's going to be okay, we'll find a way out of here," Hank said.

"I know and I think I have the perfect plan."

"I would like to hear this plan," Alice's voice said through unseen speakers.

"Shit," Gladius said.

CHAPTER 10

"SHARATI?" JOEY ASKED, DRAWING HIS gun with a shaky hand. He glanced at Poly. The last time they met, Poly had put a blade into Sharati.

Sharati glared at each of them but kept her curved dagger on her hip. "Tick, did you clear them out?"

"Yes."

"You are fools for coming here. They've been watching every stone on this planet, waiting for you to jump here, and here you are." She stared at Evelyn in Edith's arms. "So it's true. She's been born. And you," she pointed to Julie, "are with child."

"Sharati, we were just leaving," Julie said.

"You know he cleared the air here?" Sharati asked. "He predicted the world would end and it did. He gave us a new world to inhabit while he cleaned this world so we could return.

So many died that day."

Joey thought of the day they rode away from the growing cloud that would envelope the whole world of Arrack. Sharati had turned on them that day.

Lucas rushed to the stone and Joey kept his gun trained on Sharati.

"You can go, but that is what he wants you to do. He's herding you. Why not stray from his path?"

Lucas paused and looked back at Joey.

"You want to help us?" Joey asked.

"There are those who believe you didn't know what was in the package; we believe Marcus did. We are few in numbers but growing. We know he wants you more than anything in all the worlds, or more specifically, her." She pointed at Evelyn. "We can do what he doesn't think you'll do and stay here."

"This is stupid, hit the code, Lucas," Poly said.

"Wait," Joey called out, "I think she has a point. We could go to the next spot and maybe buy a week, but if we were to hide here, we might get months."

"We are not staying here." Poly put a hand on her knife.

"Fine, Lucas, get us out of here. Sharati, you need to step out of the circle."

"I was afraid you'd feel this way." She gave a quick nod toward Tick.

Joey turned around in time to see a ball fly toward them, cracking open in the sky. Bolts of electricity flew out from the stone. Joey felt a rush down the back of his neck, but the lightning bolt struck him in the chest. As Joey fell, he heard the stone humming.

LUCAS WAS NEXT TO JULIE who lay on the ground.

Joey jumped up, spun around, searching for Evelyn. She lay on top of Edith, touching her face. Edith jerked awake and looked around before clutching Evelyn and getting to her feet.

"Poly?" Joey rubbed her arm and she stirred awake.

"Evelyn . . ."

"She's fine."

"Tick threw a ball at us. You think it struck Evelyn?" Poly rushed to her and took her from Edith, inspecting her. Evelyn giggled and patted Poly's arms.

"Holy freaking moly, where the hell are we?" Lucas said.

Joey did a slow circle, looking at the wasteland. Nothing appeared to be growing in the scorched landscape. Mountains were in the distance, yet there was nothing but flat desert before them. "Where did you take us?" he asked.

"I got hit before I could finish the code . . . I might have bumped in the last digit."

"Please tell me this is a master stone."

Lucas shook his head.

"This can't be happening. Where's Sharati? She must have done this."

"I was trying to save you," Sharati hissed from behind Joey.

He spun around with his gun in hand. "Where the hell are we?"

"I don't know, but this looks like a purged planet."

"Get us out of here," Joey said.

"I can't. He was right," she pointed to Lucas, "it's a one-way stone."

Joey paced and squeezed the hilt of his gun tight. "Julie. Nearest stone off this rock."

"To the north, a long ways. Days."

He pointed his gun at Sharati. "Why did you do that? You've killed us."

"I didn't think he'd get a code off in time. We aimed to take you back to a safe house, to protect you. Not to some purged planet."

"Purged?" Julie asked. "What the hell are you talking about?"

Sharati looked at the dirt around the circle. "When you've been to as many planets as we have, you see some that look like a great wind came through and peeled a layer off the whole planet. This place feels like that. We need to get off this planet quickly. It isn't safe here." She looked to the sky.

"Great. Julie, lead the way, please," Joey said.

Julie had her Panavice out and searched the screen for a minute. "We should go through the gorge over there. There is usually a forest on the back side of it."

"What country equivalent are we in?" Poly asked.

"Chile."

Joey pointed his gun at Sharati. "You're not coming with us."

"I understand your apprehension, but you will need me. There are things on a purged planet you have to look out for."

"No." Joey said. "We are going that way, you go that way."

Sharati touched the hilt on her dagger as if by instinct. "I don't take orders from you. I will go on my own. If you find a pulser, stay far away from it. You will know it from the blinking green lights. And don't trust anything in the sky." She looked to the sky then turned and walked south.

Joey watched her for a few minutes until he was happy with her distance from them.

"Julie?"

She nodded and walked toward the gorge. "We should have kept her though. There is something on the other side of the mountain. Something powerful. It could be this pulser she mentioned."

"She tried to kill us," Joey said. "Are you prepared to have her by our side after that?"

"I'm not. She creeps me out big time," Lucas said.

Julie led the way and kept a slow pace, rubbing her large stomach from time to time. Joey remembered Poly struggling with odd pains and sore feet while she was pregnant and he wished they had some kind of cart to help Julie. It wasn't right, having her travel so much in her state. All the movement and exercise had to be straining on her and the baby, though Julie never complained.

The gorge gave them a nice path up the side of the mountain. Julie stopped periodically, but they kept a good pace up the hill. By the time the sun had reached mid-sky, they were near the top.

Joey, being tallest, got to see the city below first. He paused at the sight. The city had been enormous at one point, but now it was barren. The only true defining marks, were the concrete streets forming a nice grid pattern, crisscrossing through the old city that stretched to the horizon.

"We found another planet with a civilization," Julie said, staring at the screen and then back to the city in ruins below.

"Did someone nuke it?" Lucas asked.

Julie shook her head. "No, there's no radiation, plus look at the city. There is not a center point to the destruction. Everything seems to have just fallen down."

"There's a building still standing," Poly pointed at one in the distance. "How long do you think it will take to get here? I don't like the idea of being out here in the dark. This place doesn't feel right."

Joey felt the same way, but he wasn't sure about the single building standing in the middle of a wasteland either. They were too far to make out the details of the building but judging the distance, he thought they could get there in a couple hours.

Julie didn't appear to like what she was seeing on her Panavice. "There's something strange near that building. It's drawing a lot of power."

"You think people are here?" Joey asked.

"I don't know, but something is out there."

The unknown terrified him. Before Evelyn, he could be reckless. Now, he had a precious baby girl to protect. He watched her for a few seconds. She gazed down at the ruined city with an unblinking stare.

"We ready then?" Lucas asked.

Joey nodded. "Let's keep our weapons ready. Who knows if this is another Ryjack. Could be freaking grinners down there." He led the way down the hill and toward the city. He pulled out his second gun and skirted the crumbled buildings as he approached the first street. Seeing the destruction up close, he thought of the massive earthquakes he saw on TV and how the buildings fell to the ground in massive heaps of rubble. Crossing the street, he stepped around the many blocks of concrete covering it.

Looking down the way, he didn't spot any ambling grinners, or anything for that matter. The streets looked blank. No cars, no vegetation, no life. Nothing but rubble. He motioned for Lucas to move ahead. Lucas moved close to a building wall that hadn't collapsed and held his bow out as he did. Joey moved behind him and covered the right side.

"I don't see anything," Lucas said.

"Looks clear." Joey motioned for Poly and the rest to come out.

"What the hell happened here?" Lucas asked, looking at the piles of rubble pouring into the street. "It's like freaking King Kong came through."

"Earthquake?" Joey guessed.

"Chile *is* a hot zone, but I don't know. Look at the street . . . no cracks. And where is everything? Cars, people, plants, there's nothing but concrete."

A bird screeched from above. The sound made Joey jump and he looked to the sky. It was then he noticed how truly quiet this place was. The bird soared high above, circling over them and then turned off toward the ocean.

Don't trust anything in the sky, Sharati had told them. Joey started to feel as if he had made a mistake sending her away. "Julie, you picking anything up?"

"Just the same power source as before. Looks to be straight down this street, toward that building."

"Nothing else? No nets, no people, no Pana's?"

"Nothing. This place is a blank slate, except for that one building. I'm not even picking up satellites."

"What the hell happened here?" Lucas said.

"Sharati said this planet had been purged. I wonder what that meant." Julie looked back and Joey saw the regret on her face. Maybe they could have gotten more information from her before he sent her away. "She said stay away from blinking green lights."

"Well, if we see any, we'll be careful," Joey said, actively trying to keep his leg moving without a noticeable limp.

They walked down the street, passing one rubble pile after the next. A few still had what looked like intact walls and even what resembles shops or houses inside. Joey passed one such building and saw the children's desks lined up facing a collapsed roof and shattered blackboard.

Joey glanced back at Evelyn. She gazed at each building with as much curiosity as Julie. She seemed to be studying everything around her even pointing and making grunting sounds at a few different objects in the rubble. A red bike sticking in the pile of broken concrete sparked her interest. The red color stood out among the sea of black and grey around them.

Lucas ran through the rubble, searching for water and food, but he didn't find anything they could use. It was as if someone had already stripped the rubble for usable items. Joey eyed some of the rebar sticking out of the concrete blocks and the rust stains running down from it. *How long ago did this happen?*

The black building a mile ahead became the only reminder of what man had once accomplished here. The rest of the city around it had suffered a different fate. Did they build it after the collapse? Was it the first in vast rehabilitation project?

About a half mile out from the building, Julie halted the group. "You see that? A green light just blinked."

"I didn't see anything," Lucas said.

Joey leaned forward, staring at the black building and they all waited for the light to appear.

"I swear I saw one," Julie said, breaking the one-minute silence.

Joey looked at the group. "We'll all keep looking and if anyone sees it, let us know."

"I think we should just go around," Poly said.

"That is the only standing building in this city, if we have any chance of finding supplies, it's there."

"But something destroyed this place," Poly pointed out, "and we'd be idiots to think whatever it is won't destroy us."

Another bird screeched from above. Joey turned his hand to block the sun and looked to the sky. Two birds now flew in a circular pattern. He squinted and the sun gleamed off one of the bird's wings. What kind of birds were they?

"No te muevas!"

Joey didn't see the man holding a wooden spear until it was too late, he was upon them. The idea of his spear against his gun seemed laughable, but the man had it pointed at Evelyn. "Easy. We're just passing through."

"Americans?" he asked, looking confused.

"Yes. Do you speak English?"

"Yes," he said with a Chilean accent. "What are you doing here?"

Joey laughed. "I couldn't explain it if I wanted to, but we are looking to get out of here, so if you can put that spear down and let us pass, we'd appreciate it."

The man lowered his spear and licked his chapped lips. The dirt on his clothes matched the dirt on his face. It looked as if he hadn't eaten a thing in months and the clothes he wore hung on him like a child who got into his dad's closet. "You know a way out?"

"We do," Joey said.

The birds screeched again.

"They've spotted us. It won't be long until the cleaners come. Follow me, I've got a place we can hide."

"I assure you, we can handle ourselves. But if you have any supplies we are in great need of water and food."

"I have a few cans left. After they're gone . . ."

"That's fine, we'll find our own."

"No you won't. I've procured everything from the remains of this city. You might be lucky to find a can a day." He looked to the sky. "It won't matter anyway, because they'll be coming soon. Come with me or don't, but I'm leaving." Panic spread over his face.

"Maybe we should go with him," Poly suggested. "Sharati did tell us to not trust the sky. We could use the supplies as well."

"Fine. But if he gets all Ferrell on us, I'm shooting him," Lucas said.

They followed the man down the street and then over several piles of rubble before getting to an exceptionally large pile that seemed to surround a cave in the ground.

"What's your name?" Joey called after the man.

"Hector, but please hurry." Hector jumped down from a large concrete block to a tiled floor.

Joey gazed down at the tile, maybe a public bathroom at one point. "I'll go first. Get my back, Lucas."

"You know it."

Joey hopped down and landed on the white tile.

Hector fidgeted and kept looking to the sky. "Please, we must hurry."

Behind Hector, Joey saw a long hallway. "What is this place?"

"A mall."

The rest of Joey's group got down into the bathroom and Hector rushed down the hall. "We have to get to the vault or they'll find us."

"Who?" Poly asked.

Hector looked as if she had asked the stupidest question ever, but ignored it as he jogged down the hall and pushed open a door leading into the mall. The ceiling had mostly collapsed and rays of sunlight found their way between the cracks, shining enough light to see. Jogging down the mall, they passed several stores. Joey wondered if they had a Jamba Juice or even a functioning drinking fountain.

The mall courtyard came to an abrupt stop as the rubble piled up so high it made for a natural barrier. Hector climbed over a few rocks and jumped down onto an old escalator. He trotted down the stairs. "Come on," he called.

"Keep your weapons out," Joey whispered to his group.

Evelyn giggled as Edith passed her down to Poly over the rocks. Joey stayed on the stairs and waited for his group to get over the small obstacles.

Down the stairs, the mall got much darker and smaller as much of the building had collapsed and buried most of the first floor.

"Right over here," Hector said, pointing at a door at the end of the mall. He opened the door and Joey held his guns out, hoping his hands could still perform their magic, if needed.

Past the door, it looked much like the first hall they entered.

"Sharati is still out there," Poly said. "Say what you will, but she's helped us in the past."

"She's also tried to kill us twice." Joey held up two fingers. They ran down the hall and into a security room. A bed lay in one corner and the long dead screens stared back at them in their blackness.

"Something about this room, I think it's lined, but they can't seem to find me in here," Hector said lighting his candle. "Sorry for the mess. I didn't think I'd see another human again." He laughed. "I thought I was the last person on the entire planet."

"What happened here?" Julie asked, switching her attention from her Panavice to Hector.

"Is that a tablet?"

"Yeah, sort of."

"When I was just a niño, my mother and I would watch movies on something just like that. Before . . ." He looked at the ceiling.

Joey pegged his age at forty-five, but the gray dirt covered much of his face and clothes, so he could have gone a decade either way.

"You said you had some canned food, and maybe some water?" Lucas asked, as he adjusted Prudence.

"I have a few but to give them away would certainly mean my death. I never knew there were so many people left in the world." He stared at Poly and then to Julie. "And you have a baby and another one on the way. Wherever you are must be better than here. You have to take me with you. I will bring along the food and I can show you the water, but I want to go."

A loud pulse resonated through the building. Joey spread out his hands for balance and looked around as dust sprinkled down from the ceiling. "Earthquake?" he asked.

"It's here, stay still." Hector moved to the back wall and looked at the floor.

"What are you doing?" Joey asked as another pulse of sound blasted through the building. It sounded closer this time.

Hector opened his eyes, confused. "They're coming."

"Who?"

"Who are you?" Hector asked. When he didn't get an answer, he huffed. "Get against a wall and clear your mind. They can sense thoughts."

"I'm picking up something very powerful and it's moving toward us," Julie said.

"You guys need to get back and stay still." Hector shot a worried look at Edith and Evelyn. "I'm sorry, I can't help you."

He leaned against the wall and stared at the floor. A glazed look spread over his eyes.

"Hector," Joey called. "Hector?" He snapped his fingers and waved his hand in front of his face.

The loud pulse sounded again. This time, Joey felt it going through his body and the mall shook, stirring up clouds of dust. "Let's do what he says," Joey said. "Get against the walls and clear your thoughts."

They all picked a spot and leaned against it. Joey took deep breaths and tried to think of nothing while keeping his gun pointed at Hector.

Evelyn stared at the ceiling and then reached up to Edith's face, rubbing her cheek and making a noise with her mouth *Evelyn.* How could they expect a baby to clear her thoughts? Joey winced with each noise she made and gripped his gun. Another pulse shuddered through them and he tried his best not to think of his daughter and the danger coming. He closed his eyes and tried to send thoughts to Evelyn, to silence herself.

She went quiet and Joey opened his eyes. He realized the joy he felt and the wonder if she was indeed hearing his thoughts. He grimaced and realized his own thoughts were betraying them all. He stilled himself against the wall once again.

The pulse blasted, much closer this time.

"It's too late," Hector mumbled. "It's the baby."

"Hector, you've got to tell us what's going on. We're not from here," Julie said.

Another pulse blasted through the mall. Joey and the others cringed and Evelyn cried out. The sound of Evelyn crying shook him more than the sound coming from directly above them now. She never cried.

"What do we do, Hector?" Julie asked.

"We die." He leaned against the wall and took over his blank stare at the floor.

Joey rushed to the door and looked out into the mall. Dust stirred around and bits of concrete tumbled down a wall. Dust particle swirled around the beams of light shining through the sliver in the open roof. He searched the sky for what could possibly be making the humming sound. The ships from Vanar made a similar sound. But the sky held nothing. He looked back over his shoulder. Poly stood right behind him.

"What do you think it is?" she asked.

"I don't know. Julie?"

"It's something flying above. Its energy output is beyond anything I've ever seen. This isn't anything Marcus has ever invented."

"What does it do?"

"From what Hector said, it must read our thoughts and want to kill us."

Joey pulled out his gun and stepped onto the tiled floors of the mall. Small pieces of concrete crunched under his feet as he stepped near a high-end woman's boutique store. "Edith, stay by the door with Evelyn," he instructed, before returning to look at the gaps in the ceiling.

Something black moved over one of the columns of light, casting a temporary shadow.

"You see that?" Lucas asked.

"Yeah. Julie, can you hack it?" Joey asked.

"Been trying to, but its software isn't anything like I've ever seen. It's more organic than mechanical. It keeps changing on me."

"Lucas, I want you to—" The mall shook. Joey spread out, trying to balance himself. This wasn't the pulse sound this time, it felt as if the ground under his feet was lifting.

"There's a huge power surge coming from it. An impossible amount," Julie screeched over the growing rumbling sound.

Sections of the roof peeled back, creating a gaping hole. The pieces of roof flew off into the sky and disappeared. More rubble lifted, making its way to the top of the mall like someone had put the collapse in reverse. A small piece flew by Joey's head and shot out through the hole in the ceiling. The smaller bits around his feet rumbled on the ground and sprung out towards the hole in the ceiling. Larger chunks near the top lifted up and were carried off into the sky.

"We need to get out of here immediately," Julie said staring at her Panavice.

The smaller pieces began to pelt off Joey's body and he glanced back at Edith. She wrapped herself around Evelyn, protecting her from the debris. The sound of it all grew in volume and near the top, large chunks flew up into the sky as if a large vacuum had been turned on and was sucking out everything, yet the air felt still. A large portion of the roof tore off and revealed the object in the sky, not more than fifty feet above the mall. A black cube, maybe the size of a garbage truck, floated above and all the debris flew to it.

Edith screamed and Joey looked to her. Her arms were extended and Evelyn sat at the end of them. "Help me," Edith pleaded, yet she could barely be heard over the cacophony of sounds. Joey rushed to her and pushed Evelyn back into her arms. He hugged them both, holding Evelyn to Edith's chest as large bits pelted them. His foot began sliding on the tiled floor, pulling him closer to the rubble being lifted into the sky. Poly ran over and grabbed Joey's hand.

"Do something," Joey yelled struggling to keep hold of Edith and Evelyn. He felt the tug on his body growing with each second and the pieces or debris around them grew in size. Soon, they would be dead from contact of whatever that thing in the sky was.

Julie laid on the floor, pinning her Panavice to the ground. "I'll send every nasty worm, virus, bot, and crusher I've got. It might buy us a few seconds." She raised her finger and pushed the screen. The vacuum stopped and all the floating pieces crashed to the ground and around them. Joey held onto Evelyn and hoped to take the blow of any falling debris. One last piece of concrete tumbled down and then silence. His heavy breathing seemed loud and he let go of Edith and Evelyn.

"Get out of here," Hector said, making a dash into the hall.

Joey pushed Edith and Poly after him. Julie and Lucas were already far ahead. At the end, they climbed over the rubble and straight out the hole in the roof. Outside the mall, they looked at the black cube floating just over them.

"What the hell is that?" Lucas asked.

"Come on, I know of another place," Hector grimaced and ran down the backside of the rubble next to the mall.

Joey took Edith's hand and helped her work her way down the rubble pile, not wasting a moment looking at the black object in the sky.

The humming sound reignited. Slow at first, but growing with each passing moment.

"*Ay dios mio*," Hector said and ran down to the parking lot.

Joey trampled down the rubble, making sure Edith made it down safely.

Hector stood, staring at the ground, shaking his head. "Clear your thoughts. It's our only chance."

"If you knew how much explosive I have on these tips, you wouldn't be saying that," Lucas said, pulling three arrows out and pointing his bow at the cube.

"It's powering up," Julie called out.

"I'll try and draw it away, you get up high enough so you can hit the freaking thing," Joey said.

Lucas nodded and climbed up a pile of concrete, finding a solid place to stand.

The cube moved. It sent out a sound pulse and Joey felt it move through him. It sent painful waves into his ears and throughout his body.

Evelyn cried again.

"Over here!" Joey screamed as he ran away from the group, waving his gun in the air. He fired several shots at the cube but it didn't react. It maintained its course to his friends, his wife and daughter.

The rubble below the cube moved, and soon pieces were flying into the air and landing on parts of the city behind it like a snow blower.

Joey gave up on keeping the thing distracted and ran back to the group, firing into the cube. Sparks trailed off when he made contact.

"I got this," Lucas said, pulling his arrow back.

They watched as it trailed across the sky and made impact. The explosion struck the flying object and it veered off momentarily. A small chunk of the cube fell to the rubble below.

"*No*," Edith called out. "Not the Queen!" She ducked down, trying to hold onto Evelyn.

Joey felt the tug as well, and it gained in strength with each passing second. "Hit it again, Lucas!" he yelled above the sounds.

Lucas dove to the ground, grasping for a hand hold. "I can't, it's pulling me."

Joey grasped Evelyn with Poly and Edith and they formed a tight circle, holding her in place, but Joey felt her body moving between them.

"It's going to crush her!" Poly yelled.

The pulling got worse as Joey had trouble keeping both his feet on the ground. Hector sat, unfazed, looking at the ground with his blank stare. "It's locked in on our thoughts. We have to blank out!"

"It's taking our baby!" Poly screamed over the noise.

Joey knew, no matter what, he couldn't do what Hector was doing. He couldn't do anything else but put all his thoughts into saving his daughter.

The tug on Evelyn intensified and was more than any of them could bear. Joey felt his daughter's body slipping from his grip and his fear reached new heights as she started to slip away. Poly and Edith jumped to grab at Evelyn, but Joey had the last fingers on her. He held tight to her onesie, but the bottom button unhooked and his fingers lost purchase. She floated in the sky above them.

Evelyn cried out and turned to the machine.

"No, you can't have her," Edith yelled at the cube as she ran toward Lucas. She jumped up next to him and pulled the two arrows from his hands and ran up the rubble pile, making great leaps as the cube pulled her along. It had her. She floated toward in the air with the arrow extending out.

"Edith has the bombs," Lucas cried out while doing a handstand and hanging onto the edge of the concrete.

Joey held Poly as they slid along the ground toward the cube. Soon it would have them all, unless Edith was able to pull off a miracle. She threw the arrows out at the same moment a door on the cube opened and swallowed her up. A section of the cube broke off and shot off into the sky, toward the black building.

Evelyn floated far ahead of Joey. "No," Joey said as he reached for her with one hand. He felt his and Poly's body lift off the ground and pieces of concrete pelted his body as he floated. Lucas floated next to him and he looked back. Julie was much further away and had her face in her Panavice.

He hoped she could find another way to stop it. Joey thrust forward, trying to get closer to Evelyn.

"Get her, Joey. Use your power. *Do something!*" Poly screeched.

Joey wanted to save her, but he also didn't want to go into slow motion and watch the last agonizing seconds before his baby girl was sucked into the machine. He cursed the world and all the things that led him to this moment. It already had Edith and soon it'd have them all.

CHAPTER 11

"ALICE, OR SHOULD I CALL you Renee?" Gladius asked.

"Either is accurate," Alice replied. "What are your objectives?"

"We came to kill Marcus. Do you know where he is?"

"Yes."

"Will you tell us?"

"No."

Gladius sneered at the ceiling and searched for the speakers. She wanted to smash them in. "You told her." She pointed at Gingy.

"No, I swear," Gingy said and backed up against the wall holding her hands up.

Gladius half wanted to believe her. She didn't really think they could fool an AI like Alice anyways. She must have sensed the body heat, the extra noise, or the peculiarities of Gingy's actions. "So now what?" Gladius addressed Alice.

"We wait for Marcus to respond."

"He said to let us go," Minter chimed in.

"Negative," Alice said. "He has responded and has one question. Is Julie with you?"

Gladius looked to Hank who shrugged. "Yeah, she's here."

"Your voice patterns are consistent with lying. You are not of any use for Marcus and he has given me permission to end you."

"End us?" Hank asked, and the lights turned off.

Blackness filled the room and Gladius searched her pocket and pulled out the Panavice. She lit the room and saw Hank and Minter standing near the door.

"You hear that?" Minter asked.

"What?" Hank said.

"The air, it turned off as well." He looked at the ceiling and around the room. "It's only a matter of time now."

"Emmett!" Gingy cried out, trying to open the machine. "He's still in there."

Gladius hadn't realized Alice had probably just killed Emmett as well. *Whatever.* The guy had it coming to him in so many ways.

"Help me." Gingy pushed on the door, but it wouldn't open.

Hank rushed to her side and pushed the door until the lock broke and the door flung open. Emmett lay on the table and Gladius hesitated before shining her light on him. Blood smeared over much of his leg but no new blood was coming out of the hole in his thigh.

"He's breathing," Gingy said.

"Yeah, maybe we . . ." Hank started to say, but Emmett's lightning quick hand grasped his neck. Hank choked and pulled on Emmett's hand.

Gladius cleared the distance between them and had a knife in her hand, but Hank had it under control as he pushed Emmett's arm back down. Then Emmett went limp as he slipped back into unconsciousness.

"You're hurting him," Gingy said and punched at Hank.

Gladius felt her blood raging as she saw her hitting her man. She jumped past Hank and punched Gingy in the throat. Her stunned face tried to understand what happened as she fell to the floor, gasping for air.

"Gladius, did you really need to hit her? She wasn't hurting me."

She ignored Hank. He didn't understand the simple fact that some people just needed to be hit sometimes. Standing over Gingy, she raised her hand. Gingy cowered and covered her head. "Don't you ever touch him again."

Gingy coughed and nodded.

"Now, let's tie up Emmett before his sorry ass wakes up again." Gladius sighed, looking at Emmett's stupid chest moving up and down. With each breath, he took another breath from her and Hank. She ran some quick numbers in her head, thinking of the cubic footage they had and the average person's oxygen usage. If they got rid of Emmett and Gingy, it'd add days, easily. One glance at Hank's sympathetic face and she knew he wouldn't go for it.

Minter gathered some cord as Hank carried Emmett to a chair and they bound him to it. Gladius checked the knots and when she was satisfied, looked to Gingy. "You." Gingy whimpered. "There has to be another way out."

"There's only the one door you came in."

"No way. Marcus would have a back door somewhere in this place." Gladius pictured the whole bunker in her mind and thought of the places she'd use for a hidden escape. He would've been stupid to let Alice in on all his escape routes, and he surely wasn't dumb. As much as Marcus hated AI, he would never stay in a place where something or someone controlled his only exit. "Think, Gingy, where have you seen Marcus enter and exit?"

She looked at the floor, tears staining her ruddy cheeks. "I've only seen Marcus a couple times. He doesn't like to be bothered."

Gladius laughed. "You must have noticed his comings and goings."

She shook her head.

Gladius looked to Emmett and thought about shaking him awake to get answers, but she knew of his reputation. Getting information from him would be as likely as dogs flying. "You know you're going to die in here the same as us, right?"

Gingy looked up and nodded. "I don't know a way out. If I did, I'd tell you and get the hell out of here."

"In Marcus's room, I think I saw something," Hank said.

"Show the way."

"What about Emmett?" Hank pointed to the man strapped to the machine and a conduit running into the floor.

"He's not going anywhere," Gladius said. "Now show me what you saw in Marcus's room."

Gingy shook her head. "We're not allowed in there."

"Come on, you're coming with us." Gladius followed behind Gingy as they made their way down the hall and into Marcus's room.

"There's nothing in here," Gingy said.

"Then you won't care if we look around."

Gingy's jaw clenched. Hank pushed on a dresser and slid it a few feet. There was nothing behind it but a color of paint slightly different than the rest of the room.

"Told you," Gingy said with more sass in her tone.

"Shut it. Check the wall next to his bed." Gladius really wanted to find something now just to shove it in the brat's face.

"Nothing," Hank said and moved to the bed.

"He doesn't like people touching his bed."

Hank lifted the mattress and revealed a sheet of plywood underneath. But that wasn't what caught Gladius's attention.

"What do we have here?" she asked, pointing to a small electrical panel at the far back edge.

Minter groaned and fell to the floor. Gladius jumped back, and turned in his direction, holding her Panavice up to light the area. He lay on the ground, not moving.

Gladius raised the light to Gingy's fiery face. She raised her fists and glared at Gladius not more than a few feet away. "You were conning me the whole time?"

"I cannot allow you to leave."

Gladius saw Minter moving from the corner of her eye. Good, he wasn't dead, but how did this little woman take out such a man like Minter? "I guess we found that back door. Now, why don't you just turn around and head down the hall. We'll be gone and you can go back to your little terrible life in this hole."

Gingy took a quick step forward and kicked Gladius in the stomach. Gladius cried out from the shock of her speed and the pain radiating through her midsection. She hunched down to the ground, it was the only thing her body would allow. Looking up, Gingy jumped and her foot came down near her face. Gladius took out her knife and stabbed her in the bottom of her foot. The knife stuck in place, hopefully into bone. Gingy cried out and moved back, hopping on one foot.

Hank moved toward them.

Gladius got to her feet in one jump and held her hand up. "No. She's mine."

Gingy pulled the knife from her foot and staggered in pain. "Okay, I'll give you the code for the bed, as long as you as don't kill me," she pleaded.

Gladius saw red, getting up to attack the bitch. Gingy favored one foot but still managed to hold Gladius's knife out and take a defensive stance, awaiting her move.

Knowing her enemy's foot was injured and was holding the knife on the wrong side, Gladius kicked Gingy's leg and sent her back to the floor.

Minter got to his feet, rubbing his head. He stood behind Gingy as she squirmed away to a corner of the room. "We should kill her."

"What?" Hank looked shocked.

"She is dangerous," Minter said, pointing his gun at her. "Look at how well she lied to us about her situation. A person like this shouldn't be allowed to roam free. It's only a matter of time before she's trouble for us once again. Look at Emmett! We can end it now before it ever starts."

"No, we aren't like that," Hank said.

"Thank you," Gingy said. "I swear I won't be any trouble."

Minter fired a shot, striking Gingy in the head. Her body slumped to the ground and blood filled the exit wound, spreading onto the carpet below.

"What did you do?" Hank asked. "We don't just kill people, Minter!"

"She would have killed us the first chance she got," Minter said. "Now, please tell me you can open that bed?"

Gladius spent a while longer, staring at Minter. It wasn't as if she wasn't about to kill Gingy herself, but the man did it without a second thought. He was exactly as she thought he was, cold blooded.

Shaking her head clear, she jumped into action. "Julie gave me a few code breakers." She scanned the pages on the Panavice and found the digital lock. Then she sent the code breakers to work.

The bed clicked. "Ha! Got it." Ignoring Hank's look of shock as he stared at the dead body on the ground, Gladius stuffed her Panavice in her pocket and pulled the handle on the bed. The bed lifted up and lights lit the way down a staircase, illuminating a man wearing a black suit.

"You guys didn't waste any time, did you? Good for you. And Alice must be lying . . . she's saying you killed Gingy?"

Gladius didn't know what to say. The man standing in front of her shook her to the core. She fumbled with her knife and got it in her hands.

"Marcus?" Hank said, stepping next to Gladius to look down the stairs.

CHAPTER 12

JOEY FELT PARALYZED, LIVING A nightmare in real time as Evelyn floated toward the cube. He didn't even have time to mourn Edith, as he watched his daughter look back over her shoulder and close her eyes tight, as if preparing for something.

The cube exploded and mushroomed out before falling into the mall below.

Poly yelped as they fell. It wasn't that far, but landing on a hill of rubble made the impact more painful than necessary.

"Evelyn!" Joey screamed as he saw her plummeting to a nasty looking pile of debris, a chill running down his spine.

A silver streak rushed across the landscape and jumped into the air, catching Evelyn and landing safely on top of the rubble.

"Sharati," Poly said.

Joey relaxed, letting the feeling of going slow leave his body. All he wanted to do was get to his daughter, to hold her. He scrambled over the rubble and got to her just ahead of Poly.

He pulled Evelyn from Sharati and pressed her against his chest. She was okay.

"You are all stupid," Sharati said. "I told you to stay away from the green light."

"You saved her," Poly said holding a knife in her hand.

Sharati shifted her right foot back and put a hand on her dagger. "She is special, no?"

"Yes," Joey said at the same time as Poly said, "No."

They looked at each other and then Poly touched Evelyn on the back of her head. Evelyn kept her attention on Sharati. "She's special to us is what Joey meant."

"Yeah, our little girl."

Hector stuttered out in shock, "Wh—what is that?" He pointed at Sharati. "Are you from the sky?"

"She's not from here, pal." Lucas said dusting himself off. "You okay, Julie?"

"I think so." She rubbed her stomach.

"Who are you people?" Hector asked.

"We're from Preston. North of here," Julie said and looked up to Lucas. "We need to get moving. I'm picking up two faint signals. I bet you it's those two birds."

"You destroyed it?" Hector said in amazement, looking at the destroyed cube.

"Edith?" Evelyn said, pointing at the pile with tendrils of smoke rising from the top.

Joey then realized how well Evelyn said her name, and he felt her pain. His daughter had just lost a great friend. They all had. He hated how Eve, not even one-year old, already had a death to deal with.

"She saved us," Poly said, tears dripping.

Joey turned around and walked to the bottom of the rubble and onto the parking lot to find Lucas and Julie consoling each other. Poly walked up behind him and hugged him, he felt her body quiver against his, but he kept his attention on Evelyn. She looked up at him and he searched for the sorrow, the pain, yet she looked normal—a sweet mixture of curiosity and joy. It seemed ridiculous to expect a seven-month-old to understand death but Joey had.

"She's gone, Evelyn."

Evelyn made eye contact with him. Some of the joy left her face, but the curiosity held.

"No," Evelyn said, again clearer than she'd ever spoken.

"She's right, they don't kill you, they take you. They ship your body to their tower," Hector said still giving strange looks to Sharati.

Joey turned toward the large building he saw a piece of the cube flying toward. Did that piece hold Edith?

"She's long gone," Hector said.

"Okay, so we stick to the plan," Julie said.

"What plan?" Poly asked. "We don't even know where we are or what's happening in this world and we just lost Edith to a floating cube that tried to suck us up like the Air Bud of Roomba's."

Julie looked at her Panavice. "Moments before the explosion, a section was expelled from the cube, heading toward that building. My guess is she was on it."

"I saw it as well," Joey said.

Poly looked hopeful. "What do they do with them?" she asked, stepping close to Hector.

"I don't know, I swear, but no one ever comes back."

Poly sighed and gritted her teeth. "Who did this to this

planet? What happened?"

Hector looked confused and shook his head in small motions. "They came and started taking us, destroying large swathes of land, taking everything. Then they were gone, but they left their snatchers and watchers, looking for the last few resources."

Julie pointed to the black and green building sticking out of the rubble like a reminder of what might have been. "She's in there."

"You can't go there. They have defense set up all around it. We get too close and *bam*, gone."

"People run it?" Julie asked.

"No, just the machines."

"Machines I can control, maybe. I'll know if we get close." She looked confident.

Joey looked to Poly. She had the look of we-better-go-get-her and that is exactly the way Joey felt. Edith had become a second mom to Evelyn and a great part of the family since the day Evelyn was born.

"We should find a way in," Joey said.

"Yeah," Lucas agreed. "Just get me close and either Julie will shut them down or I can stuff another arrow into their holes. I mean, did you guys see the explosion the arrows made? Can we watch the video again, Julie? In slow motion this time?"

Julie rolled her eyes and turned toward the building. "We could be there in thirty minutes."

"We shouldn't go there. It's just death. No one returns. My parents . . ." Hector turned and looked at the tower.

"If we get there and we can't get in, we leave," Julie said. "But we need your help. You know the route there. Will you help us?"

Hector kicked the ground and rubbed the stubble on his face. "Yes. But you have to take me with you. Wherever it is you are going."

They nodded in agreement.

"I'll keep ahead of you all and make sure there are no surprises," Sharati said. She ran up the rubble pile and disappeared down the backside.

Walking behind Hector, Joey kept an eye on the sky, searching for metal birds or a giant cube trying to suck them to oblivion. His finger tapped his gun.

"This place is a bigger dump than Ryjack," Lucas said. "Why do you think these machines are attacking people?"

"They must be using us for something," Hector said. "When I was just a boy, no taller than my dad's hip, they came. A woman, who I thought was pretty at the time, announced our end on every TV, radio, and internet page. She told us they had great need of us, and that we should know we were but a moment in time; but not to worry because they would put us to use. My dad mumbled that statement for a long time after mom died. He was never the same."

"We're so sorry, Hector," Poly said.

Joey felt bad for him and wondered about this woman taking over the planet with such ease. Did this invasion come through the stones? It must have. They sent waves of these things through the stones to strip this world and leave little behind. But why? Was she the one who created stones?

They passed a fire station, a red fire emblem sat as the last reminder of the station and the color stood out from the rest of the grays and browns.

"What happened to the cars?"

"El Cubo's, as you call them, there were many more in the

beginning. They pulled the cars away, stripping them to nothingness in mid-air, taking the people from them as they did. The buildings were much the same, stripped out in the search for people. Very few things survived those first few weeks."

"No one fought back?" Lucas asked.

"We did, they all did. But it didn't amount to anything."

Joey shook his head and kept glancing at the sky. As if he didn't have enough to think about, he now had something else to add to the list. With an infinity of earths out there, what were the chances his would get picked by this purge woman?

As they approached the tower, Hector stopped. A green line had been painted in the middle of the street. Pits and chunks littered the road past the line.

"We cannot pass," Hector said firmly.

Sharati stood at the top of what looked like a bookstore. A corner of it hadn't collapsed and through the cracks, piles of books held up like last vestiges of the written world. What treasures those books could hold if this world ever got back on its feet. Knowledge of how to grow crops, or turn the electricity on, or recipes for concrete and steel . . . in a world where the digital had disappeared, books would be as valuable as gold.

Lucas got close to the books and laughed. "Porn! I can see different positions in each page." He reached in to grab one.

"Lucas, leave it," Julie said.

"These could have undiscovered truths. How dare we disregard another culture's gift to the world? Julie, you of all people should be supportive of any and all knowledge."

Julie sighed as she ran her fingers around her Panavice glancing from the tower to the green line. "Their programs here are much less sophisticated. This isn't going to be a problem."

She worked in silence for a couple of minutes.

Joey used the time to inspect Evelyn in Poly's arms. He hated bringing her around the different worlds. He wished he could have stuffed her away somewhere safe and protect her. But unfortunately he knew there were greater goals than just saving his daughter from Marcus. He needed to end it all, end his plans for Earth. His heart pounded thinking about the next stages of the plan and what they involved, what he would potentially have to give up.

No. It wouldn't come to that. He'd do what it took to make sure Marcus would die at the end of his gun or with his own hands if need be. One way or another, he didn't want phase five of the plan to ever happen.

"Done," Julie said.

"How do you know?" Hector asked, taking a step back from the line and looking at the tower. "You cross that line and you'll be shot dead."

"We cross the line. It's the only way to know for sure," Julie said and took a step forward.

"No," Lucas said.

But Julie had already crossed over the green line, standing on divots of asphalt and glaring at the tower to defy her hacking skills. "See?" She turned around. "All good."

Lucas seemed skeptical and walked past the green line to join his wife.

Hector crossed last and about a hundred feet toward the building he seemed more confident in the idea. "How did you do that?" he asked.

"I turned off the sensors." Julie strutted toward the building.

Joey jogged ahead, keeping his gun hand outstretched. He searched for a front door in all the glass on the first floor and spotted a handle. Getting close to the door, he slowed down and waved for them to stop while he checked it out.

The sun reflected off the green tinted glass and he couldn't make out anything behind the door. He took a deep breath and pulled on the handle. With nothing on the other side of the door, he flung it open and took a quick step into a lobby. A vacant desk and blank concrete walls stared back at him, as if trying to tell him, *Hey, this is just a regular building, come on in.* Another metal door stood at the far end of the lobby and had a staircase drawn on it.

Joey went back to the front door and waved his group to come in. "You narrow down where she could be?" he asked Julie as they joined him inside.

She nodded her head. "The tracker is still working. Floor sixteen. It appears to be the only floor with activity."

"Sixteen flights, you going to be okay?"

"Yeah, I'll be fine." She put her hand on her stomach.

Joey knew she'd never complain, but he saw the strain in her face when they pushed too far for too long. He'd have to watch her and keep an even pace. "Lucas, watch our backs."

"Gotcha."

Joey opened the staircase door and flashbacks of the casino hotel on Ryjack shot to him. He had been running across a mall to get to that staircase. He gazed at Poly while putting his foot on the bottom step, thinking of the dress she wore that day. He never saw her in it again and hadn't had the nerve to ask her about it. She hated everything to do with Ryjack. How could he blame her?

He counted the unmarked doors as they passed each one, taking it at a slow pace and even then, he saw the strain on Julie's face. Lucas seemed oblivious to it and walked mostly backward up the stairs, pointing his arrow at each door as they passed. Joey hoped he didn't have an explosive tip attached; they'd all be dead if one of those went off in a confined space.

"Sixteenth floor." Joey pointed at the door.

Julie spent some time getting her Panavice out and sliding her finger across the screen. "She's on this floor." She grimaced and held her stomach.

Joey nudged the door open with his foot, while keeping his gun raised. The next hallway looked much like the lobby. The difference on this floor, he heard a humming sound of power.

Stepping into the main passage way, he looked right and left. There were double doors at the end on the right, and a series of openings on the left, as if the doors had been taken off the walls.

He backpedaled away from the double doors and toward the first opening. Lucas had his back and walked next to him. One look and Joey conveyed the danger he felt to Lucas who only nodded, gripping Prudence.

Joey pointed at the opening and put his back against the wall. He gave Lucas a quick glance and then spun around into the room, holding his gun out in front of him. He lowered his gun and took in the blank room with a square bed on the floor. A pipe protruded out of the wall near where a person's head might have been. Joey backed out of the room and went to the next.

Same thing.

"She's here, maybe we can just call her name?" Lucas whispered.

"Better not, there's only a half dozen left to look in anyways."

Lucas shrugged and gripped his bow again, arrow cocked.

Joey did the same motion for the next room. A man lay on

the bed in this one and Joey kept his gun trained on the elder. His white beard ran down over his filthy shirt. Body odor emanated from the room and into the hall, killing the sterile smell of the rest of the floor. Joey cursed himself for not smelling the man before leaping in. At least he seemed docile, or maybe even asleep?

"Hey," Joey whispered, but the man didn't respond.

A clunking sound came from the wall, rattling down a metal pipe. Something exited the pipe behind the old man and struck him in the head. Joey didn't get a good look at what came out. With fear building, he pointed the gun at the man.

"Wake up and leave the room." A soothing voice called out over some unseen speaker.

The man sat up and got to his feet.

"Hey, mister," Joey said.

"*Señor?*" Lucas tried Spanish and didn't get any reaction.

Walking toward Joey, the old man didn't respond to the people or weapons pointed in his direction. Stopping just outside the door, he stood in wait.

"Go to the end of the hall, through the double doors." The smooth voice called out commands once again.

The man walked down the hall to the double doors. He pushed against them, without slowing down, and they swung in and closed behind him.

Joey and Lucas followed behind the guy and told the rest of the group to stay behind as they checked it out. Lucas took the right side and in one motion they opened the doors. In the next room stood a large silver ball, reaching from floor to ceiling. The top half opened and folded into the bottom half, as the bearded man approached it.

"Step into the egg and sit in the chair," the voice said.

"Don't do it," Lucas called out.

The man took a big step over the lower half of the egg and sat in the chair. Straps went over his hands and the egg closed down around him.

"This can't be good," Lucas remarked.

Another clunking sound came from the egg. Joey squinted as he heard the man screaming. It sounded faint, blocked by the metallic eggshell, but Joey knew it was coming from the man and they were doing something terrible to him in there. "We've got to help him!"

He ran to the egg and gripped the edges where the two sections met. Pulling as hard as he could, it wouldn't move. He kicked at the bottom and punched the top.

The man kept screaming.

He pulled his gun, momentarily thinking of shooting it open.

"Don't, that'll kill him or ricochet and kill us," Lucas said.

The screaming stopped and Joey lowered his gun. His heart pounded in his chest. The egg opened and he winced, expecting to see gruesome remains of the man. But the chair was empty. It felt like magic. Where could he have gone?

Another clunking sound drew Joey's attention to the floor. Whatever it was, it rattled down the pipe and then the sound was gone.

"So freaking weird," Lucas said.

Joey turned to Poly, who was holding Evelyn and standing in the doorway.

"You hear that?" Hector said, looking back down the hall.

Joey did, the soothing voice had just told someone to get up. He ran down the hall and came face to face with Edith. She had the same blankness as the man.

"Go to the end of the hall, through the double doors."

Edith moved toward the doors, but Joey grabbed her. "You can't go down there. I won't let you."

She pushed against him.

"Lucas, help me," Joey said.

Lucas pushed against Edith with Joey, but she shoved past them both and kept walking.

"She must work out," Lucas mumbled.

"Edith, stop!" Poly yelled.

"She's under their spell. I've seen it once before. They can control us somehow," Hector said.

Edith walked up to Poly and Evelyn.

"Edith," Evelyn said and held out her arm. Her baby hand grazed Edith. "No."

Edith stopped. She looked at Evelyn and then back to Joey and Lucas. "What happened?" she asked. "Where am I?"

"You blew up that cube and it shot you off to a tower," Lucas said. "We're here to rescue you."

"I remember throwing the arrows in the last second before the cube pulled me in. I felt the explosion and something in the cube touched my arm. The next thing I remember is your voice." She touched Evelyn's hand. "I heard you, in my head. You pulled me from the dream." Edith looked confused.

Hector raised an eyebrow and stared at Evelyn. "What are you people?"

Everyone ignored his question as Evelyn giggled and patted Edith on the arm. "Edith."

"Yes." Edith picked her up from Poly. "I'm your Edith and I'll never leave you again. You are my little queen, yes you are. Who saved me? You did."

"I think I found a way off this planet," Julie blurted, looking at her Panavice.

"Off this planet? Are you guys from the stars?" Hector asked.

Joey sighed and put a hand up to stop Hector's line of questioning, urging Julie to continue.

"The cube is a transport. They take people from here and transport them to a master stone in the north. I found a way for us to hitch a ride." She smiled and showed them the screen.

"Oh, you are my little queen," Lucas said to Julie. "Who's going to save us? You are. Yes you are." He pet her hair and she swatted him away.

"It's the next floor up," Julie said, ignoring Lucas.

Joey went to the staircase and opened the door.

"The birds are back," Sharati said running up the last few steps to floor sixteen. "You are foolish for going into one of these reclamation centers."

"Reclamation?"

"That's what Simon called them."

Joey choked down the shock of hearing she'd worked with Simon. "Come on, we think we found a way out of here." Joey bounded up the next flight of stairs. Sharati followed close behind him, keeping her hand on her dagger, bouncing her attention in all directions.

Joey pushed on the door marked *17*. The door flung open and the wind gusted down into the stairwell. The wind moved through the open walls. Only a few pillars broke up the empty floor. Several cubes sat on platforms marked with different colored lines running to them. Joey held out his gun, looking for anything moving as he moved further away from the stairwell. There were four cubes in total, but at least twenty empty platforms spread across in a grid pattern over the floor.

"We should take the red one," Lucas said, pointing at the black cube sitting on a red platform.

"It doesn't matter. Once we're in, I'll tell it to take us to the master stone," Julie said.

Sharati grunted and didn't look like she had any intention of boarding.

Hector stepped forward. "I can leave this place . . . go somewhere that doesn't have this?" He pointed at the cube.

Joey looked at Poly and Julie. They both gave him a nod. "We can get you off this planet. There is another one, I think it might be a fresh start for you. It doesn't have this."

Tears formed in Hector's eyes.

Julie walked up to the cube sitting on the red platform and punched into her Panavice. A door slid open. "Come on, we can all fit in." She stepped into the craft with Lucas running in behind her.

Joey and Poly stepped in behind Edith, Evelyn, and Hector. Julie leaned against the wall and made more room. Joey slid to the side and watched Sharati pace at the entrance.

"You coming?" he asked. With a small hesitation, she ran into the space left for her. "Get us out of here," Joey said.

The door closed and the cube hummed to life, lifting off the platform and out of the building.

"Oh, look," Julie said.

Joey turned around and faced the wall. The world below moved by, visible through small sections of what looked to be glass.

"Wow," Hector said. "There's the airport. I spent five years there."

Soon, they passed over a mountain range and many miles of desert. Another city passed by and Joey tried to find any signs of life, like in New Vegas, but this planet had been completely obliterated. He couldn't imagine something worse than Marcus and he wondered if he was somehow involved in this purge.

"Julie, can you show Hector a picture of Marcus?" Joey asked.

She shrugged and in a few seconds had a picture of Marcus on her screen. Hector leaned close and took in the image, shaking his head. Then she showed him a picture of Alice and again he didn't recognize her.

"Did the person on the message, the one who told this world they were gone, did she mention her name?" Joey asked.

"No, it was just the message. After that, everything went to hell."

Joey went back to the window and stared at the rubble city racing by. City after city they passed over looked the same. Some had the same tower and some didn't but they were all left to waste. This woman, the one on the message, stripped this world and probably moved onto the next. The number of planets is what ultimately made him feel better about Earth. What was the chance this woman would find his Earth out of all the other ones? He looked to his friends, each looking out a different window. Julie questioned Hector for a while longer, but it became evident he didn't have a clue to the bigger picture of what all this meant.

After another hour, the cube slowed and descended. They all grouped near the door and waited for it to touch the ground.

"I got it from here," Julie said.

The door opened and right in front of the cube sat a dome shape in the rubble surrounding the Alius stone. Joey took a deep breath and smiled. He wanted off Hector's planet and away from these cubes. He had enough on his plate to think about.

"Let's get the hell out of here," Lucas said and went to the stone. "Stage four?"

"Yes," Joey said. "Nothing's changed." He looked at the hills in the distance and thought about the city beyond the peaks. Nothing had changed, yet everything had changed.

One thing at a time.

"Stage four isn't what I'm worried about," Poly said.

Joey lowered his head. He didn't want to think about them failing at stage four. *No.* He shook the thought from his head. Stage four would work, he'd make sure Marcus was dead.

"Where are we going?" Hector said.

"Away from here. You can still stay if you'd prefer. I can send you back in the cube," Julie said.

"I have nothing here. Wherever we are going, it has to be better than here." He was quiet before glancing at Poly. "It's better than here, right?"

"Yes," she confirmed.

Hector crossed his arms and looked around the circle, keeping his attention on Lucas, watching his movement around the stone.

"I have a friend in LA, I'll give her a call and get you set up until you get on your feet," Gladius(?) said.

He bowed his head. "Thank you."

"As soon as we get to the master stone, I'm going back to my planet," Sharati said.

"Okay, then. Any other statements or can I get us out of here before the Rubik's Cube from Hell sucks us into nothingness?" Lucas said.

"Go." Joey moved next to Edith and Evelyn. Evelyn smiled and reached for him. He patted her head and ran his fingers down her cheek. Then he pulled out his gun and got ready for the unexpected.

"Here we go," Lucas said.

Joey mentally prepared himself before they landed in his most hated place on any planet. The stone hummed and the desert changed to the charred remains of Zach's house. His attention went directly to the spot where Samantha had died. He felt the tears building.

Poly touched his hand and rubbed his back.

"Lucas, Julie!" Rick ran over to them. "Something's gone terribly wrong at Marcus's."

CHAPTER 13

JOEY LAY ON A GRASSY bank overlooking a shanty house way outside LA. Samantha had given them the clue about this house just before she died. If she hadn't, Julie said she'd never have found it. Thanks to Samantha, they had gotten this far and Joey glanced to the sky to reflect on the amazing friend they once had.

"She loaded the program," Julie said.

"Great, we should execute it then," Poly said.

"We do that and we risk killing every person on the entire planet."

Poly huffed and went back to staring at the empty house.

"I'm going to try and get into the camera system without her feeling me poking around. It'll take a few minutes." Julie prodded her Panavice.

"We may not have long," Rick spoke up. "I've got a bad

feeling. They aren't responding to my radio calls, or cell calls. It's gone black in there."

"Not for long," Julie replied and Joey hovered over her shoulder. "Got it," she said.

An image of a hallway appeared on the screen. She swiped her finger and a black image appeared, static on the next one. "They've got to be down there." Julie swiped her finger again and a bedroom appeared. She gasped and covered her mouth.

Everyone gathered around the screen to get a better look at what elicited such a response. Joey pulled out his gun at the sight of Marcus with his friends and his dad, in the same room, not a hundred yards away.

"Don't do anything foolish," Poly said, putting a hand on his arm. She knew him well. "We can get down there before Marcus knows what hit him and end this all."

"And what if we don't?" Joey asked, moving close to Poly. "Can we really handle what comes next? Can we live with ourselves if we fail this stage? We all know the next one will be unbearable."

Poly looked hurt and misty eyed. "I'm ready to do whatever it takes to protect her, aren't you?"

Joey didn't need to answer and stared at the shack. The man who had caused all their pain, ruined numerous planets, had Earth by its collective throat, killed their parents, and wanted to take his daughter away, sat in the house in front of them. He gripped the hilt of his gun tight, and squeezed the grip.

Addressing Edith, he picked up Evelyn to give her a quick hug. "If we don't come out in fifteen minutes, get her out of here. Find Harris or Travis and just make sure to give her the life she deserves."

"As if she was my own."

Joey didn't know how to thank Edith enough, but he settled with a hug, whispering his thanks into her ear. It felt like a goodbye. He knew going against Marcus in any circumstance would be difficult, but now they were going into the lion's den.

Poly said her goodbyes and they each hugged Evelyn, kissing her and hugging her tiny body.

"We ready?" Joey asked Julie.

"Yes, the outside sensors are off," she replied.

They jogged down the bank and toward the house. Joey glanced back at Edith, barely visible at the top of the hill, Evelyn's smile beaming at them.

"We should take her," Poly said to him. "I can't stand leaving her out here."

"We all have a role, we have to stick with it. If stage five comes, we'll deal with it."

"If stage five comes, I'm killing you," Poly said.

They opened the door to the shack and saw the various bits of furniture tossed around the place as if someone had thrown a fit of rage. It gave Joey some joy to think Marcus had been living in such a hole for years.

"The stairs are over here," Julie said, walking and looking at her Panavice. A set of hidden stairs led down under the house.

They followed Julie down the stairs, until they reached a steel door standing open to a dark room beyond. The lights turned on and displayed the room with high-end furniture and decorations scattered around the wall space. It felt like a home. Not like his old sterile mansion on the cliffside. Joey held out his gun and entered the house, looking to Julie for guidance.

"The room is in the back." Julie pointed.

Joey rushed ahead and heard the footsteps behind him.

"Last room on the right," Julie whispered.

The door stood open and he spotted his dad, standing half in the door and half out. Minter glanced back at the group of people running toward him but didn't give notice and looked back into the room.

Joey slowed as he approached. Minter continued to ignore his presence and that was when he heard Marcus's voice.

"He's in the hall, they all are, aren't they?" Marcus said. "It's not like I can't hear a herd of footsteps."

Joey gritted his teeth and held both guns in his hands. He knew what he had to do, no matter the consequence. He couldn't let this get to stage five, it had to end now. He felt the chill going down the back of his neck and the sounds of the world fell to a low hum. He glanced back at Poly, she stared at him with her frozen expression of concern. She must have known what he was about to do.

Stepping past his dad, he made it into the bedroom. Hank and Gladius stood facing Marcus, Gladius had a dagger in her hand. Joey looked down at his two guns. They were filled especially for this moment, each made of a different material, each bullet built by hand. All it would take is one to make it through his shield.

His hand shook as he took aim. He didn't want to miss and stepped closer to Marcus, aiming for his head.

A bolt of lightning shot out of Marcus and struck Joey in the hands. He dropped both guns and fell back to the carpeted floor. Blood soaked into his shirt and the still eyes of a woman stared back at him. He knew her . . . Gingy, from Emmett's house. The world's sounds crashed around him as he looked into her vacant eyes.

"Joey!" Poly ran into the room and slid next to him. She didn't stop to comfort him but threw several knives at Marcus.

One of Lucas's arrows flew by. Joey struggled to get up, to do his part, but his body wouldn't respond.

Another arrow flew by and more knifes from Poly. The loud crack sound of Minter's gun filled the room. Sparks flew from Marcus as each item deflected off his shield. The gunfire stopped and Marcus stood with an arrow jutting out of his shoulder. He looked at it, confused, and then broke the arrow off in his chest.

He smiled, inspecting it. "Silk steel? Inventive," he said, pushing on his bleeding wound.

"Hank," Joey whispered, gesturing to his guns on the floor.

Marcus had a square gun out in an instant. "Uh-uh, big boy. Touch those and I'll put a projectile through her head." He motioned to Gladius and Hank backed away. "This is unbelievable!" He laughed. "You all have been chasing me for a long time, and here we stand."

Joey stared at the guns on the ground. He knew he had some silk steel bullets in there. He squeezed his eyes and tried to feel the tingling down his neck, but it wouldn't come.

"We will kill you," Poly said.

"I have no doubt you will try, but to kill me would be as good as killing this entire planet, and I think your little genius back there knows it." He pointed to Julie who stood behind Minter at the door. "You know what the stupid thing is?"

"Shut up!" Poly screamed and leaped for the guns on the floor.

In an instant, Marcus had a second gun in his hand and fired it, hitting Poly.

Joey screamed and grabbed her. The electrical charge went through him and he and Poly convulsed on the ground. The room went blurry and the yells from Hank and Lucas felt distant. When the shock stopped, he and Poly lay motionless on the carpeted floor.

They were losing and it killed Joey to admit it, but everything they planned on doing was unraveling. The most aggravating part was the killing blow was sitting in his gun, only a few feet away.

"Here's the stupid thing," Marcus said, agitated. "I haven't hurt any one of you or your families. Any harm done to you was the sole act of rogue agents. I had no idea what Isaac had done to your parents until after we found you. Then there was Simon, who was ordered not to kill anyone but took it on his own to kill Almadon. Or Max, he again stepped over the line and killed Compry and Nathen. Not to mention how Emmett decided not to finish our safe haven at the Ryjack bunker. Your children could have lived there in peace, but Emmett decided not to finish the base properly and nearly killed you all."

"And what about Samantha? You not only had her killed, you set it up for her lover to kill her. It's the sickest thing I've ever seen," Gladius said.

"It wasn't supposed to go down like that. If you hadn't killed Zach, I would have."

Joey would throw up if he had to keep listening to Marcus, but his hands had curled up and he couldn't even make his fingers straighten out. There would be no chance he could grab the gun and get a headshot.

"I'm not trying to win you over, but I want to tell you that there are other people in these worlds, people who see us and our planets as mere commodities to exploit. I've seen them."

Joey had seen one as well, but all that mattered at this point was getting his fingers straight. He could get to his gun but needed at least some dexterity to grasp the handle and sink a silk bullet into Marcus's head.

He tried to plunge into slow-mo again and the chills hit the back of his neck before it stopped. He choked and tried to gasp for breath as his whole body seized, pulling down from the top of his head, like a muscle spasm that wouldn't loosen. He stared at Marcus, unable to blink or move.

"And your daughter . . . I take it she's not here?"

"Go to Hell," Poly said.

"Thought not. Well, she is something very special, but I'm guessing you already know that. She is perfect in almost every way and you are being very cruel to her."

Joey made eye contact with Marcus and felt some of his motor skills returning as the spasm in his brain lessened.

"You're keeping her trapped in that infant body while her mind surpasses us all, including myself. You may not be aware, but you are torturing her. I can help though. I can help her see her true potential and when the time comes, she will save us all."

Hank jumped toward Marcus with his hands high. A gunshot fired and Hank fell to the ground. In that time, Gladius had grabbed the guns off the floor and pointed them at Marcus, screaming as Hank fell. "Hank!"

Marcus's eyes widened and he turned to run down the passage way. Gladius stood firm and aimed. She fired the guns and the sparks flew off Marcus's back as he ran down the hall. Joey didn't know where the silk steel bullet was in the lineup but watched as she rapidly fired the gun. A bullet made contact and sent Marcus stumbling to the ground. He recovered and kept running, turning a corner and disappearing.

Gladius ran down the hall after him, Minter and Lucas on her heels. Poly got to her feet and staggered toward the hall, falling down near Hank. Joey wanted to scream. He cursed his foul body and willed himself to his feet.

"His shield should have worked," Julie said, staring at Hank.

"Come on, we got to help," Joey said, staggering his way past Hank, and making it down the hall. Poly darted by him down the corridor. He limped as fast as his body would allow, but each step was costly. The only things keeping him moving were his wife and daughter. Lucas yelled and Joey got to the large circular room they were all standing in, searching around the room for Marcus.

"Where'd he go?" Lucas asked Julie.

"I don't know." Her shaky hand slid across the screen. "I think he got out." She looked at the ceiling to a small hole near the top.

"Evelyn's out there!" Poly said in hysterics.

Joey's eyes welled with tears, a bowling ball size lump developing in his throat.

"Awaiting orders from Marcus," Alice said over the speakers.

"We need to get Hank," Lucas said, and Gladius followed him out of the room.

"Find a way, Julie!" Poly screamed again.

"Give me a second."

"We don't have a second!"

Tears flowed from Julie's eyes and she moved her hand around the screen.

Lucas and Gladius flanked Hank as he struggled with each step. He looked up and gave Joey a weak smile as they entered the circular room. He was still alive.

"Marcus no longer needs you, but regrets the loss of Julie," Alice said.

The door in the room closed and the clanking sound of

locks made Joey realize they were in serious trouble if Julie couldn't get it together. "Get us out of here, Julie," he said.

A cloud of white gas entered the room.

"Put on your air shields!" Julie screamed.

Joey fumbled with his Pana and pressed the button marked *Air Shield* with a stiff finger. The room got quieter and he watched each of his friends get their shield on as well, Gladius helping Hank with his. They had five minutes of clean air.

The white cloud spread around the room.

"I got it," Julie said.

A beam of light shone from above and a steel ladder descended from the hole in the ceiling. Joey's heart sank, knowing Hank wasn't going to make it up that ladder. Hell, he might not be able to make it out either. "Go, Poly! Edith might still be up there."

Poly shot up the ladder, followed by Minter and Julie.

"Hank, I can't get your big ass up this ladder without you doing most of the work," Lucas said.

Hank let go of Lucas and grasped the first rung of the ladder. He pulled himself up, then fell backward, hard on the ground.

"Hank," Gladius kneeled next to him. "Get up, sweetie. You can do this." She sobbed.

"Go, get out of here," Hank said.

"We're not leaving you, Hank," Lucas said.

Joey looked up at the bright hole in the ceiling. His wife was up there, possibly facing the worst person in existence without him, and he was about as confident as Hank in his ability to get his shaky hands around those small rungs to climb the ladder.

"Hank, you've got to try," Gladius said. "We didn't come all this way to die in a hole." She cried, grasping his shirt in her fists. "I love you, Hank. Don't do this. Please, don't do this to me!"

Hank didn't respond and Joey's heart stopped.

Gladius cried into his chest and then sat up. Determined, she rummaged through her pockets and pulled out a small syringe. Stabbing it into his chest, she plunged the liquid into Hank.

He shot right up, knocking Gladius back.

"Get up the ladder, hurry!" she said.

Hank bounced to his feet and felt his chest. He grasped the ladder and climbed.

"We need to get him to a stone. That boost I gave him won't last long and without a medical team to be there for the crash, he'll die."

Gladius and Lucas bolted up the ladder behind him.

Joey sucked in for air, but the little he had left in his shield had run out. He felt lightheaded and knew he only had seconds to get outside and into fresh air. He grasped the first rung with his pointer finger and pulled. He took each rung as a personal mission to complete.

Reaching the top, he felt hands pulling him from the hole and laying him on the dirt. The whole world went black and the last thing he heard was Poly screaming.

"He got her!"

CHAPTER 14

POLY WANTED TO RUN, SHE wanted to kill. They told her about stage five, but she never thought they would allow it to get to that point. "Wake up!" She slapped Joey in the face and had trouble not blaming him for their failure. If he hadn't gone into his slow-mo crap, maybe they could have stuck to the plan better, placing that bullet in Marcus's head. "Wake up." She shook him and his head bounced off the dirt.

Crying, she fell onto his chest. She couldn't lose Joey. If he ever got up from this, she was going to get those bracelets back and chain them to his wrists. *The fool!*

"I need to get Hank back to Vanar," Gladius said.

"I feel fine. Great, really," Hank said touching the wound on his chest. "Doesn't even hurt."

Gladius sighed. "You'll be dead in under an hour if I don't get you to Sanct."

Poly jerked at this information, looking to Gladius. "Minter's getting the van."

As the van drove up to the house, dust settled around Joey, making Poly sob again. It only served to remind her of the dust grave they gave Compry and Nathen on the roof tops of Vanar.

How much could she keep giving before she broke? She shook Joey again. "You better not die on me. If you leave me, I'll hunt you to the ends of existence. I need you." She held his hand to her lips and kissed it.

Someone touched her shoulder and she glanced up to find Minter. He glanced at her and then to Joey. "He's tough," his voice cracked. "Help me get him to the van."

Once they were all situated, Minter slid the side door closed and hopped into the driver's seat.

"Where is she now?" Poly asked Julie.

"Edith and Evelyn are both nearing the stone. I think they must have had a helicopter."

"We left Emmett back there," Gladius said. "I told you we should have killed him on the spot."

"We aren't like that," Hank said and shot a look at Minter.

Minter shook his head. "He's with Marcus. I think he's the one who took her while we were messing around inside. I think this whole thing was a distraction and set up from the beginning."

"Was my bullet in his back a distraction?" Gladius said.

"We should have poisoned the bullets," Poly added. "Can you drive faster?"

"Yes, ma'am," Minter said and pushed on the pedal.

The van bounced hard and Poly kept her hands on Joey, keeping him from falling to the floor.

In thirty-two minutes, they arrived at the gates of Zach's burnt down home. Maybe in years past—before the Cough—

the house would have been immediately demolished. But the world no longer cared if a house sat in a pile of blackened sticks. It cared about getting food out to the masses and making sure they were prepared for the next epidemic. And who was the person to supply the world with the technology to facilitate these needs? Marcus Malliden, of course.

"How long has it been since they jumped?" Poly asked.

"Eighteen minutes," Julie said, giving the time since Marcus left earth with her daughter.

Poly hated hearing the number. Her daughter was on another planet with Marcus, and she could only hope Edith was handling her. The idea of Marcus touching her was more than she could bear. But deep down she knew he wouldn't hurt her. In fact, he claimed *they* were the ones hurting her, by confining her to an infant body. What had he meant by that?

Joey slumped forward in his seat as the van came to a stop. He still hadn't woken and Poly combed back his hair. "We're almost there. Wake up." He didn't and she held back the tears. Losing Joey at this moment . . . no, she didn't want to think of it. They'd get him the help he needed.

Julie left the van quickly, leaving the side door open and giving Poly a view of Zach's burnt down house. It summoned all kinds of terrible memories and she hated being there. Gladius was right, out of all the horrid things Marcus did, what he did to Samantha was beyond cruel. It showed her everything she needed to know about Marcus.

"We got the video feed," Julie said, kneeling next to a jumble of weeds near the front door.

Lucas bent over and watched the playback on her Panavice. They discussed angles and kept replaying the video. "You're right, Minter. Emmett's with him. Evelyn and Edith look fine though."

Poly sighed with a little relief and Minter didn't say anything as he grabbed Joey from the shoulders, pulling him out of the van. "Get his feet?" he asked Poly.

"House is clear. They left a while ago," Rick called from the front door. "Took everything I had to not try and send an arrow through them. You guys sure this phase five is the best of ideas?"

Poly wanted to slap him but settled for a sharp look. It was never supposed to go this far. Poly and Minter carried Joey to the stone circle and laid him on the floor. Already, weeds found their way through the soot and dirt accumulating in the exposed house. Poly knelt next to Joey and stared at his face.

"I got the code Marcus used, we can follow him," Lucas said pacing near the stone.

"What's wrong? Let's go," Poly said.

"Hank and Joey," Lucas pointed to each of them. "They're in a bad way and I don't know this code he used. He went somewhere different."

"Joey would rather die than let that man have her for one second longer than necessary. She could be right on the other side."

Lucas took a deep breath and she saw the struggle in his eyes. Anger built in her as she watched the argument build in his expression. "This is the *plan*, Poly. You knew at some point, Marcus had a very good chance at besting us. Now we have the upper hand. He thinks we're dead. Julie's program worked and Alice sent the false information to Marcus. His guard will be down. If we jump right now with Hank and Joey like this . . ." his words dropped off and he shook his head.

Gazing at Joey, he looked back to Poly. "We can't lose our

only advantage and reveal ourselves. Not yet, anyway. We need to be a strong five here to stand any chance."

The number five stung. Another reminder of the friend she lost not fifty feet away from the spot she stood.

"I'm fine," Hank said and then collapsed to the ground.

"He's crashing!" Gladius yelled and glared at Poly. "We need to get them help, now."

"Fine," Poly said and Lucas typed in the code.

The burnt house turned into a magnificent mansion, overlooking the ocean with spectacular views. Jack ran up to them.

"Get medical teams going," Gladius ordered.

Jack jumped and typed into his screen.

Men and women in white shirts with oak trees on the chests flooded the room with their floating gurneys. They lifted Hank and Joey onto them and carried them off. Poly followed Joey down the elevator and to the medical wing under the house.

"Harris here?" she asked Jack.

"No, but I told him you were all here and he's on his way."

They pushed Joey into a small room with the makings machine. One nurse put a hand on Poly's chest to stop her from entering. Poly grabbed the woman's thumb, twisting it and sending her to the floor. The nurse grabbed her hand and yelped, but Poly didn't care. She wanted to make sure Joey was going to live.

They slid his body off the gurney and into the machine. The doctor pulled the door down over him and stepped back. "We shouldn't be in here while the machine's running."

Poly nodded and reluctantly stepped out of the room. "Sorry," she mumbled to the nurse who was still rubbing her hand. Without waiting for a reply, Poly looked through the small window on the door. *You've got to make it, Joey. I can't do this without you.*

The nurses left and the doctor studied the screen, rubbing his chin.

"What is it?" Poly asked.

"I've never seen anything like this. His injury . . . it's as if he's damaged every cell. But that's impossible. He couldn't be alive—" He stopped. "I'm sorry but I don't know if this machine can fix this."

"He's different. Run the machine."

"He may not handle what it does to him."

"Run it!"

The doctor nodded and pressed a button on the screen. From behind the door, she heard the humming. She watched the window, staring at the small space between the two doors where she could see Joey's arm.

"Hank's going to be okay," Julie announced, entering the room. "How's Joey?"

"They don't know," Poly said, starting to sob.

Julie wrapped her up in a hug and she embraced her best friend. Feeling her baby bump pressing against her, she cried even harder. Julie brushed her hair back and kissed the side of her head. She wanted her mom there as well. She wanted to collect everyone she loved and stuff them away to some far off place to keep them safe. The worlds seemed determined to take from her with open abandon; and the more she fought, the more she lost.

Poly didn't speak. She didn't have words, and the grief over the possibility of Joey not being there… Not being able to see his face, feel his touch, their daughter wouldn't know him. She leaned on Julie and Julie held her, not speaking but just being there.

"Thank you," Poly said.

"For what?" Julie asked.

"Just being a friend. If something happens to Joey and Evelyn . . ."

"Don't say it. We're going to make it through this," Julie said. "We're going to win. We have to."

Poly nodded her head and leaned back to see Julie's face. Tears streamed down her cheeks as well. "No matter what, we will get her back. We will get her back."

Joey screamed and Poly jerked away from Julie and Poly rushed to the window. His arms shook and he continued to shriek in pain. She pulled on the door handle, but it was locked.

"You can't go in there," the doctor warned.

"Julie, open the door."

"You'll be exposed," the doctor said.

"Julie, help me. He's dying in there."

"The machine is attempting to repair him," the doctor explained. "We've never had a—no one's ever had an injury like this before. It's going to be painful to repair the damage, *if* it can be repaired at all."

Poly punched at the door and watched Joey convulse and scream. She heard him like this once before, back when those detectives tortured him. Even then, she was pinned to a chair and forced to listen from afar. "How long is this going to take?" she asked.

"I don't know."

Poly glared at him and pulled a knife out.

"Maybe a couple of hours, possibly a lot longer."

Her heart sank and she dropped the knife. *Hours?* Not only did her husband have to be under torture for hours, but every minute that passed meant she was just that much further away from Evelyn.

She slumped down, leaning her head against the door, listening to each of his tormented noises. She felt numb and the whole world seemed distant to her.

The hours moved by, people she loved came and went and she might have responded or might not have, nothing mattered until Joey was better and they could get their girl back.

Some of the time she spent standing and staring at the arm. It gyrated with his screams and went limp in his silence. After more time passed, he stopped screaming and his limp arm became stationary. She pressed her face against the glass, wanting a scream from him. Something to acknowledge his life.

The beep from the monitor gave her the only reprieve from not tearing down the door and checking him herself.

She didn't notice the doctor touching her arm at first and when she did finally acknowledge him, she shook her head and he seemed concerned.

"Is it done?" Her face felt saggy and she wasn't sure if she was ready for the answer. She wasn't sure if she was ready to enter that room and see what kind of husband she had left.

The doctor took back his hand and closed his eyes for a second before looking at her. "After sixteen hours, it's done all it can do."

"Open the door," she demanded.

"We don't know what the machine did to him. Maybe I should go in first," the doctor suggested.

Poly glared him down and he opened the door. She rushed in, not sure of what to expect as she lifted the door on the machine. "Joey." She touched the sides of his face. Sweat covered his body and soaked his clothes. She wiped her hand on her shirt and touched the side of his face again. "Joey?" He opened his eyes and she laughed and cried at the same time. He blinked. "Poly?"

His voice made her smile while tears streamed down her face. It might have been her name or anything else in existence, but the light in his eyes and the fact that he still knew her meant she still had him. She didn't have to face the next phase alone.

"Yes, it's me," Poly said and held his hand.

"Did we get Evelyn back?"

"No."

He squeezed her hand and closed his eyes. Tears dripped down his temples and into his already soaked hair. Wiping his face, he looked at her again. "What are we waiting for then?"

With Poly's help, he got off the bed and up into a standing position outside of the machine. She took a lot of his weight on her shoulder and walked him out of the room.

They all cheered and applauded as Joey and Poly appeared in the waiting room. Poly was taken aback from the large group of the people she loved looking back at her with smiles and tears. She hadn't even realized her mom, Julie's mom and the rest of the parents were there. Joey received a hug from Karen and Minter. Then Hank walked up.

"You okay, Hank?" Joey asked.

"Yeah, how you doing?"

"Better. I thought I broke myself back there."

"Tough to break a kid like you," Harris said as he made it through the crowd.

"Harris," Joey said, hugging him. "They got her."

"I know and we are on the brink of getting her back and ending this all." He hugged Poly and then stepped back and addressed everyone in the room. "We have planned this out for over a year, and for some of us, our entire lives . . . and just now, we are at the precipice of the end. This was the part we all knew would test our resolve, push our faith to the limits, and the next step may be more than some can handle. But together, we will finish this and put an end to Marcus. Soon, we'll honor those who have fallen in our quest."

They cheered again and Poly watched Joey raise his hands and join in. Happy to see him with a functioning body didn't assuage the thoughts racing through her mind. Thoughts of Evelyn with that man. They had to make their move now.

"We need to prepare," Harris continued. "Restock the guns and arrows. I doubt silk steel will work again. We have a few other materials we hope can get through."

"I'm not going to throw knifes at him next time," Poly announced. "I'm going to walk straight up to him and choke the life from his body with my bare hands."

Harris turned to a grim expression, and the corners of his mouth pulled back in a sick smile. "I hope we can deliver that outcome to you, but can you give us one day to resupply before you go on attack?"

"Eight hours."

"That's enough time," Harris said. "You heard the lady. Bring your weapons and follow me to the armory."

Poly sighed and watched everyone file out, many saying goodbyes. She hung back with Joey until the last person left the room. "You doing okay?" she asked.

"Yeah, a bit stiff but," he wiggled his fingers, "These are working again."

"The doctor said if you do it again, the machine won't put you back together. There is no wiggle room. If you do it again, you die." She pursed her lips and stared at him. It was hard to put into words the way she felt for him and how much he meant to her. Tears flooded her eyes for the umpteenth time that day.

"Don't cry," Joey said, hugging her.

He felt sweaty and smelled like burnt hair, but she relished in his touch, embracing his body and losing herself in his chest. He wiped a tear from her face and pulled her chin up, kissing her on the lips and then again on the forehead.

"Whatever happens next, we can make it through it if we have each other," Poly's voice wavered.

"We'll get Evelyn back."

"I know," she said, but wasn't convinced. After so many attempts to get to Marcus, they had only managed to wound him.

"We should go help prepare," Joey said and sagged against her.

She pushed him back upright and he stumbled back. "What's wrong?"

"Nothing, just feeling tired." He gave her a don't-you-worry look that made her do exactly that.

"Should I get the doctor?"

"No. How long was I in there for?"

"Sixteen hours."

He gripped his chest and squeezed his eyes shut. "He has had her for sixteen hours?"

"I know."

"And you agreed to another eight?"

"Joey, you can barely stand. I can barely stand. We need to regroup and be ready for Marcus with our best."

He took a deep breath and looked at the door. "I can rest when we have Evelyn back."

Poly saw the look building in his eyes and knew he was

about to get stubborn on her. She only had one card to play. "I need the rest. I've been staring at your body in that machine for nearly a day. I haven't slept or ate in I don't know how long."

He walked back and hugged her. "I'm sorry. I just can't stand thinking of him having her."

"We need to be somewhat rested if we are going to have any chance of besting Marcus."

"We'll sleep for a few hours, then we go."

"Okay."

Her and Joey found a room and slept for the next eight hours. Poly made sure to not set the alarm clock and it was Lucas who woke them when it was time to go.

One by one, they gathered near the circle in the house, some sporting new weapons. Minter held a large rifle with a scope and Harris hand delivered Joey his guns.

"These are loaded with a deadly party pack," he said.

"Thanks." Joey put the guns back in their holsters.

Poly looked over her man. He looked better, a lot of the shakes he tried to hide were missing and some of the color was back in his face.

Lucas walked into the circle alone and stood next to the stone. As discussed, he was going to jump ahead of the group to find the path Marcus took, and then jump back to get the rest.

"I'm going with you," Joey said, stepping away from Poly. "You'll need a second person to cover you, giving you time to portal back out if needed."

"If it's a master stone," Lucas said. "It'd be good for someone to have my back."

"It'll be a master stone," Harris said. "You've got the specialized Panavice Julie made for you, correct?"

Lucas tapped his pocket. "Yep."

Poly moved forward to touch Joey's arm. She didn't want him going with Lucas, but she knew he had to. As horrible as it sounded, they couldn't allow all of them to be in a single place they didn't know. If Marcus set up a trap, Lucas and Joey should be able to handle it well enough and get out of there.

He turned and kissed her on the lips. It shocked her for a second because he never showed much affection in public, especially in a room full of people, but she got lost in his embrace and kissed him back. It felt as if they hadn't had a moment together in a long time and now she wanted to get away from it all and take her husband somewhere private.

He took a step back and she tugged on his sleeve.

"I'll be right back," Joey assured her.

"You better."

Not to be outdone, Lucas got up from the stone and grabbed Julie, dipping her into a long kiss that Poly couldn't stop staring at. Once finished, he nodded to Joey and returned to the stone. "You ready?"

"Yes."

"Julie knows the code as well, but if we don't return in a week, you'll know our fate. Here we go."

"A week!" Poly ran to the circle, but they were already gone.

CHAPTER 15

TREE'S LIKE HE'D NEVER SEEN before towered over them. The jungle canopy blocked so much of the sun it felt as if they were in the twilight of the day. Joey took a few steps and fell to his knees, unable to keep the charade going.

"Joey?" Lucas ran to him. "What's wrong?"

He grabbed his stomach with his shaking hand and threw up on the jungle floor. Sweat dripped from his face as he heaved again and again.

Lucas paced next to him. "We should go back, man. You're sick."

"No." Joey held out a hand. "I was just holding it back for too long."

"You faker! I knew you looked off."

"I can't let Poly see me like this. She has enough to worry about."

"That machine didn't fix you all the way, did it?"

"I feel better. I do." Joey pushed up to his knees and got to his feet. On his way to the edge of the circle, he wondered if Lucas got the code right. Marcus wouldn't bring Evelyn to a world like this. Just getting over the enormous roots spreading over much of the forest floor would have been an obstacle too large for a person carrying a baby.

The Panavice confirmed his suspicion. "She's not here."

"This is a master stone, he probably jumped, thinking he'd lose any trackers."

Joey took a deep breath and knew Julie had sent Marcus the report through Alice that they were dead. Did Marcus always cover his tracks this efficiently, or did he know they we're still alive?

Lucas held his Panavice close to the stone and scanned the top of it. "I got the next code."

"Let's go."

"We should get you back to the doctor."

"No."

"You should be resting."

"Lucas, you better never tell any of them about me. Let me deal with it. It passes over time. Besides, they know what we are doing and until we find her, there's no reason to go back."

"I don't like this, Joey, not one bit."

"If your baby was taken, I'd do whatever it took to get it back."

"Him," Lucas corrected.

"Him?" Joey smiled. "You're having a boy?"

"Yeah, Julie got a scan while you were . . . healing."

"I'm so happy for you. Why didn't you tell us?"

Lucas walked to the stone. "Julie didn't want to take

anything away from what you guys were going through. The pregnancy was kind of a shock for us in the first place. Guess my boys can't be stopped by mere modern day protection." Lucas laughed. "You ready?"

Joey nodded and stuffed his shaky hand in his pocket.

"Here we go."

The stone hummed and Joey glanced at his shield, making sure to capture enough clean air in it before the jump.

The midday jungle turned to darkness. Rain poured down on them and Joey ran the scan on his Panavice, locating the signals. His heart leapt at the sight of the two red dots on his screen. They were only a few miles away. He gazed into the darkness, in the direction of Evelyn and Edith. He had no idea what planet they were on, or where he was in the world, but it didn't matter. He was closer to Evelyn, closer to having a family that wasn't perpetually endangered. "Got her. Three point two miles that way."

"Great. Now we just need to figure out where we are."

Joey spotted another marker on his screen and knew exactly where they were. "Sharati's not far from here."

Lucas wiped the rain back from his face and flung the excess water on the ground. "Just great. Out of all the planets, Arrack is where he's keeping her?"

"This is also what we've been looking for, his headquarters outside of Earth or Vanar. This is the last stage," Joey said.

"I got bad news," Lucas said looking at the stone.

"One way stone?" It wasn't a question. He knew and turned back to face Evelyn's direction. They'd have to find another stone to get the others.

"Yes," Lucas said.

Joey glanced down at his Panavice and pinged Sharati. She

accepted and her face appeared on the screen. Joey tilted the screen and let the water fall off.

"Joey?" she asked.

"We know where she is."

"I see her on my screen as well. I'm coming to you. Meet me half way." Sharati's camera turned away from her as she turned it off and Joey saw a group of Arracks around her.

"We better play it safe with her," he said to Lucas.

"I don't trust her either."

Joey watched Sharati's red dot on his screen as she moved toward them. He began their trek in Evelyn's direction and hoped the rain would let up. He couldn't see more than a hundred feet ahead.

"Should we use our lights?" Lucas said loud enough to be heard over the roaring rain.

"Better not."

Lightning crashed and lit the landscape. More desert looking than anything else, rocks, dirt, and sloping terrain were laid out before them. They could manage it.

"Come on, we're meeting Sharati."

Lucas kept his bow out with an arrow clipped in place, constantly scanning their surroundings. Joey kept his guns holstered and wished he had worn rain appropriate clothes. The shield didn't do a thing for water and it soaked into his clothes, weighing him down. His feet might as well have been stepping through a shallow pool. Streams ran everywhere, and in the first hundred feet, he'd plunged into knee deep puddles. Taking big steps, he climbed from a deep puddle as a lightning strike lit up the terrain just enough for Joey to get his bearings and keep on course toward the hill on the horizon.

Checking the red dots, Sharati made much more ground

then them. Joey ignored the warning calls from his body and pushed harder, getting some distance from even Lucas. "We've got to pick it up, Lucas," Joey said, looking over his shoulder.

"Pick it up? I've got twenty freaking pounds of water I'm carrying here. My socks are soaked. My socks!"

Joey sighed and started to jog. He made it ten feet and fell, face planting into the mud. He pulled his foot out of the water hole it went into.

Lucas laughed. "Watch out, that first step's a doozy."

"Let's just get to the top of the hill so we have the higher ground."

"You think something's up?" The smirk left Lucas's face and he looked out into the darkness.

"Always."

Joey crawled up the hill, not even bothering with trying to walk up the embankment; after several falls, Lucas joined him. The soft mud caked on his hands and knees, making the climb that much more difficult.

At the top, Joey stayed hunched over, breathing hard and letting the rain pour down his face, dripping from his mouth and nose. The effort took more out of him than it should have and he struggled to get back on his feet. He stared at the dark sky and watched another flash light up a distant cloud.

What were the chances of getting caught in a desert downpour? Two, maybe three times a year this might happen. He thought of Evelyn and knew Edith would protect her from the elements. He glanced down and saw Sharati's red dot close by now. She should be visible from the hill they were perched on. He stopped and turned to face her direction.

As if on command, a bolt lit up the desert.

He had been right about Sharati. She didn't just have a few

Arracks with her, she had a small army. Joey's heart picked up and he gripped guns in both hands. She'd saved them on a number of occasions, but she also tried to kill them. Which one would show this time, friend or foe?

He might have yelled, or asked the group to stop running at them, but the rain and wind drown out any chance of that. With each passing second, the urge to run straight to Evelyn became stronger. If he could just get close to Marcus, he could stop it all. He didn't want to put one more person at risk if possible. The Arracks moved as a unit and if they had ill intentions, Joey knew there was nothing he could do to stop them.

"She's got company," Lucas yelled.

They waited and watched, hoping this interaction would be to their benefit. Sharati took lead and had her group halt at the bottom of the hill. She didn't have any troubles in the mud, easily making her way up the embankment. She reached the top and gave them a toothy smile as if out of practice.

"You're fortunate to be here on a raining day," Sharati said. "The city has been praying for rain for months and when Marcus showed up, it started to rain. You are very blessed indeed to be here for this." The rain slid off her silver skin and made her look shiny and smooth.

"Well, aren't we the lucky ones," Lucas said, wiping his face in futility.

"She's that way, not far from here," Joey said. "Will you help us?"

Sharati looked back at her group, a mixture of male and female Arracks, some with the yellow streaks on their shoulder. "That's why we are here. We know Marcus didn't make the rain, just as we are sure he is the cause of all our pain since he arrived here."

Lucas stepped to the side and slipped. He slammed onto the muddy surface and then scrambled, trying to get back to his feet and falling again. Joey reached over and helped him up. Lucas tried to shake some of the mud off, but it stuck and smeared all over his clothes. He lifted his hands in the air and shook his head.

"You okay?" Joey asked.

"Just . . . no."

"Sharati," Joey said. "If we leave now, I think we could be to her in a half hour."

"No, there's a flash flood river between us and her. There are no bridges for miles, and no way to cross safely."

Joey turned and looked at his Panavice. Evelyn hadn't moved since their arrival on the planet. Lightning cracked in the distance and the wet landscape ahead revealed itself in the flash. How bad could a desert river be? "We'll go it alone then," he said.

"Joey," Lucas said. "That's not the plan. We are supposed to go back and get everyone."

Joey kept his back to Lucas and looked out into the darkness.

"It's tough to *stand* in this stuff," Lucas continued. "You really think we can cross a river in it? You sure you're fine?"

Was he fine? No, but at what point had he been fine? Maybe before any of this started, but fine was a luxury of a distant life and a future goal. He'd give Poly and Evelyn their *fine* if it killed him. He stomped away from them, toward Evelyn.

"This isn't the plan, Joey," Lucas yelled over the rain.

Joey spun around. "Really? The *plan?*" Joey slapped the water off his face and glared at Lucas. "When has a plan with that man ever worked? What, you think we should go gather up your wife and yet to be born child, or my wife or our best friends and take them to him? Should we keep delivering our people on a silver platter?"

"This is about Samantha, isn't it?"

Joey turned away from him and ran his hands through his hair. He screamed at the sky before turning back to Lucas. "We just have to go there and catch him by surprise. He can't track our Pana's and Julie said it would be impossible for him to trace Evelyn's and Edith's trackers. This is our chance, Lucas, you and me could end this now."

Lucas didn't answer and Joey threw up his hands and walked away. The mud slid under his soaked feet as he walked past Sharati and down the back side of the hill.

"It's suicide," Lucas called from behind.

Joey kept stomping through the mud and water.

"He's a stubborn one," he heard Sharati say.

Joey didn't look back and kept in a straight line toward Evelyn. He didn't want to bully his best friend into anything, but he wasn't going to risk the ones he loved anymore.

"Wait for me, for Pete's sake." Lucas splashed through the water and caught up to Joey. He put his hand across his shoulder and walked with him. Joey looked over to his friend and stopped.

"I want to end this as well, you know?" Lucas said.

"I know," Joey said and felt bad for questioning Lucas. "We just need to get past this river and we're there."

Lucas nodded and they turned to walk toward the two red dots.

The rain lessened as they moved down the hill and back to the flat terrain. Water filled up the desert like a sponge, but the sponge couldn't take any more and the water seeped everywhere, filling every hole and depression. Joey glanced back and saw Sharati and her group following closely behind.

It took twenty minutes to get to the river Sharati mentioned and Joey stopped at its edge. The water roared with turbulence and shred through the parse land, carrying with it a heavy mixture of mud and rock.

"No freaking way," Lucas said with his arms crossed.

Joey paced at the edge and pulled his hair back with both hands. Sharati kept her distance but he spotted her with each lightning strike. "We have to get across."

"No, this is nuts. We just can't. Look at the water, Joey."

"It doesn't matter. Some water isn't going to keep me from getting my daughter back." Joey stepped to the shallows and felt the foot deep water pushing against his legs. He gauged the distance and figured if he swam hard enough, he could make it across, even if the river swept him down a mile, he'd get across.

"Get out of there. You're going to get killed, and then where would we be?" Lucas yelled.

"He's right. There's no way," Sharati said. "Shudi, Shudi." She gestured to Arracks behind her and down the river.

Small pebbles peppered his legs and he took another step, sliding his foot down the sandy bottom of the river's edge. Waist deep, he felt the force of the river. The idea of crossing started to feel foolish and the larger debris rolled over his feet and slapped his legs. Joey took a deep breath and eased into the river, neck deep. The cold water slammed against his whole body and for a brief second, he thought he might be able to walk, maybe it wasn't that deep.

A large rock struck him in the thigh and he cried out in pain. The impact knocked him off his feet and into the full, raging force of the river. He tried to swim, but the water churned him around like rolled dough. He went under and the sound of rock clanking against other rocks roared beneath the melee above him.

He fought to get to the top and flung his arms manically to keep above the rapids. A rope struck him, tightening around his forearm. He couldn't see the shoreline as the torrent of water continually splashed his face, but he felt the tug toward it.

"No, I can get across," Joey called out, knowing very well they couldn't hear him. He turned and tried to fight against it, but his arms were already getting tired and the rope pulled him harder. He gave in and felt the edge of the shoreline.

An Arrack with many necklaces rushed to him and grabbed at his wrists. Another Arrack joined in and they both pulled him ashore.

The rain continued to pour down as he lay on his back, next to the raging river. He felt the squishing mud underneath him and gripped it with his hands. He felt like crying. A lightning bolt high in the sky formed a jagged streak directly above. The thunder that followed rumbled through him.

"Joey?" Lucas called out. "What the hell, are you crazy?" he said, trying to catch his breath. "If Sharati hadn't called out Cowboy Arrack here to rope your stupid ass, you'd be dead right now."

Joey couldn't tell if he had tears or if the rain just flowed over his face. Evelyn was so close and he couldn't get to her.

"You listening?" Lucas asked.

"Get him up," Sharati said.

Several Arracks crowded around him and got him to his feet.

"Now you understand, you can't cross, right?" Sharati said.

Joey nodded. "Where is the nearest bridge?"

"Thirty miles to the north."

He walked past Sharati and slipped on the mud as his leg shook. His head hurt as well, but he squeezed the muscles in his leg and got it back under control. Where the rock struck his thigh ached in pain.

"Where are you going?" Lucas asked.

"To the bridge." It didn't matter if they followed or not. He'd find the bridge and get to her.

He heard Lucas and Sharati talking, but the rain clouded their words. Didn't matter, he'd get there with or without them.

One hour into walking next to the river, his feet hurt and his legs felt like gelatin masses, begging for a break. He pushed on. Long ago, he lost sight of Lucas and Sharati and the rest of the Arracks. He thought he spotted lights in the distance, but it could have been the lightning. The downpour had lessened and turned into a light rain with a spattering of showers. The river on the other hand, seemed to strip through the desert with more vigor than before.

Watching the river for the last hour, gave him a chance to clear his head. He was foolish to try and cross it. His left thigh ached from the boulder that struck him in the water, and with each step, it throbbed in pain. But that was only one of his problems.

Sneakers weren't the best form of wet weather wear and while they kept grip on the slick landscape, he felt his feet softening and rubbing through the muddy socks. Small pains in his feet were turning into larger pains. When daylight came, he thought of taking them off and inspecting his feet for blisters and cracks.

He wasn't sure which direction was east, but he desperately awaited the rising sun. With the sun's rays, he hoped he might have a chance of drying off and increasing his speed to this bridge.

How much had he already walked? Two miles? It was going to take a day or more to get to the bridge at his current pace. He stopped on a small hill above the river. The rocks clacked around at the bottom and the top formed heavy rapids making a soothing sound. He resisted the urge to sit down and take off his shoes and instead took out his Panavice.

The Panavice displayed Evelyn's red dot. It still hadn't moved and sat right next to Edith's. It did give him some comfort, knowing the two were still together. At least, Evelyn had a friend with her. She was probably sleeping next to Edith.

"I'll be there soon." He took a step and slipped, falling on his side in the mud. He lay there, shaking his head and wondering why the worlds were so against him. Standing back up, the mud slid off his hands and he shook his legs, trying to get as much off as he could.

Cleaner, he took a deep breath and sped up to a jog. The shoes squished with each step and the mud tried to pull him back down but walking wasn't going to get him to his daughter any sooner. He jogged faster. It felt good, getting some wind on his face and even the water seemed to run away from his eyes and mouth.

He wished he could've said he ran the entire time over the next six hours, but many horrible things happened and mainly to his feet. He had taken off his shoes hours ago and ran across the mud barefoot, a decision he wished he'd made from the start. But the soggy shoes and socks had already done their damage by way of blisters and a crack near the heel of his left foot. The leg that had an encounter with a flowing, river rock had a large bruise that went bone deep and swelled out, feeling hard to the touch. He felt his mind slipping as well, he couldn't tell if it was a side effect of the slow motion or just being hungry and dead tired.

None of it mattered. He had to find a way to her, the pain in his body would go away with time but if anything happened to her, he didn't know how he could go on. So, he kept jogging, not as fast as a few hours ago, but a steady pace nonetheless. His lungs burned with each heavy breath of the rain-filled air.

Dawn broke across the horizon. The impending sun gave him hope and he ran harder. His body couldn't handle it, but he'd never pushed it this far, so maybe it could. What he wouldn't do for one of those jet packs Julie mentioned.

He slowed down and looked back. He'd hoped Lucas would be there, trudging along with him, but in the daylight, he saw how hopelessly alone he actually was. The desert spread out as far as he could see, with nothing but shiny pools of water and a smattering of bushes and cacti dotting the landscape.

He slipped. If his body had been working normally, he might have had a chance to recover, but instead he braced for impact. The muddy ground rushed to his face and he slammed into it, his shoulder taking the brunt of the damage.

He groaned and rolled onto his back. It wasn't the first time he'd fallen during his run, but definitely the hardest. Pain shot through his sides and he gripped his shoulder. An especially dark cloud moved over him, and with it, a downpour of rain. It blocked much of the sun and he felt the heavy drops peppering his face.

He laughed hysterically, and then screamed at the sky and laughed some more. The water pooled around his body and diminished any chances he thought he had of getting dry, yet it all seemed to be the funniest thing he'd ever experienced and continued to howl.

"That all you got? Bring it on! That can't be all you have."

Next, came the tears. He sat up and buried his head between his knees. The idea of finishing the thirty miles crashed around him. He should have tried to cross the water again. Damn Sharati for pulling him out. He could have made it, he was sure of it. He glanced at the raging river and it hadn't showed any signs of slowing down. The storm had moved to the north and he figured it would be feeding the river for quite some time.

"I'm sorry." He didn't have an exact reason for the apology and knew there wasn't a person in the world to hear it, but he said it anyway. He had to hear it with his own ears, an apology for every stupid thing he'd done over the last few years. If he hadn't gone to the forest that one day with Bull, if he hadn't convinced his friends to join him. And then there was Samantha. If he hadn't led her on, then cast her aside for Poly . . . if he hadn't found those earrings . . . she might still be here with them. He sobbed into his knees and squeezed them tight against his chest.

He'd never felt so alone in his life. He was glad to have his friends and family so far away. This was his battle to face, his fight to the end. No matter what, he wasn't going to allow Marcus to live another day. That was his mistake from day one, involving his friends. If he'd only taken Simon's deal, or just given himself up, he could have eliminated his friends from the equation and Samantha would still be alive.

The rain mocked him and showered down with glee. He slapped his face, but it wasn't good enough and he struck harder. He slapped again and again, until his vision blurred. He screamed out and got to his feet, or at least tried. His weary legs crashed from under him and he fell back to the muddy surface.

He tried again, barely succeeding in his second attempt. Stopping had been a mistake and his body felt stiff. It took great effort to take the first step. But once he did, he kept moving, nothing could stop him. How long had he traveled? He had to be getting close.

The left leg trailed behind as he tried to speed up to a light jog. Toes dragging through the mud, he couldn't get it lifted to a full stride. After a few minutes, his body loosened and he felt his hip joints and thigh muscles working. He lifted his legs and ran. The rain cloud moved past him and the sun crested over the distant mountains.

He ran, knowing full well he couldn't keep up the pace, but it didn't matter. His heart got to its peak quickly and his breath came in rapid, shallow bursts. He pushed harder, sprinting and feeling the mud barely making contact with his bare feet. If he fell at this speed, he wouldn't be getting back up.

The wind blew his face dry and he felt a bit of the heat radiating from the sun. The sky held a smattering of dark clouds, each one raining down a column of liquid. He screamed. He'd get there if it killed him.

Running up a small hill, he saw it—the bridge. Joey ran the rest of the way and fell down on his knees in front of the large timbers making up the bridge. The mud clung to his hands and knees in large clumps and he reached for the wood, feeling it with his filthy hands. He crawled a few more feet and welcomed the rough wood on his face. He slid up onto the edge of the bridge and lay there. His body beyond exhausted, he couldn't believe he'd made it. The idea of death filled him and he closed his eyes, welcoming the blackness.

The sound of clanking wheels and chattering reigns woke him. The sun blared its power over him. He jolted upright and cursed he'd fallen asleep. A band of wagons approached and any plan of going unnoticed left long ago as an Arrack stared at him from a few feet away.

"Marundi," it yelled out.

He'd made it this far, given everything that he had, and it was all for nothing. He would never be able to defend himself against the band of Arrack's approaching his position. Laying back down and closing his eyes, he left it to the greater powers to decide his fate.

CHAPTER 16

POLY FLUNG THE DOOR OPEN on the caravan to see Joey laid out on the bridge. His mud covered face contorted with pain. She hopped out of the vehicle and ran. *What did he do to himself?* She slid up to him and grasped the sides of his head. He opened his eyes, tears forming and falling as soon as he focused on her.

Pulling Joey's sobbing face into her chest, Poly rocked him like a child, tears flowing freely down her cheeks and landing in his wet, muddy hair. Sharati said thirty miles he'd have to travel to get here. They thought it would be best to get to the bridge and then split, sending a party down river to meet up with him . . . but here he was, on the bridge, looking a wreck. Had he ran the whole way?

"Joey."

"Why are you here?" he asked.

"We do this together."

She felt his arms wrapping around her waist, pulling her tight. She stayed there, waiting for him to come to the realization he wasn't alone, and nothing in all the worlds would ever make it so. They were all going to kill Marcus as one, as planned. Evelyn would be in their arms soon.

He released her and lifted his head to take her in, grinning when she smiled at him. The whole group had gathered behind her while she embraced Joey and the sight of them took her breath away.

Julie, Lucas, Hank, and Gladius stood closest, and behind them Harris, Jack, Sharati, Travis. To the right, Rick, Minter, Beth, Opal, Karen, Gretchen, and Trip. Even further back, she spotted the mutants, Kris, Maggie, and a few others.

The sight gave her chills and she glanced at Joey. His mouth hung open and she saw the same reaction from him, shock. They were all there. The fool of a man had thought he would face Marcus by himself, yet Marcus had hurt too many for one person to end his horrible life. Each face Poly gazed at had been destroyed by the man not thirty miles away.

"Can you walk?" Poly stared in horror at his purple feet. Where were his shoes?

"Yeah." He pulled himself to his feet and took one step. Pain shot through his face and he crumpled to the ground.

She rushed to his side. "Stay down. What hurts?" She looked over his body, searching for injuries.

"My leg." He pointed to his left leg.

She pulled off his pants and gasped at the hematoma sticking out of the side of his leg. "Julie," Poly called. Julie and Lucas came running up. "He's hurt."

Julie pulled the bag from her shoulder and set it next to Joey.

Lucas leaned down. "You're one crazy bastard, Joey Foust."

Joey smiled and patted Lucas on the shoulder. "You did all this, didn't you?"

Lucas nodded.

"You're a great friend," Joey said.

"You know I am. You think I'd let you take on the big baddie all by yourself?"

Julie rubbed the cream on his leg. He winced from her touch but quickly relaxed as the cream did its thing.

"Anything else hurting?" Julie asked.

Joey shook his head and sat up, but quickly laid back down, grasping around his whole body. Poly took the cream from Julie and began to rub him down. Lifting his shirt, she saw the bruised shoulder and started there. Soon, she'd rubbed the cream over his whole body, like a conscientious mother might for her child at the beach. It wouldn't last forever but with each application, she watched the relief spread across his face.

"This guy," Lucas told Poly, "tried to jump into the river over there in hopes of crossing it. If it wasn't for Sharati, his bloated carcass would be floating out to who knows where."

Poly glanced back at Sharati. Poly had stuck her in the chest with a knife once and hoped that was water under the bridge.

Joey got to his feet with the help of Lucas and he tested his leg with a smile.

"I got to get a picture of this." Lucas held up his Panavice and snapped a picture of Joey, barefoot in his underwear, and covered in a mixture of mud and cream Poly had spread over him. Joey made it a point to get his clothes on directly after the picture.

Hank and Gladius then came over to greet Joey and his face filled with joy at their sight.

"Let's get one big shot," Julie said, rushing to the bridge to set her Pana on the railing. She waddled back and gathered everyone close in. Poly put her hand around the waist of Joey and smiled for the camera. Julie rushed back to the camera and showed the picture to the rest of them in a projected hologram.

Poly hadn't seen such a display since the double wedding. After the picture, the parents gathered around Joey, his dad and mom greeting him with hugs and tears. Minter didn't seem to want to let his boy go.

Poly relished in the sight. Her mom walked over to her with a smile.

"Your dad would have been proud of you. He'd be amazed, actually. You have turned into the best daughter we could have ever asked for."

Poly nodded and stared down south, somewhere out there *her* daughter was with Marcus. The urgency struck her. "We should get going," she said, but the joyful conversations continued and everyone ignored her. "We need to go!" she screamed.

This silenced the crowd.

"Anubi, hardi," Sharati said and twirled her hand in the air.

"Joey, come with me," Poly said.

He said his goodbyes to his mom and dad and followed her to the wagon. She got in first and he brushed off her attempt to help him in. Lucas, Julie, and Hank piled into the wagon with them.

"Where's Gladius?" Poly asked.

"She wanted to ride with Travis for a bit."

Poly nodded and took a towel, doused it with water and leaned forward to wipe the mud from Joey's face. He took it from her and wiped his own face down and then his hands and arms. The towel turned brown from the mud, but seeing his beautiful face again made her heart melt. She wished the rest of the Six would have given this cart to just her and Joey. She wanted him and took in a deep breath in an attempt to tame her desire.

"Sharati said there's an abandoned city a few miles outside of Marcus's fortress," Julie reported. "We're going to regroup there and formulate our plan."

"Our final plan," Hank said.

"Yes, this is it," Poly added.

"You doing okay, Joey?" Julie asked.

"Yeah, that cream's helping out a bunch."

The cart lurched forward.

"I can't tell you how good it feels to have you guys next to me," Hank said.

"Aww, Hank's getting all mushy," Lucas said.

"I'm serious, being with Gladius has been amazing, but there is nothing like the five of us in the world. I love you guys."

"Gladius has turned you into a big softie, hasn't she?" Lucas asked.

"I think its sweet, Hank," Julie said. "We all love you too."

"So, you and Gladius doing it now?" Lucas asked Hank.

Going red in the face, he shoved Lucas. "Shut your pie hole, dude."

"Okay, okay! Just answer me this . . . does she bring that doll, you know, into bed?"

Hank grabbed Lucas, shaking him against the wall.

"Help, Julie, an ape has escaped the zoo and is attacking me!"

They laughed and it felt so good to have the five of them in the same space. Poly got teary eyed and looked out the window as they passed over the bridge. She knew they were going to a place that could very well be the end of them all. Marcus might still think they were dead, but it wouldn't take long for a man like him to figure out what was really going on.

Over the next hour, Hank did a lot of talking for once, telling them of his adventures with Gladius, romping across the cities of Vanar. Poly hugged Hank and thanked him for all they did for her daughter. She started to feel as if she'd asked too much of her friends.

The wagon stopped and an Arrack opened the door.

It felt good to get up and walk around, after spending hours in the wagon. She tried to help Joey down, but he again waved away her hand and jumped to the ground.

She turned to take in the small town consisting of just a few buildings arranged around a circular dirt road. The plaster on the building had cracked long ago and the holes for windows and doors were vacant.

Joey walked up and wrapped his arms around her, hugging her from behind. She touched his hand and looked back at him. His lips came close to her ear. "Do you know why we aren't going right now to get Evelyn?"

"Sharati and the Arracks have an idea. We are going to assemble here and then form our attack."

Joey sighed and squeezed her harder. "She is only a few minutes away . . ." He left the thought hanging, but she knew what he wanted. She wanted the same thing. The very idea of her being with Marcus was unbearable. Edith was the only thing keeping her from going insane.

"We'll unload the carts and get the weapons set up," Harris spoke up.

"Weapons?" Joey perked up at the information.

"You think I'd come to a fight with just my hands?" Harris

laughed and walked away.

"We're going to wait, Joey. Okay?" Poly asked.

"Yes." His hand shook and he pulled it away from her.

They gathered in the large structure and stood on sandy floors. Harris and Sharati went into detail about each person's role, making sure everyone knew what to do and when. Most of the plan predicated on Marcus acting in a predictable manner. Poly didn't like much of it because it gave Marcus openings to escape, or chances to harm Evelyn. She gripped her knives and listened intently to the part involving her and her group. She nodded and took in the information.

"Where is the part where we kill him?" Joey asked.

Harris lowered his head. "This is a rescue mission first, destruction comes second. If we can, I will push with my group to kill Marcus."

"We all need to push, rescuing her is futile if Marcus lives. He will find her again. We will always be on the run," Poly said.

Harris rubbed his chin and glanced at Sharati. "We think we might have found a way for you to live away from Marcus. Sharati tells me her father found a human planet, much like your Earth. He kept it from Simon and MM after seeing what they did to Ryjack. She knows the code."

Poly gawked at the idea. "You're suggesting we should just flee? Hide somewhere, forever looking over our backs?"

"We have to prepare for a plan in case we don't kill him."

Poly shook her head as she thought it all over. The idea of going to another Earth was enticing. "We would all go?"

"Whoever wants to, but yes, I would say all of you."

"And we leave our home planet to fall to his will?" Lucas said. "You know he's implanted every person on our planet with a device we have no idea what it does?"

"I have control of Alice now," Julie said. "He won't be able to broadcast the signal anymore. We solved that."

Joey held his fists at his sides and glared at the crowd. "Are none of you getting it? We rescue Evelyn and then we *kill* him. That is the end of the story, period. I don't care about you guys destroying his toys, or data, or whatever else you want to destroy of his; we don't leave until he is dead."

Harris nodded. "We all hope it comes to that. We'll use the cover of night to start. Are you ready, Sharati?"

"Yes," she said.

Travis walked in the middle and took in the crowd around him. "We have a mission. Each one of us has our own reasons for being here, but I think we can all agree, we are here today for you five. You have come into our lives and left large footprints behind, and I mean that in the best possible way." He looked at each of them in the eye. "Tonight, we will honor you and take everything back that Marcus has taken from us."

"Hell yeah!" Lucas said.

"We should all get something to eat and take it easy for the next few hours while we set up the final part of the plan," Harris said. "Let's take this time to enjoy one another's company, as some of us will not make it to morning."

Poly didn't like the notion of any of them dying. The idea of losing another friend couldn't be rationalized. Sure, she would risk her life to save Evelyn, but she didn't know if she wanted to risk the lives of everyone else.

She stared at the two red dots on the screen. They were apart now and seeing the distance between Evelyn and Edith sent her heart racing. What could they be doing to her baby girl?

CHAPTER 17

JOEY LAY FLAT ON THE dirt bank, watching as Sharati led a large group of Arracks straight down the road toward Marcus's compound. They approached slowly and by the time they reached the gates, darkness covered the desert.

"They're there," Julie said and held her Panavice close to them so they could all watch the camera mounted to Sharati's necklace.

The building Sharati faced was built into the side of a mountain and had a giant door. She stood a hundred feet back from the entrance. The door opened and a man walked out from the door with his hands held up and a smile on his face. Marcus Malliden.

"Take the shot," Joey said even though Sharati couldn't hear him.

"To what do I owe the pleasure of such an unannounced

gathering at my front door?" Marcus asked.

"We know it was you who blew the poison over our lands."

"If I remember right, Harris and his stooges delivered this poison to you, not me."

"Kill him," Joey urged to the screen. He could be there in minutes and kill Marcus himself.

"I've seen it on three planets now," Sharati pushed on. "You nearly killed us all and then came in with the cure, playing the hero. You find it the easiest way to push us under your will."

Marcus laughed. "And what if I did? What are you and your little gathering going to do? Insight a revolt?" He raised his hands up and looked around. "I am a god. You think the rest of the Arracks are going to go against their god? No, and I will give you this single chance to turn and leave here now."

"We aren't going anywhere."

A light went out from a lantern the Arrack had been carrying, and Joey knew that signal set in motion his parents, floating down the river and soon, Harris's weapons would ignite.

"Thidius!" Sharati cried out.

Gunfire sounded from the Arracks. The sight of it shocked Marcus. He stumbled back as bullets crashed into his shield.

"Where did you get guns? They are forbidden." Marcus raised up two guns and fired into the Arracks. Sharati jumped to her right and ran in a sweeping circle.

The door opened again and out came a flood of Arracks. They ran past Marcus, wielding long knives. The gunfire crashed into many of the front liners, but they kept coming out, trying to protect their god. Marcus backed up, making his way to the door and behind the flow of Arracks.

"Okay, you guys better move," Julie said.

"If anything happens to us—" Lucas started to say.

"Just go, you'll be fine," Julie said and hugged him. "I love you."

Lucas knelt down and talked into her pregnant belly, rubbing it.

Gunfire let Joey know the Arrack fight was still going Sharati's way. Out gunned, they would have to send out every zealot Arrack in the building to deal with them. He gazed down at the encounter, seeing the flashes of gunfire. The front doors closed and he spotted a large ball arching across the sky like a beach ball on fire.

"Tell them to get out of there," Joey said.

Julie shook her head. "I can't."

He watched the ball hover over the entrance, before it exploded. A wave of fire came from the explosion and crashed through the Arracks below. Joey rushed to Julie's screen, seeing if Sharati had somehow made it, but there was nothing but blackness.

The bomb made it brighter than the sun ever could and he felt the intense heat from it. He looked to the river and spotted the parents floating in a clump to their location. He hoped Marcus wasn't looking for more people in this attack.

"He just killed them all, his Arracks and ours," Lucas said.

Joey sighed and gritted his teeth. Another life Marcus had ended. It didn't change the plan, Sharati had done her part. "Let's go," he said.

They left Julie at the hill and jogged behind Marcus's fortress. The back side looked like the hill they'd just come from, more rocks, with no distinctive markings.

"You sure this is the place?" Joey asked.

Lucas held the Panavice near his face. "It should be right around . . ." he searched around them, "here."

Behind a rock stood an opening covered with a metal grate.

It was about two feet wide and the tunnel turned to darkness before he could tell how deep it went.

Hank took off his bag and pulled rope out, fastening it to the rock.

"You sure that rope is thick enough to handle your sheer mass?" Lucas asked Hank.

"Sharati said it could hang a Niddi, whatever the hell that is. But it sounded heavy."

Lucas laughed. "I better go first." He took off Prudence and tugged on the rope, looking down into the hole.

"Use the gun in close range," Joey said.

"I got it." Lucas touched the gun at his side.

Hank pulled the grate off the hole and dropped the rope into it. It zinged along the narrow path and a thunk sounded at its end.

Lucas clipped Prudence to his waist and adjusted his quiver. He smiled, but it didn't reach the rest of his face. "I . . ."

"We know, and we'll be right behind you," Poly said.

He nodded his head and slid down the rope and into the darkness below.

"I'll go next," Gladius said, leaving no room for discussion as she slid down the rope.

Joey followed behind her. Using the gloves Harris gave them, he slid down the rope. Heat built up around his hand and he tightened his grip as he slid into complete darkness. A single green dot from Lucas's Panavice appeared when his feet struck the bottom.

Poly was right behind him and he made room for her in the darkness. He pulled her out of the way as Hank came down hot.

"Gladius?" Hank whispered.

"Shh," she responded.

Lucas lit up the space with a small amount of green light, to see a door at one end of the vent room. It couldn't have been more than a few feet tall.

Joey lifted up his Panavice and stared at the two red dots on either side of the building. They had separated the two since the attack started. Poly glanced at the screen and moved to the door.

She opened it without a word. An Arrack stood on the other side. It turned and Poly jumped from the door, stabbing it in the neck. It gargled and fell to the floor, grabbing at its gaping wound.

"Dang," Gladius whispered.

It wasn't surprising to Joey. If an alarm sounded, the whole plan would go up in flames. They couldn't ask questions first, or give warnings. Not this time.

"Come on," Lucas said, walking down the hall. A few dim lights lit their way, but the extra light also meant it'd be tougher if an Arrack appeared.

Hank grabbed the dead Arrack and stuffed it in the vent room.

Joey kept his gun out and hoped he didn't have to use it. One loud burst . . .

"Edith isn't far from here," Lucas said.

An Arrack rounded the corner and jumped at Lucas, stabbing at his face. Lucas's shield deflected the blade and a throwing knife from Poly struck the thing in the eye.

"Jesus," Lucas said and took a deep breath. "Thank you, Julie." He patted his chest and checked his face for blood.

"I helped you out there a *little*," Poly said.

Lucas led the way down several flights of stairs and into a large room with white walls and shining LED lights. A man in a white coat with an oak tree on the chest stared at a screen while typing, not noticing their arrival.

Lucas tiptoed up to the man and smothered his face with a rag. The man went limp in his arms and Lucas rested him on the floor.

"Who are you?" another man asked from the door.

"Shit." Lucas in one motion pulled Prudence from his side and fired an arrow into the guy's head. The man's paper cup fell to the floor and he landed next to it.

Hank dashed over and dragged the man behind a desk.

Lucas took deep breaths, and glanced a few times at the man lying dead behind the desk. He took out his Panavice while holding Prudence. "Come on, Edith should be over here."

A large explosion rocked the building. Glass vials rattled in the cabinets and a monitor fell over.

"Harris," Joey whispered. Good, it meant another part of the plan was happening, drawing all of Marcus's attention away from them.

Lucas nodded and pushed open the door.

A medical room of sorts, with large clear vats of liquid, appeared before them. It felt familiar to Joey, like he'd been there and then it struck him. This was similar to the room they used to pull the serum from him. Those large cylinders would hold people in stasis for Marcus and it didn't take long to count all six of them. Maybe Marcus had a plan of his own in securing them and the thoughts of it sent his heart beating hard. He searched for Poly and she stood directly behind him.

"She should be over here." Lucas walked closer to a wall of frosted glass. "I hope Julie has this alarm shut down." He cringed and touched the glass. It instantly went clear and Edith stood on the other side, shocked to see the group staring back at her.

She ran to the glass and pounded it, yelling something, but

the sound didn't come through.

"Open it," Poly said.

Lucas pulled on the handle and the door opened. Joey knew Julie was behind the unlocking, working her magic from afar.

"Edith," Lucas said.

Edith crept to the door and exited, looking around as if none of it was real. "They have Evelyn. I tried to stop them, but they kept doing things to her."

"What did they do?" Poly asked.

"They kept her in these machines, I heard her screaming. I don't know, they wouldn't let me near her until afterward." She lowered her head and tears flowed from her eyes.

"What did they do to her?" Poly asked.

"They changed her . . . she's different now."

"Different *how?*" Joey moved close to her and she cowered from his aggression.

Edith opened her mouth to answer and then collapsed to the floor. Staring at the ceiling with a blank glaze over her eyes.

"What the . . ." Gladius darted to the floor next to her. "She doesn't have a pulse."

Joey scanned the room, looking for anything that could have killed her.

Julie's voice sounded from Lucas's Panavice. "He killed her. He must have had something implanted. Lucas, I had to do something about her door, it would have killed you if I didn't shut off the security on it . . . but he knows now. I'm sorry. He knows only I could do what I just did. And if he knows I'm alive, he knows you're all alive. I'll do everything I can to protect you."

Joey grimaced at the news and knelt next to Edith. How would Evelyn handle the news of her godmother dying? He wanted to weep for her, but got back to his feet and glared at

Lucas instead. "Let's get Evelyn."

Lucas nodded and looked at his Panavice. "She's on the move, to a corner of the fortress. I don't think there's an exit over there."

"He better not have hurt her," Poly said glaring in the direction Lucas pointed.

CHAPTER 18

HARRIS DROPPED ANOTHER MORTAR INTO the chute and ducked. It shot out and landed on the edge of the building. Travis matched his movements, sending his mortar to the far side, where they knew Marcus kept a landing pad for aircraft. Harris fired another barrage of smoke canisters around the whole building, creating a thicker smoke cloud and cover for the parents as they ran toward the front door.

Julie had turned off all the sensors and the smoke left Marcus all but blind to the attack.

Once the parents were inside the building, Harris sent another mortar into the sky and it landed on the back side of the building, near an escape hatch.

"We should go in," Travis said.

"Soon." He wished he could use his computer controlled weapons and set them on autopilot, but Marcus would hack those so quick, he'd have them blown up before they got the first shot off. These antique weapons worked just as well, but required manpower.

Travis grunted and launched another mortar to his second location.

MINTER STEPPED PAST THE SMOLDERING front door with Rick on his heels. A silvery figure rushed at them in the darkness and he fired three shots into it. "Come on." He knew they needed to continue pushing into the building, keeping up as many fronts as possible.

Karen stepped up next to him holding a gun. She looked nervous as hell. "Where's Joey?"

"He's doing his part, don't worry."

"We are on planet Arrack, facing Marcus Malliden and you tell me not to worry."

Minter sighed and fired into another oncoming Arrack.

"This way," Beth said, pointing at a flight of stairs leading up.

Minter bounded up the stairs two at a time. Reaching the top, he glanced back down at Karen, momentarily wishing he'd left her back on Earth. She wasn't a fighter like the rest of them. He sighed and felt a dagger fly by his face and strike an Arrack stalking him. It slumped to the floor next to the top step.

"Thanks, Opal," Minter said.

She nodded and had another knife in her hand.

Rick pointed past a pair of open doors and moved to one side, waiting for Minter to take the other side. Once into position, Minter glanced into the next huge room. Arracks were scattered, rushing around and picking up bits of concrete, possibly to use as weapons. He knew from his limited view, these weren't organized soldiers. He'd be able to kill each and every one of the bastards.

KRIS STOOD NEXT TO AN air hole, looking past the grate. According to the scouting reports, this pipe would lead down into the bowels of the fortress. "Go for it, Maggie," he said.

She smiled and ignited the bag of debris in her hands, a flammable cocktail courtesy of Harris. She got the mixture smoldering and coughed at the rancid smell.

"Don't breathe it in, sweetie."

She nodded and turned her head away from it.

"Why don't you send them a present?" Kris said to Jasper.

Jasper took the burning bag and set it next to the grate. He took a deep breath away from the bag and then blew the smoke down into the grate. It whistled and bellowed as his immense breath blew the smoke deep into the fortress. He took a quick breath and blew again, sending the smoke deep into the bunker.

"That should keep the bugger out of there." Kris smiled.

"Maggie, grab another bag. Jasper here is going to blow through that one quickly."

Maggie bounced with excitement and with red hands, ignited another bag. "When do we get to go down?"

"Soon. We've just got to wrangle this cat first."

CHAPTER 19

JOEY WATCHED THE RED CIRCLE move to the back corner of the building. Marcus was being herded there by everyone on the outside and he was grateful for their involvement. It gave him the chance to kill Marcus once and for all.

"If we keep moving down this hall and through the kitchen, we should end up close to where he and Evelyn are," Lucas said.

"Let's go then." Poly urged Lucas to get moving.

Joey gripped his rail gun tight in one hand and his Colt semi in the other. The Colt had the party-pack of ammo, especially built for Marcus.

They jogged down the hall and past a double swinging door. The kitchen looked bright and clean. It smelled of soap and burnt chicken. An Arrack stood near the dishwashing station, paralyzed at the sight of the intruders.

Joey raised his gun but then lowered it after looking at the fright in his eyes. "Get in that cabinet." He pointed to the cabinet, but the Arrack seemed confused. He opened the cabinet door and pointed at the Arrack and then in the cabinet. The Arrack slid his feet across the floor, never blinking and climbed into the cabinet. Joey closed the doors and shoved a wooden spoon in the handles. If it spent enough time, Joey was sure it could break the spoon and get out.

Lucas led them past the kitchen and into a cafeteria of sorts. Tables and chairs were scattered around and knocked over, the tables filled with half eaten food. They must have caught them at dinner time. They probably weren't expecting a regimen of Arracks knocking on their front door tonight, let alone a whole army of highly trained people.

Lucas kept low and moved around the chairs. They all made their way to another hall and down several flights of stairs. An Arrack walking up froze at the sight of Lucas. Joey hoped it was another kitchen type. Unfortunately, the Arrack pulled out his dagger and screamed. Gladius lunged forward and killed the Arrack with her dagger, but the damage was done. The sound of many Arracks moving up the stairs sounded from below.

"We didn't expect it to be easy the whole way there." Gladius shrugged.

Lucas backed up, holding out his gun. "If we can get them as they round the corner, they'll have a tough time getting close to us."

"I'll get the left," Joey said.

"I'll take the middle," Poly said.

The sounds of many feet rumbled on the stairs, vibrating tendrils of dust loose from above. The first Arrack rounded the corner and Joey shot the thing in the head, sending it falling back down the stairs. Six more ran past their fallen comrade and

Joey made quick work of five, firing the rail gun. Lucas took the other one out.

Lucas looked over at him in admiration and shook his head.

"I've practiced," Joey said.

"I can see that."

A large group of them filled the whole staircase, but it was just a slaughter for Joey and his gun. Each projectile ripped through the Arracks, six deep. And in a matter of seconds, they had filled the stairwell with dead Arracks.

Joey moved slowly next to the first Arrack and peered down the stairs. "I don't see any."

They made their way over the pile and descended further.

The stairs ended at a large room, lined with beds stacked three high. Joey inspected the beds as they walked by, making sure each lump didn't have a living thing behind it.

An Arrack leapt from the top bed, and Hank grabbed the thing in midair, slamming it on the ground. It didn't bounce or move, black blood trailing from under its head.

"Nice," Lucas said. "Thanks."

Hank looked at his hands in disgust.

At the end of the hall, stood an open door and Joey glanced at his Panavice, the red dot stood just fifty feet in front of them. Evelyn was in that room, which meant they'd found Marcus as well. The last encounter nearly killed them all and resulted in losing Evelyn. This time would be different. He wouldn't allow Marcus to escape, the man had nowhere to go and they had all made sure of that.

Joey resisted the urge to run straight into the room and kill the bastard. Marcus had even left the door open, an invitation. He felt the cream Julie put on him wearing off or maybe the pain was so severe it didn't help it anymore. The weariness in his muscles and his bones was great. He could still shoot better than most, but he didn't know much about Marcus's ability—other than Harris saying he could beat any man, living or dead, including himself. But he was still a man. He had weaknesses, he would make mistakes.

"What should we do?" Poly asked, looking at the open door.

"We split, three in, two out," Lucas said.

"Okay, Lucas and Poly, come with me. You guys," he looked to Hank and Gladius, "come in behind us."

They nodded in unison.

Joey walked down the hall, leading the way. He kept his Colt in his right hand and waited for Marcus to make an appearance. Past the ornate wood door, it looked similar to the rooms in his bunker on Earth. His bedroom had a bed, a dresser, and was devoid of any personal effects, and a family room with a couch and fireplace on the other side.

A little girl's face popped up from the couch and ducked back down.

"Was that . . ." Poly asked.

It couldn't have been. That girl was a two-year-old, not a baby.

"Come out, sweetie," Marcus said walking out of a bathroom attached to the bedroom. He dried his hands with a white towel and tossed it on the back of a chair. The little girl came out from behind the couch and ran up to Marcus. He lifted her up and smiled, tapping her nose. "They're here. Just like I promised."

"Edith is dead," she said.

"I know, it was a terrible accident, I'm sure."

Joey raged at the sight of his daughter aged a couple of years in only a few days. Is this what Edith had talked about? Is this what they did to her?

Joey rushed forward, Lucas and Poly flanked him. He hit a solid wall a few feet into the room. His gun bent back and he reached his hand out, feeling the invisible wall.

"I knew you wouldn't act rational." Marcus said, casually turning to look at them. "That's why I have the wall up. Don't bother trying, you can't get past it unless I allow it."

"Give her back," Joey said.

"You don't deserve her. You have no idea how important she is to the worlds."

"This again?" Joey asked. "Give her to us, now."

"What did you do to her?" Poly asked.

"I helped her. I did what you couldn't and probably wouldn't do. She had the mind of a giant, stuck in a baby's body, it was cruel. I set her free and now she'll grow up as quick as her mind does."

"You bastard, I'm going to kill you." Poly used different knives and stabbed at the wall but nothing got through. She flailed against the wall, crying and reaching for Evelyn.

Marcus looked concerned and adjusted Evelyn in his arms. "I obviously could have killed all of you a hundred times over since we first knew of each other, but I haven't. Don't you want to know why? Your beautiful daughter here understands the why, but she wants her momma, her papa, and her friends to know why. She won't help me without you."

"You tried to kill us back in your bunker." Poly seethed with rage.

"Yes, I did. You've become most irksome to my plan of saving Earth. Curious though, how Alice reported you dead when you are obviously alive. Something I will no doubt figure out in time. Where is Julie?"

"She's gone back on Earth," Lucas said.

Marcus laughed. "I know she is near. She is one of the most fascinating people in all the common worlds. I will be truly interested in seeing what you and her produce for a child."

Lucas fired an arrow against the shield and it bounced off.

"Come on in, Hank and Gladius. This regards you as well."

Hank and Gladius hung around the door and stayed there.

"Very well. I've been searching for you all since the day I made a journey to a purged planet. Do you know how many mutants I've created, trying to invent something as special as all of you?"

Joey paced near the shield and gave Lucas the look. Lucas typed into his Panavice and nodded his head. They had figured on a shield from Marcus, and Julie had linked her Panavice with Lucas's. Lucas looked down at his Panavice and showed Joey the screen.

Ten minutes.

He cringed at the idea of waiting another ten minutes while this putrid man spewed his poison for his daughter to hear.

"How many mutants did you create?" Lucas asked and Poly sent him a hateful look.

Marcus continued, ignoring Lucas's ploy to keep him talking. "You know, each of them are related to me in some way? I took my own superior DNA in an attempt to create special people like you."

Joey rolled his eyes and sighed. He couldn't listen to this man for one more second. "Why don't you just kill yourself? Save us the time here and we can move on with our lives. If Evelyn is so important, don't keep her from her parents."

"What I'm trying to say is, Isaac used a serum based off of my DNA to help create you. Now, I'm not saying I'm your dad or anything, but we are definitely related. Evelyn has even taken to calling me Grandpa."

"Gramps," Evelyn said. "It's funny because you don't look older than thirty-two."

"Dang, have I already hit the thirties?"

"If he doesn't stop . . ." Poly punched at the wall.

"Come on, Julie," Joey whispered to himself.

"Now I am sure Julie is trying to tear this wall down, so I will be quick with my story." Marcus set down Evelyn and she jumped on the seat next to him.

"Evelyn, come to Mommy."

"You need to hear what he's going to say," Evelyn said.

"Thank you, my dear." Marcus took a few steps closer to them. "You know, I didn't send Isaac to kill your parents. I actually had no knowledge of his actions until much later. He was trying to win back my favor after I punished him for ruining Ryjack.

"And Simon, well, he overstepped my orders and killed Almadon, but to be fair, I'd only told him you were off limits. He was merely trying to bring you to me so I could keep you safe and help create her." He pointed to Evelyn.

"I suppose Samantha was just an accident?" Poly said.

Marcus sighed. "Her death was an unfortunate side effect of bringing in a man I knew little about. Zach picked me up in his big rig the first day I arrived on Earth. I told him I'd make him a person of great importance and power and I would only require his complete obedience until our task was complete. But Zach had flaws and disobeyed me. I believe he thought he had surpassed me in some way. In the end, he acted on his own in killing her."

"So we are to assume you are an innocent bystander of

multiple unfortunate circumstances?" Joey asked.

"For the most part, yes. There is a threat out there like nothing else in all the worlds. There is a society with technology I could only describe as magic and science weaved together. But they need human bodies to sustain themselves, and from the wrecks of worlds they leave behind, it's apparent they need a lot of them. I think there might even be two such of these greater beings, battling each other. I've noticed differences in purged worlds."

"Hector's world?" Lucas said.

"You've seen one of these worlds then?" Marcus asked.

Joey glared at Lucas. "Yes."

"Good, then you will understand when I show you this. It always starts the same. A woman appears on every TV, phone, radio, intercom, and walkie-talkie, delivering a message to the world. To save our limited time, I'm just going to show you her video."

A projection of the woman appeared on the invisible wall. She looked to be in her late thirties. Pretty, but had a look of stone determination. "It is my deepest regret to inform you that although your lives seem important to each and every one of you, you're entire civilization is but a mere blip in time and space. I have a great need for you. Your lives, your essence, will push me on, and therefore, your existence will have meaning.

"Our culling will begin immediately. You may resist with all the vigor your world can muster, but none of it will matter in the end. Take solace in knowing there are many of you in existence, so no matter how far we reach, there will always be a *you* somewhere in the worlds. I thank you for the gift you are giving us. You matter more than you know."

The screen blanked out and Marcus stood closer to the wall,

walking the edge of it.

"What the hell was that?" Gladius asked.

"Please listen to him," Evelyn said.

Hearing Evelyn's support of this man invigorated Joey's resolve to crush down the wall and kill him. He pushed on it with his hands and tried to get Evelyn's gaze. She looked so much older.

"This is who I believe created the stones," Marcus continued. "She uses them to wipe entire species off the map. I'm not sure what is behind her motivation exactly, but it's only a matter of time until she finds Earth. And when that happens, there is nothing you can do to stop her."

"What does any of this have to do with anything?" Lucas asked.

"The Cough. You think I used it to take control of Earth, and there is some truth to that, but ultimately I am trying to save it, maybe save all the worlds. The tech they possess—" Marcus shook his head. "Don't you guys get it?" He pointed at Evelyn. "They're coming and they'll take all of you, unless she is ready for them."

"Evelyn, come here sweetie," Poly said.

"No, Mom. You've been scared of me since the day I was born. Don't think I don't see the way you look at me. Even now, I can hear it in your breath and see it in your eyes."

"That's not true."

Evelyn hopped off her chair and walked to the edge of the screen. Poly knelt and Joey stood behind her, keeping his focus between Marcus and Evelyn. Seeing his daughter walking stirred emotions of pride, fear, and anger. Marcus changed her, made her body grow into a little girl, but her eyes looked the same.

Poly reached for her, but the invisible wall stopped the

mother-daughter embrace.

"*He* hasn't lied to me." Evelyn pointed back to Marcus and Joey felt his anger hitting its zenith. Changing his girl's appearance was one thing, but corrupting her heart and mind was completely another. "So you don't lie to me now, Mother. Are you afraid of me?"

Poly sobbed and wiped her eyes. "I wasn't afraid of *you*, but of what you meant. This horrible man," she pointed at Marcus, "has destroyed all of our lives, and if you were just a normal little girl, he wouldn't try to take you away from us. But you are right, I knew the first second I saw you, you were different."

"You think I'm strange."

"No." Poly placed her hands on the wall. "No, I thought you were the most wonderful thing ever to appear on Earth. But that knowledge sent deep fear into me because I knew he'd be coming for you."

Evelyn smiled and looked from Joey to Poly. "I believe you."

"Then end this now, Evelyn. I know you can stop this. Stop Marcus and take this wall down."

Evelyn looked back at Marcus and then to Poly. Joey gripped his gun tight and readied himself for what Poly asked Evelyn to do. "You still don't get it, Mom. I was made for a purpose. I have a specific task I need to complete, and Marcus is going to help me with it. We need him."

"No," Poly sobbed. "He's evil. You can't trust him."

"I can tell when a person is lying; he has not lied to me."

Joey glanced at Lucas and his Panavice. Lucas gave him a slight nod.

"I headed to this room on purpose," Marcus stepped in. "I knew it'd give me the opportunity to explain things. Now that you know what is at stake—the entire planet and every other one just like it—you need to know Evelyn is our best chance at stopping them and taking the fight to them. I am constructing an entire facility dedicated to Evelyn back on Earth. But she needs a mom, she needs a dad. I want you to join her there in preparation."

Joey reeled from the offer.

"We aren't going anywhere with you," Poly said.

"This is what you wanted . . ." Marcus said. "This is the chance for it all to be over between you and me. No more chasing, no more fear of who is behind you, no more wondering if your family is safe. You and your family can live together and when the time comes, we'll save all the worlds, with Evelyn at the front line."

"What can a little girl do to save the world?" Gladius asked.

"I implanted a nanobot into every person on planet Earth and when the time comes, Evelyn will be able to access every one of those."

"Why don't you just do it yourself and leave us alone?" Poly asked.

"If I could, I would. This task is solely in the hands of Evelyn."

"What?" Lucas said, looking at his screen. "No, no, no . . ." Panic spread over his face. He pursed his lips and stared at Joey, trying to convey a message without words. Something had gone terribly wrong, and the way Lucas looked at the Panavice, it must have been Julie.

"I'm sorry," Lucas said before running out of the room.

Hank moved to follow him, but Gladius put a hand on his shoulder. "I'll watch his back," she said and ran after Lucas.

Hank raised his hand in protest, but she was gone.

"Just the three of us now, and from the looks of it, Julie isn't breaking my wall down anymore. Hope she's okay," Marcus said with a wry smile that made Joey want to slap it off his face. If he'd done anything to Julie . . .

Joey pulled out his Panavice and looked at the screen. A message from Lucas said, *Julie's having the baby*

No, it's too soon, he thought. Poly got up and peered at the screen. She couldn't hold back her gasp.

"Bad news?" Marcus asked.

"Julie's having her child. I can't wait to finally see him," Evelyn said.

"How do you know that?" Poly asked.

CHAPTER 20

JULIE GROANED AND GRIPPED HER stomach as another contraction hit. Her pants were soaked from her water breaking. She punched in a message to Lucas, and then looked around for another person to help. But in the dark of the night, all she saw were glowing rocks and embers from a few cindered bushes around Marcus's compound. *Not now, anytime but now, it's too soon.*

She gripped her Panavice and sent another bot into his system, trying to find the weakness in his code. Another contraction and she dropped to her knees. The Panavice slipped from her hands and fell into the dirt.

The contraction passed and she picked up her Panavice. She'd break down the wall if it killed her; she owed it to her friends and to her rapidly arriving baby. She didn't want a child to be born in a world where Marcus still existed.

OMW, Lucas texted her.

She knew he'd come running and regretted telling him, but she couldn't let them keep thinking the wall was coming down any second. She used her moment of comfort to double her efforts, searching and probing the edges of his program. It was as complex as anything she'd seen, except for the purge people's tech.

One of her bots sent back a green light message, meaning it found a way in. Her fingers flew across the screen, looking at what the bot found. She opened up her nuke program when another contraction hit. She reeled in pain and dropped her Panavice again.

"Didn't expect to find you alone," Emmett said, reaching down to pick up her Panavice.

HARRIS RUSHED INTO THE BUILDING with Travis. The parents were expected to take the left side and they would take the right. He spotted Evelyn's dot, deep into the bunker and hoped the kids were able to handle Marcus. He had another place to go.

The entry didn't have a moving Arrack in sight. The parents did their job well.

"It should be near the main power source," Travis said.

Harris nodded in agreement and ran to the back of the entry and through a double door, held open by two dead Arracks. Past the doors, another room, a banquet room perhaps. It didn't have any tables or chairs, but a few tapestries hung on the walls with various fruits and vegetables.

He dashed across the room and shoved open another door. Lucas ran into him.

"Whoa, what happened?" Harris asked.

"It's Julie, she's having the baby." Lucas tried to move past him, but Harris pushed him back.

"What of Marcus?"

"They are in a standoff in his room. He's got a barrier up. Spouting all kinds of junk, saying Evelyn is going to save the world from those purge people. It was his plan all along."

Gladius ran up to them. "Jeesh, man, you are fast. Hey, Dad, Harris."

Lucas pushed past Harris and ran toward the front of the building. Gladius raised her brows and ran after him.

Travis stepped toward Gladius, and Harris thought the man might be considering going with her.

"Come on, we've got to do our part," Harris said.

Travis took a deep breath. "I hate she is involved in this. If anything happens to her, I won't be able to honor my agreement with Poly."

Harris nodded. "I won't fight you if that time comes." He ran down the stone stairs and through many corridors and rooms. The passage became narrow, forcing them to walk sideways to get past the last hallway and then crouch down as the ceiling got lower and lower.

A steel door stood at the end of the hall. There was nothing particularly secure about it but enough to keep out any wandering Arrack who may happen upon it. Harris pulled out his Panavice and typed into the screen. The lock on the door turned green and the door swung in.

The white walls and stainless steel of the interior room felt in sharp contrast to the stone structure they'd been running around in. Marcus was a never ending supply of surprise. How he could have a room like this, made so far from anything remotely considered technological, was a feat in itself. Harris walked into the room scanning for, and not finding, any traps.

"You sure she's in here?" Travis asked.

"Oh yeah, this is it. The last stored version of her in any world we know of."

A single black stand sat in the middle of the room, about the size of a filing cabinet.

"Is she . . . active?"

"No, she's in stasis."

"You sure he doesn't have another version out there?"

"I don't think so. We just need to destroy her here, leaving the last remnants on Earth. And Julie has an end game set up for her as well." Harris felt his jacket pocket. "You got the card?"

"Yeah," Travis said and handed Harris a red card with a green dragon on it.

"Nice design. I know of a lady who'd love it."

Travis nodded but didn't say a word as Harris slid the card into the slot. He then pulled a Panavice from his jacket pocket and placed it next to the card. The bar on the screen ran up to a hundred percent. Harris pulled the card out.

"This is going to set our worlds free," Harris said, shaking the card in the air. "And you should have it." He handed Travis the card.

"I thought this was your whole reason for coming here, to pillage all of Marcus's knowledge."

"I trust you will put it to good use." Harris watched Travis take the red card. "Now," he turned to the black tower, "we destroy her and everything Marcus ever created." Pulling a vial from his jacket, he placed it on top of the black cube. He then set a catalyst right next to it, strapped with a small explosive. "Okay, it's set." Harris backed away from the device. "Thirty seconds."

Travis backed up with Harris until they were out of the room and shut the door. Harris watched the seconds count down on his Panavice until it reached one. A small explosion sounded from the room. It was no louder than the firecrackers he played with in his youth, but it wasn't the explosion that would kill Alice, Renee, or whatever version Marcus created for her here.

He stepped into the room and watched as the liquid vials spilled over the metal cube. It melted the sides and created a hole right through the middle, dripping into the stone floor. In under a minute, the entire cube melted into a black pool on the floor.

"She's gone," Harris said. For him, this was the second to last part of their plan and for the most part, it had gone better than he ever could have hoped for.

Now onto the last stage. However, Marcus wasn't going to go down easily, and from the sound of it, he'd taken to psychological warfare with the kids. He hoped they had the will strong enough to ignore the man's words until he got there.

Harris rushed back down the stone hall and up the stairs.

"I have an idea," Travis said as he stopped, halting their progress. "He's formed a wall that I imagine only Julie can get through."

"Yes, that's safe to assume."

"What if we find a workaround? You have another one of those vial set ups?"

Harris smiled and pulled the vial from his jacket. "I like the way you think, Denail."

MINTER GRIPPED HIS GUN AND fired into an oncoming Arrack. The building seethed with them and he felt around his jacket for more clips. They protected this part of the building more than any other they'd encountered so far. "Rick, to the left!"

Rick shot an Arrack only a few feet from plunging its dagger into Karen's back.

"Thanks," Karen said, holding a gun of her own. Minter tried with all his might to get her to stay behind but she'd insisted.

"Harris gave you the okay, Beth?" Minter called.

"Yeah."

"You ready?"

Beth walked forward, holding her Panavice. She nodded and placed it on the desk. She pulled out a cord and plugged it into a wall full of panels. A green light lit above the cord. She picked up her Panavice and typed into it. "The download's going to take ten minutes. Why don't you guys go help the kids while it's—"

Minter fired three quick shots into a group of Arracks rounding the corner. Rick fired two more and finished them off.

"We stick together," Minter said. "If we don't kill everything this man has, another might take his place. It ends here."

CHAPTER 21

JOEY PACED NEAR THE CLEAR wall holding him back from his daughter.

Marcus hadn't said anything in the last few minutes, but the expression on his face said all Joey needed to know. The creases between his eyes grew deep and his lips went razor thin. Something bad was happening and it made Joey smile. His parents and Harris were doing their part and at the very least, they silenced Marcus.

Poly tried to get Evelyn to talk to her, but she seemed to be giving her mom the silent treatment.

"Fine," Joey said to Marcus. "We'll go with you if you can guarantee you won't harm any of us here, and we have control of Evelyn."

Poly faced him, stunned.

Marcus looked up. "No harm will come to any of you, but

I have to be in control of what Evelyn is taught and the way she is taught. I cannot have any interference in this."

"No," Poly said, shaking her head at Joey.

"Agreed."

"I'm glad you've come around. I really feel she needs her parents."

Evelyn jumped from the couch and walked close to the wall. Joey watched her prying eyes and felt a tingling in his head. He squinted and pushed his thoughts down. He wasn't sure why, but it felt as if she could actually read his thoughts and might even pick up on his lie.

"I'm so happy," Evelyn said. "We can be a family again."

Poly sobbed and covered her face with her hands. "How can you do this?" she mumbled.

"This is how it has to be, Poly."

"No!" She stood up and attacked him. "You don't have the right to make this decision." She peppered his chest with punches.

He wrapped her up in a hug, squishing her arms against his chest. He kissed the side of her head and whispered, "Trust me."

"How do you feel about this, Hank?" Marcus asked.

"I still want to kill you."

"He's telling the truth," Evelyn said and laughed. "I can't wait to get to know you, Hank."

"Joey, place your weapons and Pana on the floor and I'll allow you alone to enter the room."

"Let me in there!" Poly yelled, pounding against the wall.

Joey set his guns on the floor and stared at the Colt with its party pack in it. One of those bullets was supposed to be the end of Marcus, and now he needed to find another way. He set his

Panavice, and a multi-material dagger Poly had made for him, on the floor.

Walking to the wall, he nodded to Marcus.

"You are allowed to move through it now," Marcus said.

Joey put up his hand and felt nothing but air where the shield had been. Poly rushed to his spot and tried to get through, but the wall held for her. Joey sidestepped her and entered the room with Evelyn and Marcus. Poly grabbed his hand before it crossed through the wall, and he turned around to stare at her. Tears formed in her eyes as she shook her head.

"I love you, Poly. You have to let me go now," he said, squeezing her hand.

She squeezed back before letting go, turning away to compose herself. Hank pulled her into a hug and whispered into her ear.

Evelyn ran up to him and he knelt down, hugging her. Her body felt so big now. Just days ago, he'd held her as a baby, and now she was the size of a two-year-old. He wanted to cry at what Marcus had done to her, but held it back and gave her a smile.

"What's wrong?" she asked.

"Nothing, just missed a few milestones with you is all."

"Don't feel bad, I like it this way. Being in that tiny body, my muscles wouldn't work properly, my throat couldn't form words in the right way. This *is* better."

"You're so smart."

She smiled. "The smartest."

"Telling jokes already?" Joey brushed her hair back. It had grown several inches as well.

"I learned from Lucas."

"Another joke?"

She laughed. It was the first time he heard her new laugh and he hugged her again, wanting to spend every last second he had with his daughter.

"I love you so much, Evelyn."

"I love you too, Daddy."

"Can you go over to the corner of the room and take a seat, facing the wall?"

She stuck out her bottom lip and looked to Marcus. "You have to try, I know that now. But, Daddy, you might not do it, and even if you do . . . I may not be able to save you all in the end."

"In time, you'll know."

Evelyn nodded her head.

"Now go on, get to the corner and don't look back."

He held her hand for a moment and then she pulled away, taking a seat, facing the wall in the corner of the room.

"This is a mistake, Joey," Marcus said and put his Panavice in his jacket pocket. "All I want is for you to raise your daughter in the safety of my protection. If you end me, then all is lost for your world. They will come and they will take everyone you've ever cared about, including Evelyn."

Joey glanced at Poly, her hands pounded against the glass again, screaming, "*No!*"

Past her, he spotted Kris entering the room with Maggie.

"The more the merrier," Marcus said.

Kris touched the invisible barrier. "Maggie, do your thing."

Maggie's red-hot hand touched the barrier. The clear wall shimmered under the extreme heat.

"She might actually get through," Marcus said in admiration. "I've always loved the mutants."

"Don't do anything, Joey, we'll be in there soon," Poly

pleaded.

Behind her, Hank looked distraught. Joey met his gaze. Sharing a heavy look, Hank nodded his understanding, a tear rolling down his cheek.

"Yeah, Joey, don't do anything," Marcus mocked and tossed a silver ball onto the floor.

Joey turned to stare at the device, the same ball that kept him from saving Samantha. He took a deep breath and looked back to Poly; he had to end it before she came through. And from the looks of Maggie, it might not be long. The clear wall had an orange tint to it now and some of it sagged around her hands.

Joey rushed to Marcus who took his approach with an amused smile. Within a few feet of Marcus, Joey swung for the man's stupid face, but he shifted a few inches and dodged it.

"No need to get violent," Marcus said.

He swung again and missed. Swinging for his stomach next, Marcus blocked his hit with a hit of his own. He gave up the punches and jumped onto Marcus, but the bastard grabbed Joey's arm and slammed him onto the ground.

"Don't hurt him!" Evelyn said from her chair, still looking at the wall.

Marcus sighed and took a step back from Joey, holding out his hands.

Joey rolled over and struggled to get to his feet. Not just from the fall to the ground, but from the punishment his body went through the night before. The cream had worn off, his muscles were aching and telling him to lie down and sleep for days.

"Joey!" Karen yelled.

He turned to his mom and dad as they ran into the room

with the rest of the parents.

"My, oh my. You even brought the originals out to play? Well, this *is* a treat. I've never been able to meet you. Hello." Marcus waved and Joey used the distraction to rush him.

Marcus side stepped the attack and sent Joey face first to the floor, right next to the steel ball. Completely ignoring him, Marcus walked closer to the wall. "I recognize you all from the videos. Who would think, after all these years . . . here we are, together in one room?"

Joey picked up the ball and gripped it tight in his hands as he got to his feet.

Marcus glanced over his shoulder, sensing his approach, but Joey walked wide, getting closer to Maggie. The wall had turned as red as Maggie's hands and sagged in heavy clumps around her two hands.

"As I was telling dear Joey here, this doesn't have to be violent. Evelyn is in agreement. You all don't have to die in some attempt to take me out."

A pop sound came from above, sounding like a single shot from a gun. Lucas had a gun, but he should have been on his way to Julie. That meant Harris or Emmett. No one had seen Emmett yet, but knowing Marcus, he was somewhere creating the most trouble possible.

"We can't let you have our queen," Kris said.

The room felt like a warming furnace and sweat beaded on Joey's forehead. He kept near Maggie, taking the heat and waiting for the moment the wall would come down.

A crack sound drew Joey's attention to the ceiling again and something dripped down from above. The liquid fell to the rug on the floor and hissed, dissolving a section. More drops fell from above, splatting on the ground and destroying the rug. A hole formed in the ceiling from the drip and it grew each second.

"What the hell?" Marcus said, looking at the ceiling.

Joey glanced back at Maggie. The wall shimmered and her hand plunged into the room.

"Catch this." He tossed the ball and Maggie caught it with her fiery hand, the ball melting between her fingers.

"Wait!" Marcus held out his hands and froze in place.

Joey gritted his teeth and shivered. He didn't know how long he had to kill Marcus, but he wasn't going to waste it.

The ceiling hole had enlarged to the size of a person and as he rushed by, he spotted Harris getting ready to jump in. Joey couldn't have timed it better, he'd be rid of Marcus before the rest of his friends and family were killed. And maybe if he did it fast enough, he'd live through it as well.

The sounds of the room dulled to a low hum, and he glanced back at the people he loved, watching him with frozen expressions.

He threw a punch at Marcus and this time it landed, but Joey screamed out in pain as the shield blocked his blow. Wringing his hand, he grabbed Marcus by the jacket and pushed his body to the floor, face up. He picked up the wooden chair and smashed it over his face, but it didn't cause damage like it should have. He tossed the broken chair to the floor and picked up a glass vase, breaking it into a sharp piece. Getting on top of Marcus, he pressed the blade against his eye; the makeshift blade doing nothing but slicing through his own skin. He dropped it and looked at his bloody hands.

The stretch on his mind started, not as bad as last time but he felt the pull, felt his body melting from the inside. He didn't have much longer before he damaged himself again. His legs and hands shook and he fought the growing urge to release. "There has to be a way!"

"Daddy," Evelyn stood in the corner, facing him.

He darted his attention to Marcus, but he stood there, still, and the sounds were dull; they were both in slow motion together. "You shouldn't be here, Evelyn."

"I can't watch you die, you have to let go before it's too late. I had to come here to tell you that." Tears built in her eyes.

"Tell me how to kill him then," Joey pleaded, feeling the pull of time so much his vision distorted and Evelyn shifted into three people before consolidating.

"It's too late." She cried and shook her head. "You're not going to make it now." She ran up to Joey and hugged him. "I'm sorry, I should have known you'd not let him live. I should have ended this long ago and now I'm going to lose you."

"I'm still right here," he strained to stay holding onto his daughter. "I'll never leave you."

"I won't forget you. If you can last a few more seconds, I can show you how to kill him before everyone else I love dies." Evelyn turned his head up and pointed at the ceiling. A drop of the liquid was falling from the hole above, only a few feet above the floor.

"Of course." Joey struggled to get his aching body moving again and pulled Marcus, dragging him underneath the floating drop, positioning him just right. Joey lay on him, putting as much weight on the man as he could. "Evelyn?"

"Yes?"

"Take care of your mom, you're going to need each other."

"She's not going to do well without you."

"I know." A lump formed in his throat, making it hard to get the rest out. "Tell her I love her and I love you as well. I'm so sorry, Evelyn. I wish it could be different, but I had to protect you both."

"I will, I'll tell her. And Daddy . . . I love you too, so much."

Seeing her teary face, he released from the void and saw the horrible realization in Marcus's eyes as the drop struck him in the head, dissolving a tiny hole through his skull in an instant. A blood trail streaked over his forehead and the blank stare from Marcus told Joey everything he needed to know.

Marcus was dead.

He collapsed on his body, no longer able to move and saw Poly screaming and running up to him. He tried to mouth a few words, but they wouldn't come out. His whole body felt liquefied, and the bands holding his mind together, erupted.

CHAPTER 22

THE SECOND MAGGIE CAUGHT THE ball and destroyed it, Poly knew she'd lost Joey. Seeing the room destroyed in an instant did little to console her. Even when the blur ended with Joey on top of Marcus and Marcus dead, it did nothing to stop her agony.

She pushed past Maggie and felt the burning heat scorching her arms and legs, getting to Joey. He looked at her in his last moment. She captured his gaze and slid to the floor, pulling Joey off Marcus. "Help!" She rolled him on his back and screamed as her heart broke, holding him to her chest. "We need to get him to the machine! Marcus has to have one here."

Harris dropped into the room from above, with Travis right behind him.

"Travis, help me," she pleaded.

Travis rushed down and picked Joey up off the floor.

"He's gone," Evelyn said.

"Oh, Evelyn," Poly ran and picked up her little girl. Tears ran down the sides of her little face and she quivered, looking at her dad in Travis's arms. "We're going to fix him. We've done it before."

"Not this time," Evelyn sobbed.

"I know where the medical wing is," Hank said.

"Go. I'll take care of this," Harris said, gesturing to Marcus.

Poly didn't need an okay from Harris, she pushed Travis along to follow Hank. The parents cried as Joey was carried by, and Karen held onto Minter, both running right behind Poly.

Hank took them through multiple corridors before finally getting to the same wing where Edith lay dead. Poly held Evelyn's head against her chest, blocking the view of her godmother as they moved by. They entered a small room with the makings machine. Travis lay Joey down gently, before closing it and turning it on.

"Come on." He pressed on Poly and ushered her out of the room. He closed the door and looked through the small window on it.

"Is he going to make it?" Poly asked.

"I don't know, he was getting cold . . . there are limits to what our technology can do."

Poly didn't like the answer and hugged Evelyn tighter. Putting her daughter down, she collapsed in front of the door and leaned her head against it.

Evelyn got up and looked back to where Edith lay. "I knew when Edith died. It called out to me like a faint scream. I think it was her soul releasing."

Poly perked up. "Did you hear your dad?"

"No. He's holding on. He's holding on for you. Mom, you

have to let him go."

"No, I need him, I can't live without him. We've been through too much to end like this." Poly lost control and sobbed against the door.

"It's not for you, but for him. He needs to move on. He needs to go to the place beyond and wait for us. We will see him again," Evelyn said.

Poly wiped the tears from her face and looked up to her daughter standing over her. She barely recognized her face. "How do you know?"

"I feel things. And I feel him screaming in pain."

Poly stood and looked through the window. He'd pulled through last time, and she had faith he'd make it again. She put her hand on the door. "I'm sorry, I can't let him go."

"Then he'll stay, but what we are going to get isn't what you want," Evelyn said. "It's not what any of us are going to want." Tears flowed from her face. "You have to let him go. He'll be free, with his soul intact."

She turned from her daughter. "I can't." *Fight it, Joey. I'm right here for you.* She wished she could feel him, she wished she had the extra sense of him that Evelyn had.

If you did, you wouldn't be doing what you're doing, Evelyn's voice sounded in her head.

"Was that you?"

Evelyn looked away.

No one said anything as Poly leaned against the door, crying her life out from herself. She knew deep down what Evelyn meant, but she couldn't let go, even if she wanted to. Letting go of Joey would be letting go of her own life. If there was even the slimmest of chances, she'd take it. She'd hold on until there was nothing left to grasp and then she'd keep reaching, trying to find him. It wasn't a conscious decision but one her own soul made for her.

She wasn't sure how much time had passed, but she felt Travis touch her shoulder.

"It's done," he said.

CHAPTER 23

LUCAS RAN ACROSS THE SCORCHED ground in front of Marcus's fortress. It killed him to be split between his wife and his friends. They both needed him and he hoped he didn't just leave them to their deaths.

The hill they'd left Julie on felt distant. He checked his Panavice again and wondered why she stopped responding. His mind went wild with child birth complications. He cursed himself for leaving her alone.

Shapes formed as his eyes grew accustom to the darkness. The bodies of Arracks, charred and smoldering lay everywhere and he dodged a few, jumping over others, while running as hard as he could. He glanced back to see Gladius still trailing him. He didn't think she had it in her to keep up but she looked as determined as he felt.

He stumbled over a burnt Arrack and took a few steps to

get his footing before continuing to run. At the bottom of the hill, he kept pace, even as his lungs and heart protested the exertion. He knew she should be at the top of the hill and kept pushing through the soft soil.

Reaching the top, he searched around, frantically trying to find his wife. He thought about calling out her name when he saw her pants on the ground. He picked them up and they were soaked. He tossed them to the ground and looked at the soil, checking for the impressions from her departure—any clue as to her whereabouts.

"She couldn't have gone far," Gladius panted out in a whisper, looking at the ground. "Look, heel drags." She pointed at the two lines in the dirt.

They led down to the abandoned town. Wind gusted up, bits of sand hitting his legs and stinging the tears in his eyes.

"Someone took her?" He faced the wind and ran into it, down the hill.

"Wait," Gladius whispered, grabbing his arm. "We've got to be smart about this, you might get her killed."

Lucas slid to a stop. "What do you mean?"

"One, she's in labor. Two, she's been taken by someone for reasons we don't know. Bottom line, we need to approach with caution."

"Fine, we go in silent, but not slow. The wind is in our favor."

Gladius nodded.

Lucas ran down the hill. He avoided a few large rocks and jumped over a small bush as he kept his max pace. The first roof tops came into sight. It didn't take long, even with the wind gusting against him, to get to the edge of the first house.

He waited for Gladius and she ran up next to him, breathing

hard. He bent over, thinking he might throw up, but fought it back down. "I can't catch my breath," he said.

"You're telling me."

A scream sounded from a building across the street.

Lucas stood erect and faced the noise. "Julie."

"Wait," Gladius said grabbing his arm again. "Let's split up, you take the right and I'll flank the building from the left."

"Okay." Lucas slid next to the wall and heard Julie scream again. He took out Prudence and held a few arrows. Staying close to the wall, he stepped into the building through a hole in the wall. Julie screamed again and he heard the mumbling of a man in the room. This sent Lucas into a flurry of emotion. He rounded a corner and crept up to the busted out opening that once probably held a window. He saw the man behind the voice.

Emmett knelt near the bottom of Julie's spread legs. "Come on, you can do this," he said.

"It's too soon," Julie cried.

"Marcus wants this baby, so you can either push it out or I can take it out."

Lucas spotted Gladius on the other side of the room and he directed her to go to the back door. She disappeared around the corner and he waited for her distraction.

His sweaty hand held the arrow and then he heard the knock on the door at the back of the house. Emmett stood up and looked toward the noise. Lucas jumped up and fired two special arrows meant for Marcus, in quick succession. Emmett didn't even see him as the arrows crashed into his chest. He slumped forward, stunned at the sight of them sticking from his body and fell in between Julie's legs. She screamed and scrambled backward.

"Lucas?" Julie called out, panicking.

He jumped through the window, pulling back an arrow, waiting for Emmett to move.

Gladius came through the door, holding a large knife.

The dirt floor ground under his feet as he approached Emmett's body. Lucas kicked him and rolled him onto his back.

Emmett coughed, blood spewing from his mouth and down his face. He reached for his side, but Gladius stepped on his arm. "So this is how it ends?" he asked, coughing again. "I'm okay with it, I'm ready to go. Finish me off, I don't want to bleed out like this."

"I . . ." Lucas held his bow steady on Emmett's face. The man didn't deserve a quick, clean death.

Julie screeched in pain, making his decision easy. His wife needed him. Letting the arrow fly, it landed with a thud in the middle of Emmett's face. Slinging Prudence over his shoulder, he turned to Julie.

She groaned and grabbed her bare knees, face strained. After a few seconds, her face relaxed and she said, "I don't want to have my child here. Not on Arrack."

He wanted to grant her wish and ran his hands through his hair, pacing next to her, thinking of a way. "We are too far away from anything. Can you stand?"

"This baby is coming, Lucas," Julie said.

"Julie, I'm going to check your dilation, okay?" Julie nodded and Gladius went between her legs. "I'd put you at a seven. You think you can move?"

Julie nodded again.

"Let's get you up then," Gladius said and reached down low. She put Julie's arm over her shoulder and Lucas took her other side. Together, they lifted her to her feet.

She cried out and hunched over.

"The building next door is cleaner and doesn't have a dead body in it. How about we get you there?" Gladius suggested.

They helped Julie walk out of the room and into the next. Gladius had been right, the room felt cleaner and the dust hadn't settled much on the floor. Gladius took off her jacket and laid it out.

"Okay, we're moving to the floor now," Gladius said.

"It's too soon," Julie said. "I'm not due for another couple months and then some. Something's wrong."

Lucas gave her a smile and took off his shirt. He placed the shirt over her bare legs. "I hope you know about childbirth." He looked to Gladius, pleading.

"I do, but it's been in hospitals. Not in . . . whatever you'd call this place."

"What do we do?" Lucas asked.

"Did you kill him?" Julie asked.

"Yeah, we just killed him in the last room." He wondered if she was losing her mind.

"Not Emmett, you imbecile, Marcus."

"I don't know. The whole rest of the place has been cleared out though." He looked at his Panavice and sent Poly a ping.

"Was there a hospital in the fortress?"

"Yeah, a real fancy looking one."

She grabbed his shirt and pulled him close to her face. "Take me there."

"We ran for two miles to get here."

"There are wagons outside." Julie groaned and got to her feet, holding onto Lucas's shirt.

"You sure?"

"I'm not having my child in this shit hole!" She walked out

of the room and into the windy darkness of outside.

They found a wagon with decent padding and set up Julie in the backseat. Lucas climbed in with her. "You okay?"

"You ask me that one more time and I'm going to stab you."

Lucas knocked twice on the wood paneling and Gladius got the wagon moving.

"Okay, we're moving." He leaned across the wagon and kissed Julie on her sweaty forehead. "You look great."

"Liar." But she smiled.

Lucas got a message from Hank and felt the blood fleeting from his face. "Marcus is dead, but something happened to Joey." The thought of something happening to Joey made him nauseated. If he'd been hurt because Lucas left his side, he couldn't imagine how he'd ever live with himself.

The bumpy road jostled Julie around and she cried out each time. Lucas attempted to stabilize her, but she didn't want to be touched. He looked out the windows and saw them passing the hill he ran up. Next were the bodies of Arracks, or speed bumps as he now felt they were, each one making a sickening crunch sound.

"What are we driving over?" Julie said.

"Nothing, just some bushes I think."

Another minute and they were at the gates. Gladius flung the door open and helped Julie out of the coach.

"I'll take care of her," Lucas said. "Just make sure the path is clear in front of us. We're going straight to the medical wing. You think you can find it?"

"Yeah." Gladius rushed to the front gate, dagger in hand.

Julie screamed out again and squeezed Lucas's bare shoulder hard enough to leave marks.

"You sure—"

"Just move!"

He walked her to the front gates and into the main room.

Gladius was hugging Hank just past the front door. Hank, the damned savior, had brought a gurney.

"Thank you, Hank."

Hank let go of Gladius and set the gurney on the ground. It wasn't anything more than a few poles and a thick fabric, but it was better than asking a mother in labor to traverse through a dark fortress full of dead Arracks.

Lucas and Hank got her on the gurney and lifted her up. Hank led the way with Gladius next to them, keeping an eye out for Arracks. In a couple minutes, they made it to the double doors of the medical wing.

Hank slowed down and pushed the doors open with his back. He took a quick right and Lucas saw the gathering of people down the hall, his dad and all the other parents. He even saw the little girl who was supposedly Evelyn, but he still didn't know how that was possible.

"Come on, they have a room over here I found," Gladius said.

They took Julie into a private room with a sanitary bed and running water. After they got Julie onto the hospital bed, he hugged her. He didn't think they were going to make it in time, but she held out. She was such a trooper.

"Get my mom," Julie said.

Hank ran out of the room and soon, Beth and Gretchen returned. Lucas took a deep breath of relief at their arrival. He was way out of his depth in trying to birth a child and then it dawned on him, what Emmett wanted with Julie. Marcus wanted his child as well and even knowing the man was dead, it sent a wave of fear over him. He now knew what Joey felt. He'd die to protect his son. He'd have crossed that river.

The mothers rushed into action, washing hands and setting up towels around her.

"Okay," Beth said brushing the hair away from her daughter's face. "I'm not going to sugarcoat this, it's going to be uncomfortable. Just focus on the fact you are bringing a life into this world and that is what you are going to work so hard for, okay?"

Julie nodded and her face strained. She gripped the bed sheets and Lucas stood next to her head and grabbed her hand. Tears fell down her face. "Something happened to Joey, didn't it?" she grunted out.

"I don't know, they put him in that healing machine," Gretchen said, before going between her legs with gloved hands. "She's ready," she announced. "It's going to hurt, but your baby is counting on you to get him into this world. You ready to do this?"

"Yes."

"Then push, baby girl. Give me all you got."

Lucas stayed up near Julie's head and held her hand. She bared down and squeezed his hand harder than he thought possible and he squeezed back trying to send some of his strength into her.

"Again," Gretchen called out.

Julie whimpered and blew out some of the sweat pouring into her mouth. Her wet hair clumped against the sides of her face. She squeezed hard and grunted.

"Almost there, don't stop!"

Lucas glanced down and saw the baby come out into Gretchen's hands. Bloody and slimy, she handed the baby to a waiting Beth, who held her grandson with tears in her eyes.

"After birth, just a second, Julie." The placenta and the rest of it all came out into a bucket.

"You want to cut the cord?" Gretchen looked to Lucas.

"No, go ahead."

He wanted to hug Julie. They did it, they'd made a child. He felt so emotional, he hugged her tight, feeling her sweaty body against his. He cried on her shoulder. This child wouldn't have to be born into a world where MM would hunt him down, where Marcus would manipulate his life and make him forever look over his shoulder.

"We did it," Julie said.

"*You* did it." Lucas heard the sink running and a few whimpers from his boy. He tried to get a better look at him as Beth cleaned him up. "How does he look?"

She didn't answer and kept washing him.

"Beth?" Lucas demanded, a ball of worry hitting his stomach hard. "Is something wrong?"

She wrapped him in a towel and turned with tears in her eyes. "He's a perfect baby boy."

Lucas let out a long breath of relief and stared at his new baby's face. "He's so small." He'd never seen anything better in his entire life and just seeing the little guy looking back at him melted him. "Julie, look at our boy."

"Can I hold him?"

"Of course you can, he's yours." Beth lowered him into Julie's awaiting arms and he looked up at her, silent and intelligent, looking much like Evelyn when she first came out.

Lucas pushed his thoughts away, as none of it mattered. His friends killed Marcus, he killed Emmett, and it was over. Their kids could be different and not fear some mad men coming after them.

The door swung open to the room and Evelyn walked in.

Lucas, surprised by the little girl's entrance, watched her walk around the bed and get close to Julie and the baby.

"I finally get to meet him," Evelyn said, as the baby turned to face her. She laughed, shaking her head. Then she took a few steps back, her eyes going wide with fear, pointing at the bundled baby. "He's going to kill us all if we don't kill him first."

CHAPTER 24

POLY GOT UP AND STEPPED back from the door. There'd been a brief commotion and some of the parents were missing, along with Evelyn. But she couldn't focus on that now. The machine was done and she stood next to Travis, gazing through the window. He went to the screen next to the door and typed into it. Opening the door, he walked in and Poly rushed in behind him.

"Don't expect much. He's alive, but—"

"Get out of the way." She lifted the lid. "Joey?" She couldn't stop smiling. "Joey, can you hear me?"

"He can't. He's non-responsive to stimulus. It's on the report."

"What do you mean, like a coma?"

"No, after what he just put his body through, this machine doesn't understand it all. It only repairs what it sees as broken.

What we have left now is . . ."

"What? Like he's a vegetable?"

"This machine is struggling to keep him alive, Poly."

She noticed a few wires and tubes running into his body.

"I don't think it'll be long now. I'd use this time to say your goodbyes."

She felt the panic building and stared at Joey's face. He looked like he was sleeping. She pushed on him and then shook him. "No, you can't leave me. Not like this. Wake up, Joey!" she screamed. "*Wake up!*"

Travis took a few steps back and Opal came into the room, then Minter and Karen.

Poly spotted her mom and fell into her. "Where's Evelyn? I want my daughter!"

"Shh," Opal petted her head, "she's fine, just went to see the new addition."

"What are you talking about?"

"Julie just had her baby boy."

Poly felt like she was floating. Her body had become disconnected from reality as her mom kept speaking. She heard the cries from Karen and the sobs from Minter, but they felt as distant as the constellations. Evelyn told her to let him go, but how could she? She couldn't live without him.

Voices floated in space and she felt her whole world go black. Gravity left and she fell. She wasn't ever going to get her Joey back. His body might have hung on for a bit longer, but his mind had stilled. Maybe if she fell far enough, she could find him. If she fell deep enough, he'd be there, waiting for her just like Evelyn had said.

"Mother," Evelyn called out, loud and above all the other distant noises. "I still need you, come back to me."

Poly didn't have the will. She'd already given into the darkness, hoping she could find Joey. If she searched far and long enough, she'd find him again. They were meant to be together for eternity. This wasn't how it ended.

The cool floor chilled her cheek and the soft screams around her didn't register as reality. The hands lifting her felt unreal. They'd beaten Marcus and won, but she never felt so much loss in her entire life. She was broken, and didn't want to be put back together.

POLY SCREAMED AND JERKED UP, pulling at the restraints on her arms and legs.

"Poly, I'm right here," Opal said.

The bright lights blinded her vision and she kept screaming. It had to have all been a dream. She couldn't have lost Joey. She felt him, just a whisper in the wind, but he was there and she grasped hard to keep him. She screamed, because none of it mattered, let the world hear her screams, let Joey find them and come to her.

She stopped screaming and her eyes adjusted. Taking in the room, she knew she wasn't in Marcus's fortress. She wasn't next to Joey. "Where is he?"

Her mom looked pained. "Same place as always, dear."

"Why am I tied down?" She pulled at her wrist restraints.

"You've attempted to kill me, twice. And you've tried to do other things . . ."

"I want to see him."

"You don't want to do that, not this time. Let it be different today. I love you too much to see you do it again to yourself."

"I want to see him!" The door opened. "Evelyn?" Poly

asked but it couldn't be, the girl walking toward her looked closer to seven than a baby.

"I heard you from across the building. Grandma, may I?" Evelyn moved to the vinyl wrist straps and untied one.

"How are you so old? How long have I been here? Where am I?"

"These questions don't get old to you, do they?"

Poly shook her head, trying to understand her daughter.

Evelyn sighed and walked to the other side of the bed. "You've been here for three months, and it's been the same thing each time. Every few days, you wake from your self-induced coma and want to see Dad. We show you and you relapse, hard. You know how many tears you've put on me?"

Poly shook her head, she couldn't understand it; she'd been there for months, doing the same thing? "Where am I?"

"We're just outside Sanct. Travis has been very generous with his resources."

With her next hand free, Poly reached out and touched Evelyn's long hair. She'd only had tufts last time . . . no, that wasn't right either. Marcus had accelerated her growth. The memories flooded in and she felt the blood leaving her face and the room faded.

"Here we go again. *Mom*, stay with me!"

Poly jerked upright and looked at Evelyn's snapping fingers. She was turning into a beautiful little girl and she hated how she'd already missed so much. "I won't relapse this time," Poly said.

With the leg restraints gone, she got off the bed and wobbled around. Opal moved next to her and stabilized her with an arm around her waist.

"There are a few things you should know, Mother."

"What's that?"

Evelyn walked with her through the hospital room door and into a brightly lit hall. Poly squinted and looked down the hall to an oval opening, with a woman sitting behind a desk. The lady looked up and saw Poly, her eyes going wide as she dashed around the desk.

Evelyn sighed and stopped walking. She gazed up at her mother with intelligent eyes, far beyond her youthful appearance. "After all this time, nothing seems familiar?"

Fear built in Poly and she felt something deep within, something she didn't want to grasp yet. "Can you take me to your dad?"

Evelyn pursed her lips and took Poly's hand. She nodded and started walking. The woman behind the desk approached, but Evelyn waved her off with her free hand. The woman with an oak tree on her chest turned and scurried behind the desk. She typed into her Panavice and watched as Poly strode by with her daughter in hand.

"You said some things have changed?" Poly inquired.

Evelyn gave a slight nod to the woman behind the desk. "I've been going through the details of Marcus's information." She laughed. "He amassed a great knowledge of the worlds."

Poly hated hearing his name. "Tell me, how is Joey? Is he awake yet?"

"I found things . . . things he kept hidden from everyone— even his mother. Oh, do you remember how Julie trapped Alice within her special program?"

"Yes," Poly said, staring at the clear doors at the end of the hall, sunshine and greenery visible beyond.

"I compartmentalized her and placed her in a special Panavice. She can never get out unless I need her."

Poly gazed down at Evelyn's Panavice. It looked huge in her

small hands. "Is Julie around? How about the others?"

Pain shot across Evelyn's face or maybe it was a wince. "They are around, but they have a child now, so they're probably tending to it."

"Him," Poly corrected.

"Yes, *him*."

Poly wanted badly to see Julie and Lucas's child, but it didn't register high on her scale of needs. Right now, she was focused solely on seeing Joey.

They approached the clear doors and Evelyn slid her hands over one of them. A few green dots bounced around on the glass and it swung open.

"Where are you taking me?"

"You need to understand this isn't easy for me, as I've taken you on this walk many times in the past few months. Sure, some things change, and sometimes you even have a couple of different questions, but the end result is the same."

Evelyn pulled Poly outside and onto a stone path surrounded by grass. Poly thought of the terrible place Emmett put her with Samantha and Joey. But that never felt real, this felt vivid and the colors were bright, the sunshine warm and the person she walked with, precious.

Poly touched Evelyn's hair, brushing her fingers down its length, to the tips reaching below her shoulder blades.

"You're doing it again," Evelyn said, looking sad.

"What?"

"You're avoiding the subject."

"I'm not, I don't even know what we're talking about."

Evelyn sighed and gripped Poly's wrist. Poly's face lit up at the strength behind those small hands. Her grip felt like a vice at first, but lessened as Poly's hand fell to her side. Evelyn slid her hand into Poly's and pulled her along the stone path. The path led down and away from the large white building behind them.

None of it seemed familiar, yet it kind of did. Poly momentarily felt dizzy. "I don't remember Sanct being like this."

"Yes, you do. You just don't want to acknowledge the memories. It's not much further."

Her heart pounded and she gripped her daughter's hand tighter. "I don't think I want to go. Let's go back to the white building and talk. I've missed so much with you."

"Come on, you said you wanted to see him, right?"

Poly felt tears building in her eyes and nodded. She hesitated and Evelyn pulled her along. How had she become so strong, so amazing? She couldn't even be a year old. At that thought, she stopped. "Have I missed your birthday?"

"You haven't. Come on, I have many things to do still."

Evelyn pulled her along, down the stone path, meandering on a gentle slope. Poly tried to walk slower but Evelyn tugged at her hand, using her body weight to keep her moving. They rounded a corner of rock outcroppings and Poly froze in place.

"It's beautiful."

"You described this to me in one of our longer days. I wish I had more time for days like that."

Poly gazed at the meadow with bright green grass, rolling upward to a knoll. A perfect oak tree, much like the one on the woman's shirt, or as Poly realized, the one she made for Joey in the scene generator—the location of their first kiss. She rushed ahead of Evelyn, feeling the grass on her bare feet, walking under the oak tree's round canopy. Getting dizzy, she lay on the grass and gazed up into the leaves moving in the slight breeze. The sun glittered through the gaps and swayed in and out of sight as the leaves moved with stronger gusts.

She sat up as Evelyn approached. "Is he coming here?"

Evelyn sat down next to her, her Panavice sitting in her lap. "Mother, you are the bravest person I've ever known. I watched the videos and did all the analysis on you, so it surprises me every time when we get to this point."

Poly wanted her to stop talking and felt tears building in her eyes again. She gripped her daughter tightly and held her for a while. "I love you so much, Evelyn."

"I love you too, Mother." Evelyn's eyes misted up. "Let me take you back to the moment, after Dad killed Marcus."

"I don't want to—"

"We put Dad in the healing machine, remember?"

Tears flowed down Poly's face and she nodded.

"Afterward, we discovered his mind was gone, only his body remained."

"No."

"Mom, listen." Evelyn sighed. "I want to tell you why I think you are the bravest person I've ever known." Her little kid voice was filled with wisdom and Poly sniffled. "You are special, all of us Six are. We can feel on a deeper level, with connections I cannot identify yet, but you knew . . . you knew you were keeping him from moving on. You were the only thing keeping him from finding peace."

Poly's body shook and uncontrollable tears fell from her face. Ragged breath and a shaky chin didn't deter her from glaring at Evelyn.

Evelyn took her hand and wrapped both of hers around Poly's. "You are the one who gave him that peace. I felt it the moment you gave in and let him move on; it was the most beautiful thing I'll ever witness in my life, I am sure of that."

The words crushed against Poly like a train against her

chest. She pushed back at it, her effort futile. She went back to the moment in Marcus's fortress. The feeling she'd been suppressing deep in her gut since the moment she awoke, erupted to the precipice and she leapt up with it. The void filled her again, a world without Joey, without her soul mate.

"No, there has to be a way. We can still save him."

"No, Mother. He's gone."

Something in her wouldn't accept it, even though her mind screamed it true. "You lie. This isn't happening, this isn't real. Who are you?"

Evelyn stood. "Don't do this. Fight it."

She watched Evelyn's mouth move, but the words came out in a mumble and her face distorted and swayed. The black void came to collect her and she welcomed it. Joey wasn't dead, she couldn't accept it.

CHAPTER 25

EVELYN FELT THE GRASS BLADES with her fingertips and the morning dew seeped into her black pants. She watched her mother's limp body be carried away after the men put her on the gurney. Evelyn had done a few different things this time and wondered if she would ever get her mother to accept his death.

"She relapsed again?"

Evelyn rose up and wiped a few bits of loose grass from her knees. "Yes."

"It's not your fault. Maybe I should give it a try again."

Evelyn laughed at him. "Travis, you had the worst run of all of us. We're getting to her, she'll eventually find her way back to us."

"It kills me seeing her like this." He glanced at her and then away.

Evelyn looked up at Travis, such an interesting man. Like

many of the people on Vanar, he had lived a long life filled with despair and triumph. Now, he ran the world. Such a fascinating arrangement he and Harris had. It gave Evelyn hope in humanity that a man like Travis could forgive a man like Harris. She wanted to ask him about Maya, another mystery, and one that had been erased from all the servers she searched. In time, she planned on discussing it with him, among countless other things.

"Have they arrived?" Evelyn asked.

"Yes."

Her mom left her view and she turned to Travis, holding his hand. "We should go."

They walked to the rock outcropping and Travis placed his hand on a smooth section of the rock. The rock slid open and they descended down the stairs and into the elevator.

"You know, your grandparents have been trying to visit again."

"They want to see Poly, not me."

"Evelyn, you know that isn't true."

She did, but she wasn't prepared to let them back in to her life yet. So much had to be done and she already spent all of her available family time with her mother. Once she got Poly rehabilitated, she could bring in the rest of the family.

Travis looked thoughtful. "She asked about Julie again, didn't she?"

"Yes."

"We should make contact."

"You know how I feel about that." Evelyn adjusted her footing as the elevator moved.

Travis shifted his feet and looked at the wall.

Evelyn didn't say anything else as the elevator traveled

across the compound and back up into the building. The doors slid open and Travis's opulent house appeared. She gazed out of the window across the room, taking in the expansive ocean view. She loved the ocean and could spend a great deal of time watching it, trying to figure out the endless intricacies of what made it work. Marcus had written a few papers about the oceans. They were what made the worlds livable. Without the oceans, life would not have made it past the microbial phases.

"You coming?" Travis asked, standing outside the elevator.

Evelyn didn't answer and walked out, taking in the guests who'd convened in his house, all sitting on the couches and chairs in his family room. They stood as she approached.

"Harris," Evelyn nodded to him. "Hank, Gladius, a pleasure. Jack."

"Hello, Evelyn," Harris greeted.

"I called this meeting because I didn't want a digital copy of our conversation. I must ask we all turn off our Panavices and place them on the table." Evelyn moved first and placed hers on the glass coffee table. Everyone else obliged and set there's down. A quick scan from her and she verified they were turned off.

Hank made to get up, most likely to hug her. She didn't want to procrastinate on this meeting any longer, so she put her hand up and motioned for him to stay seated.

"Good to see you, Evelyn," Hank said. "You are truly growing like a weed."

Evelyn let the pain in her bones register. It reminded her of her dedication to get rid of her child body and reach her full size. She didn't like the bright looks from Hank and Gladius, like they were regarding a child.

"Thank you, and I see you are strengthening your connection

with Gladius," Evelyn said.

"What do you mean?" Hank asked.

"Your bond is growing, getting stronger by the day."

"Well, I keep him busy," Gladius said in a sly way, touching Hank's leg.

Sex, she'd heard so many adults allude to it, all of whom probably thought she was too young to understand the concept. But the mechanics were simple enough, and Evelyn knew when she had her adult body, she'd explore this thing so many held in such high regard.

Evelyn sat in the only available seat, one of Travis's oversized chairs. She hated how she had to climb up on it and her feet didn't reach the floor as she sat.

"Thanks for inviting us here, Evelyn," Harris said. "How is Poly doing?"

She liked Harris, always straightforward with his wants and questions, not wasting time. "Still relapsing."

"I've seen a lot of wonderful things in my life, but one of the most astonishing is the times I've spent when the Preston Six are together. I think if we got the remaining ones together to be there for Poly, we could get her to snap out of it and start to heal."

"Thank you." Evelyn let her reply fall flat and Harris sat back in his seat. "I brought you here to discuss what I've found going through the information kept at Marcus's fortress."

They leaned forward and Harris shifted uncomfortably in his chair, shooting a look at Travis.

"While Marcus made many discoveries, I've kept my focus on this one threat, the whole reason he took me . . . the purge people." She dangled her feet and regretted taking the seat to begin with. "The threat is real and Marcus's plan was very detailed and well thought out. He found these purged planets early on, and was almost killed several times by these 'greater beings,' as he refers to them. He believes they are the ones who created these Alius stones. But let's get to the present.

"Marcus knew that when Vanar was purged, it wouldn't be able to put up much of a defense. With Earth, he had a chance to put in everything he had learned since the disasters at Ryjack. So he infected our population with a disease, for which he had the sole cure. With this cure, as you know, he implanted a nanobot, one that I can control under the right circumstances."

"What do you mean, 'you can control'? There are a few billion people with these nanobots. And to what purpose?" Harris asked.

"With the help of Alice, I can link up with every person on the planet."

"Why?" Hank asked.

"When they come, they search for the conscious mind. We met a man, Hector, he knew the tricks to keeping his mind clear enough to avoid their detection. First, I want this man. I need to speak to him about the purge."

"I'm sure we can find him," Harris said.

"Let me know when you have him."

Harris crossed his arms and leaned back.

"Evelyn," Gladius said. "There is a good chance, even in his notes, Marcus could be manipulating you."

"Thank you for the warning," Evelyn said, feeling Gladius's doting eyes on her. "The first step in my plan involves moving me and my family back to Earth, to prepare for the inevitable."

"Whoa," Travis said. "You want to take Poly back to Earth?"

"Yes."

"But she is making progress and is in a safe environment

here."

"She hasn't made progress and I am starting to question your true motivation with her," Evelyn's gaze leveled on Travis.

"What can we do to help?" Hank asked.

"Nothing at the moment, but I do enjoy seeing you two around." She smiled and crunched up her shoulders. "Travis, and now Harris, have suggested that having friends around Poly could help, and I was thinking you could be there when we make the move."

"Of course, whatever we can do to help Poly," Hank asked.

"Speaking of friends, do any of you know where Julie and Lucas are? They seemed to have disappeared."

They all shifted in their chairs.

"We don't know their location." Harris ended up being the mouth piece and Evelyn held back her contempt. She hated people lying to her.

"I have no intention of harming them."

"And what about their boy?" Gladius asked.

"He's going to end us all. I sensed his soul in the moment my father passed on; his fate was revealed to me. I will not falter in my opinion. Time reveals all."

Harris sighed and glanced at the others. Evelyn didn't like how much time they had all spent with each other. She loved Lucas and Julie like second parents, but their child was a problem she had wished she had taken care of sooner. But now, she knew hurting the child would cause too much pain on the ones she loved. It didn't mean the threat couldn't be compartmentalized, but she wasn't lying about not harming them.

Harris put his hand in his jacket and Evelyn sent the chills down the back of her neck and the world in front of her froze in place. She hopped off the chair and inspected the contents of

Harris's jacket. It was a letter from Julie.

Dear Evelyn,

It felt prudent to inform you we will be taking a long sabbatical from it all, and plan to raise Will in a safe environment. Please stop trying to find me and my family.

Aunt Julie

Evelyn sat back on the chair and released time. The dull hum changed to the noisy environment of the room.

Harris pulled at his jacket and realized the letter was in her hands. "Sneaky."

"I don't like to waste time, Harris. I know you appreciate that. I've read the letter and I think they are going too far with this. I have changed my mind and don't want to harm him."

"You've made aggressive attempts to find them, Julie is careful and very smart. I'd be cautious if I was them as well," Harris said.

She took a deep breath and set the letter down on the chair. "I was considerably younger when we first met, and my past actions don't represent my current intentions toward Will." They were never going to understand and trust her the way they trusted each other. Joey and Edith had been the two who truly took her for what she was and didn't expect anything else from her but to just be herself.

"When is the move then?" Travis asked.

"Immediately. I'd like her to wake up in her own bed, the bed she grew up in, where her mom is making breakfast or whatever common routine they had."

"I'm very happy to hear you are reconsidering including the family," Harris said.

"It's time," Evelyn said.

"I agree," Travis said and patted her on the shoulder.

"No, it's time." She hopped off the chair and stuffed the letter in her pocket. "The meeting is over."

Travis nodded and stood. The others did the same, exchanging looks.

Travis walked next to her and she reached out, holding his hand. She liked the contact with him. He had become the one constant in her life, but she knew it wasn't because he enjoyed her company, it was because of Poly. She watched the way Travis looked at her mom and felt the connection between the two when they were close. It was nothing like Joey and Poly, she'd never felt something like that, but it grew stronger each week from Travis. The move was as much because of him, as it was from keeping Poly away from them. Maybe a planet of separation would sever the tie.

"I want you to keep *him* here," Evelyn said.

"Okay," Travis said

"I think it will help my mom," Evelyn said. "I want to visit him, alone."

Travis nodded and let her enter the elevator on her own.

She used her thumb and pressed the unmarked button. The elevator shifted to the right and then dropped a few floors. The doors opened and she stepped into the blank square room with stainless steel walls and white lights reflecting off the glass floor. She touched the panel on the wall and a large drawer slid out, hissing and sending a cold gust of air over her.

"Hello, Dad," she said, touching his cold hand. His face held a tinge of blue and frost formed around his eyebrows. "I may have found a way, but it will involve risking the entire world." She reached for his mind but came up blank. "I wish you could hear me, talk with me. You always knew what to say. I hope I'm doing the right thing, but only time will reveal that answer."

She knew he couldn't hear her, but it didn't make it any easier to say the words. "Mom isn't getting any better. She needs you and I think somehow, she still feels you and I know you still feel her. I'm going to take her back to Earth, so you might not feel us for a while, but know we aren't gone. I need her to start healing."

She brushed a few bits of frost off his face. "This may be the last time I visit you for a while, maybe forever, depending on how my plan goes." Getting on her tiptoes, she kissed the side of his face. "I love you."

CHAPTER 26

"THAT LITTLE GIRL CREEPS ME out," Gladius said, taking Gem out of her case. "Oh, Gem, I've kept you locked up for way too long."

"You know what creeps me out?" Hank started.

Gladius typed in the coordinates on the aircraft and it lifted off from her dad's beachside mansion. From the increasing height, she spotted the new building inland—the hospital he'd built solely for the purpose of housing Poly. If the media found out about it, they'd thrash him for such spending on a single person. Though, if they knew that person was Poly, they might change their minds; they might even wonder why Travis had not done more for her.

Gem patted her arm and looked up with her plastic eyes.

"You were talking about Gem, weren't you?"

"What? No, I like Gem."

"She creeps you out, admit it. It's not her fault you grew up in a world without Your Doll."

"I don't know, it's been just me and you for a while, and now we are bringing in Gem? She stares at me when you aren't looking."

"Oh, ha-ha, so funny. You know I had her custommade? She's a part of me, I've told her my every secret and the things she's seen me do . . ." she trailed off.

"I know she is important to you and that makes her important to me, but she's not coming into the bedroom."

"Like I'd risk getting her dirty. You learn a lesson once the hard way and you never forget it."

Hank sighed.

"Fine, I'll put her away for now." She turned off Gem and put her in her case.

The aircraft soared over Sanct and Gladius looked down, feeling a sense of pride at the city's resilience. In a way, what Poly and Julie created had turned into a blessing. It prepared them for what Marcus was about to inflict on the world.

"You think she's telling the truth about Marcus's plan?" Hank asked.

"Yes. It makes sense. The dude never really went without a plan." She glanced over at her man and saw his somber look. She knew he was thinking about Joey and Samantha, and probably Poly as well.

"I want to move back to Earth. I think I need to be there for her."

Gladius squinted and glared at Hank, but he wouldn't meet her eyes. "You want to help Poly?"

"Yes, but she isn't who is going to need our help, it's Evelyn. You're right, she is getting creepy, almost robotic in her actions. She is starting to remind me of Marcus. Even Marcus did endless charity work and cured most the diseases of the world for free, before his mother died." Hank looked worried, and shook his head. "I think these hyper intellects, like Marcus and Evelyn, need human contact and not just yes men following them around."

"Are you calling my dad a 'yes man'?"

"No. Well, sort of. We all know he has other motives, as staying in Evelyn's good graces keeps him close to Poly."

Gladius closed her eyes and shook her head. Her dad couldn't see Poly as single right now, it was too soon. But he did have a woman in distress disability . . . always had. "You think my dad's going to move to Earth?"

"If he does, we'll know how far he's willing to go. And if he does, it's all the more reason to move to Preston. It's a great town, I think you'll find it interesting."

"I'm not a small town kind of girl, Hank." She crunched up her mouth at the idea of it. What did they do there, milk cows and herd chickens around all day? The idea of doing laundry terrified her.

"I know, but we can build a house there to suit your needs. Did you know we hand-build houses still? There are no printers."

"You're not selling it very well."

"How about this then, it's a great place to start a family."

Her heart raced and her eyes went wide. She stared at Hank, letting the meaning of his words sink in. "You want to start a family with me?"

"Of course."

Gladius felt tears building in her eyes and she unbuckled her seatbelt to straddle Hank's lap. She embraced him in his chair and felt the aircraft descending without anyone controlling its flight path.

"I didn't think you'd like the idea," Hank said.

"It's the nicest thing anyone has ever said to me." She played around with her hair in his face because it annoyed him, but he brushed it back with his hands and kissed her.

"We'll need some money to make it on the other side."

"Gold. It's valuable everywhere it seems and I've got tons of it."

"Wow. Are we really going to do this?" The excitement built in Hank's voice.

"Yes," Gladius squealed out in joy.

"You know when you scream like that . . ."

Gladius smiled and reached back, putting the craft in hover mode. She returned and started unbuttoning her shirt.

"Gem's put away, right?"

Gladius laughed. She couldn't believe they were going to start this new chapter of their lives together in Preston of all places. It would take some getting used to, but what was life without some risk and change?

CHAPTER 27

POLY AWOKE IN HER BED, reaching around for Joey, but he wasn't there. She sighed and rolled out of bed. Placing her feet on the floor, she briefly considered rolling back under the covers.

"Hey, Mom." Evelyn called from her open door.

"Hi, sweetie, is Grandma cooking breakfast?"

"No, she went to town to get eggs."

"You sleep last night?" Poly asked.

"No need."

Poly nodded and walked to the doorway. "I wish I could condition my body to eliminate the need for sleep." She bent down and hugged her little girl. "Can't you stay small for a bit longer?"

Evelyn laughed. "I'm limited to the growth rate of my bones, so you're in luck. If I could, I'd already be as big as you are, Mom."

"Well, I'm not considered a tall person by any means. Maybe you should aim for higher."

"Dad was six-foot-one."

Poly nodded her head and the mention of Joey sent a wave of guilt and pain through her. "Maybe you'll be tall like him."

It'd been two months since they moved back to Preston and after a few weeks of waking from the coma, she could mention him without breaking down into a mess. The doctors and her daughter told her *time heals*, but that wasn't exactly true. Sure, she'd found a way to live with it, but it hurt just as bad every day. She'd just found ways to hide it more from Evelyn. She had a special girl to raise.

A beeping noise sounded from outside, like a dump truck backing up.

"What did you get?" Poly asked with her hands on her hips.

"Just a three phase power supply, I need it for my work," Evelyn said in a rush.

Poly walked downstairs. Out the front door, a group of electrical trucks parked around the house, with a few men working on the power pole and others tearing out the old electrical panel on the house.

"Good day, miss," one worker in a hard hat said.

Poly closed the door and turned to Evelyn as she approached. "How are you paying for this?"

"You know."

Poly took a deep breath through her nose and closed her eyes.

"Mom, I *need* this power upgrade. The old power supply couldn't run half the stuff necessary. Besides, you know this is me trying to save the world, don't you think that's worth a bit of fudging the bank accounts?"

"It's stealing."

"No. I'm creating money, it isn't coming from anyone. I just channel it so it becomes harder money. Really easy actually."

Poly felt weaker and looked at her daughter. What was she going to be like in a year, ten years? Poly already lamented everything she was never going experience with Evelyn. The idea of sending her to school seemed ludicrous considering she'd learn everything in a matter of hours, find mistakes in the texts, and then make corrections.

"I know you are thinking you're doing the right thing here . . ." Poly couldn't come up with an argument but then realized what Evelyn really needed, something she hadn't had—life experience. "How about we go on a road trip, just me and you? I could take you around and you could visit places you've seen online, actually meet some of the people you are saving."

Evelyn crunched up her brow as she tried to rationalize Poly's request. "I get all the information I need on the internet."

"Seeing a picture means nothing compared to seeing, smelling, and touching something in real life."

"Can I bring my Panavice?"

"Sure."

"Okay, when do we leave?" Evelyn said, sounding excited.

"We'll tell Grandma about it and then head out. Go pack a few things."

Evelyn nodded and ran back upstairs to her room. Poly watched her leave and waited for her door to close. Hearing it shut, she rushed to the back bedroom Evelyn had converted. She pushed the door open and gazed at the dark room, filled wall to wall with monitors and different computers. Wires ran across the floors with extension cords plugged into every available outlet.

Each monitor had scrolling information across it, stock markets, web cams, traffic cams, random web pages. But one monitor, off to the left looked different than the rest; it was clearer and didn't have any text filling parts of the screen. The whole screen showed a construction site, a large dome building of some sort, mostly done, with a few sections left exposed.

Poly leaned in closer to see the men on the side of the dome. They looked miniscule in comparison to the behemoth complex.

"Mother?"

Poly jumped at Evelyn's voice.

"What are you looking at?"

"What is this?"

Evelyn walked over. "It's something I'm building, well, it's actually something I'm finishing. It's going to help me save everyone."

Poly's mouth hung open and she shook her head. "This isn't just some shuffling around of a couple stocks, this is a *major* project, Evelyn. This is costing what?"

"One point two billion."

Poly fell on the seat next to the screen and her heart pounded, staring at her daughter. "Evelyn . . ."

"It's got to be done. When the Purgers come, they aren't going to be negotiated with, they are going to take everything. If I have to create a few billion to help save Earth, it's worth it. In fact, we can take our road trip there. That way, I can show you what I've built."

Poly didn't know what to say. A kid takes some money from the change drawer and they get grounded . . . what did you do to your one-year-old baby girl who just stole a billion, or billions as she put it, from the world?

"Sweetie . . ." Poly felt a tingling in her mind and she

resisted Evelyn's attempts. "Don't do that."

"Do what?"

"You're trying to change my mind, to make me see your side of it. Don't do that to me, or anyone else, it isn't right."

"I don't know what you're talking about." Evelyn turned off a monitor.

"What was on that?"

"Nothing."

"Turn it back on."

Evelyn blurred for a split second and the monitor turned on.

"I know you just went fast. Don't keep things from me."

"Ugh, fine." She hit a few keys on the keyboard and the monitor switched to Lucas, Julie, and their child eating breakfast at a diner.

Poly stumbled back, with her hand over her mouth. "Why are you watching them?"

"It's not them, just him." She pointed at Will. "I get feelings with people. It's hard to explain, but I know how people are from the moment I meet them. When I first met Will, seconds old, I knew he'd be the end of us, it screamed to me. Even just looking at him on the screen, I can't shake the feeling."

"You can't . . ."

"I'm not going to do anything to him, Mom. I'm just watching, that's all, I swear. Don't you think if I wanted to hurt him, I could? Like in minutes, I could call a missile to strike that very diner, but I don't and won't."

Poly struggled to find a way to communicate with her. Just the fact she'd thought of a missile strike as an option was disturbing. "Maybe we should meet with Julie and Lucas, so

you can get to know Will. I'd sure love to see the little guy."
Poly stared at the screen and tried to get a better look at him.
He sat up in his baby chair at the end of the table while Lucas
played an airplane sort of game to feed him. What would he be,
six months old? Was he a normal boy, or was he like Evelyn?

"I'd like to meet him. Maybe I can talk with Aunt Julie and
see if he's exhibiting any dangerous behaviors."

"I bet he can't even walk."

"For now. Can we go on our road trip and stop talking
about this?" Evelyn whined.

"Yes, I think it's even more important now that we do, and
no more spying on them."

Evelyn shrugged and left the room with a backpack on.

When Opal got home, they helped unload the groceries and
had a light breakfast together. Opal thought the road trip idea
was fantastic and helped Poly pack a few items.

Saying their goodbyes, they got into the car. "You ready?"
Poly asked Evelyn.

"Yes."

She peeled out on the dirt road, sending a cloud of dust over
the construction crew. She laughed and Evelyn looked out the
back window. "Oops, forgot about them," Poly said.

"I'll send them extra money."

CHAPTER 28

"HERE COMES THE PLANE," LUCAS said, making a propeller sound.

"Please don't," Julie said, looking at her Panavice under the table. She hadn't touched her eggs and only ate half a slice of bacon. "She's gone." She breathed out a sigh of relief.

"Good, little creeper," Lucas said, shoving another spoonful of mashed bananas into the baby's mouth. "You're a hungry little guy aren't you, Todd?"

"Come on, we need to check on Will."

Lucas shook his head and smiled. "He's fine, you worry too much."

"I'll never stop worrying." Julie got up and slung the diaper bag over her shoulder and then used the bib to clean the baby's face.

"I'll get him," Lucas offered and stuffed a piece of bacon in his mouth before lifting the baby and adjusting him with one arm. Walking out of the café, he realized he'd already forgotten the town's name. He thought to ask Julie, but she was already ten feet ahead of him and setting a fast pace.

A few more blocks and out of the way of any cameras, Julie entered a two-story brick building with a *Douglas Inn* sign situated over the door. Lucas caught the door with his foot, right before it closed on him. He spotted the bottom of Julie's feet as she bounded up the stairs.

"She's getting faster in her old age," Lucas said and smiled at Todd, before waving at the woman watching TV behind the desk. She never looked up.

Lucas sighed and walked up the carpeted stairs. He didn't like keeping his boy in a place where you had to put a sheet on the floor if you wanted your little one to move around. And the smell had hints of smoke and mildew, maybe mold. It had been their home now for a few weeks. Julie liked it because it only had internet in town and only the café had a connected camera. It made it easy to set up the ruse.

Lucas hit the second floor and looked at the closed door marked *201D*. He turned the handle and opened the door. Across the room, he spotted Jess. She lay on top of a comforter, spread out like a person who'd lost consciousness because of a large amount of booze.

"There's Mommy," he said to Todd. He walked past her and stepped over a bottle of vodka. Tin foil wrappers littered the nightstand and he sighed. Jess had been doing well the last couple of weeks and they thought she might be turning a corner, but she must have found a local dealer. Lucas wasn't sure where she got the money, but he shuddered at the speculations running through his head.

Pushing open the next door, he heard Julie talking with

Beth. They both stopped talking when he entered.

"She's fallen again," Lucas said. He was glad the baby he held couldn't understand the consequences of his mother's actions in the next room.

"We should get rid of her," Beth said. "She's not the kind of person we want around Will," she spoke in a low whisper.

"Daddy." Will ran up to Lucas for a hug. "You bring me anything?"

"Not this time. Your mom had a feeling and we rushed to get back to you."

Will smiled and looked to his mom. Each day he appeared to be weeks older and bigger. Lucas questioned Julie's decision to accelerate his growth, but she agreed with Marcus in that it was cruel to keep him trapped in a baby's body. Lucas didn't share Poly's wanting of a normal child, he was thrilled to have such a special guy. And to think, *he* created him—with Julie's help, of course.

Beth came over and took the baby from Lucas.

"So, what have you been doing while we were out to breakfast?" Lucas asked Will.

"I've been going through the Panavice Mommy gave me." He looked back at Julie with a bashful expression.

Lucas wasn't the best at guessing ages, but he thought Will looked to be maybe two years old. Lucas knew he was special from the first moment he got to hold his baby boy.

"And what did you find?" Julie asked.

"Oh, not much, just learning how to code. I think we can adjust the shield so no one ever has to get hurt again."

"Don't worry," Julie said. "We won't let anything happen to you."

"There were six of you, and now there are four."

"Not true. We have Evelyn and you, that makes for six again, now doesn't it?" Lucas said.

"Speaking of her, when do I get to meet Evelyn?"

"In due time," Julie said, but Lucas remembered the weird little girl coming into the delivery room and announcing Will needed to be killed. What a morbid thing to say about a newborn.

Lucas's smile drooped when he stared at the stunned look on Julie's face gazing at her Panavice. "What is it?"

"Poly just texted me . . . she wants to meet."

"What do you mean? With Evelyn? You sure it's Poly?" Lucas said.

"Yeah, it's her. I took a quick snap shot of her from her Panavice."

"Ask her what it's about."

Julie typed into the screen and Will looked on with excitement. "She says it's time to get back together. It's what Joey would want."

Lucas let out a long breath and just hearing his best friend's name put a weight on his chest, making his heart beat faster. Lucas felt he never should have left them to face Marcus. He could have done something, he had arrows tailor made for Marcus. He could have shot through the hole Maggie made in the shield or any other number of things. He didn't regret it, as leaving them behind saved Julie and Will from Emmett, but it still hurt. The anger at the situation he was put in, simmered at a constant boil.

"Maybe it's time. She looks like she's got it back together. She's even driving a car," Julie said and Lucas knew the look of optimism on her face.

"Which child are you going to show her?" he asked.

"I'm sure as hell not going to let them see Will."

"Come on, Mom." Will pouted.

"No, not yet. She might see you as a threat or who knows what. I don't want to risk it."

Will looked to Lucas. "Let me talk with her. I think she'll see I'm not going to hurt anyone."

"How do you know she would even think you would?" Julie asked and her question struck Lucas; they'd never told Will about Evelyn's prophecy.

Will looked at the brown carpet and kicked at it with his little sneakers. "I sort of looked through your notes."

Julie looked stunned and walked closer to Will. "Those are encrypted, by me. How did you get into them?"

"I just wrote a program to emulate yours and was able to migrate the files across."

Julie closed her eyes and cocked her head. "That's almost impossible."

"I'm sorry, but I just knew there was something about her, I could see the way you look when her name is mentioned. I want to meet her."

"No, we bring Todd. He's our baby as far as they know and it's going to stay that way."

"I agree," Beth said.

Will crossed his arms and ran to the bed, climbing up and flopping himself onto the sheets.

Julie raised her eyebrows and nodded to Lucas, making him follow her into the adjacent room with a snoring Jess. "My guess is, Evelyn manipulated Poly into this trip. I think we should meet with Poly and Evelyn and show them Jess's baby."

"And if she spots the fake?"

"We beg for mercy."

CHAPTER 29

"LOOK, MOM, A COTTON CANDY machine!" Evelyn dashed ahead and Poly rushed after her.

Her daughter gazed at the large bowl and watched with anticipation as the man smiled and poured the sugar in. Threads spun around the bowl and the man used a paper stick to collect up the goodness.

"Two dollars, miss."

Poly handed over the money and watched Evelyn take the stick from the man. She pulled on the cotton candy and then pinched it between her fingers. Some of it dissolved on her finger and she looked up with wonder.

"It's amazing!"

"Yes, it is," Poly said and offered a smile.

The noises of the carnival surrounded her and the people skipped by, laughing and conversing about what ride they wanted to spend their tickets on, or where their child had gone. She stole some glances at other families, a dad cheering for his boy at the dart throwing booth, while another dad carried his girl on his shoulders. She felt tears building and a sticky hand touched hers.

"Mom?"

"Yes?"

"Can I eat it?"

Poly laughed and wiped a tear from her face. "Of course. It's what it's made for."

Evelyn took a bite directly from the ball of pink and pulled a piece off with her teeth. Her eyes went wide and she smiled big, looking up to Poly.

"Can we go see Aunt Julie now?"

Poly took out her Panavice and checked the time, 4:32. Thirteen minutes early. "Sure, we can head over to the food court."

Evelyn kept nibbling on the cotton candy as they walked past different games. "Oh, I want to play this one!"

Poly stopped in front of the game, a rope leading up to a button located high on a wall. A kid currently was on it and was taking his time on the wobbly rope. A few dowels had been placed on the rope, giving a sense of it being possible, but Poly knew the game. "Sure, we have a few minutes."

The kid on the rope crept along on his stomach, sliding up the rope. As he got higher, it got wobblier. A few more feet and the boy fell to the bouncy pad underneath.

"Come on up, missy. You want to give it a go? Three dollars."

Poly ponied up the cash and lifted Evelyn onto the platform.

"She's a bit small, miss. She's going to have—"

Evelyn held up her hand to silence the man and placed a foot on the rope, getting a feel for it. The game attendant laughed and waved Evelyn on.

She took another step onto the rope and then two. The guy looked on with a confused expression. Evelyn targeted the button at the top and ran up the rope. At the last few feet, she leapt, striking the button and sending a flurry of sounds and a red light flashing.

Evelyn landed on the bouncy surface underneath and rolled back down to the platform.

"In all my time, I've never seen anything like that. She some kind of kid tight-rope-walker?" The guy said as he handed Poly a large stuffed panda bear.

"She was blessed with good balance."

Evelyn hopped off the stage and gazed at her prize. "Give him the prize back, Mom. It's not fair, me doing these challenges; they are built for you guys."

Poly hesitated, but Evelyn insisted, so she handed the panda back to a thoroughly confused man. "Thank you," she said as they left the stand.

Arriving at the busy food court, they found a table littered with empty paper baskets of leftover French fries and what looked like a pizza crust.

"What did you mean back there, those challenges aren't fair?" Poly picked up some of the trash and set it on the heaping mass around the stuffed trash can.

"You know, for normal people."

"You're normal."

Evelyn gave her a sideways look.

"Mostly normal," she amended.

Evelyn rolled her eyes. "You were right though."

"About what?" Poly took a seat next to Evelyn.

"Experiences. I've looked at videos of fairs around the country, studying them. I even understood how cotton candy is created, but to actually touch it . . ." She rubbed two fingers together. "To taste it and smell it, brought so much more detail into light. To experience something is much better than reading about it. Thank you for getting me out. And now, we get to meet Julie, Lucas, and Will. This day couldn't get any better."

Poly smiled and enjoyed watching Evelyn experience the world, but she couldn't help being anxious about seeing Julie and Lucas. She hadn't even met Will yet.

"Hey."

Poly jumped from the seat at Julie's voice. She held a large diaper bag and looked tired, but Poly was so happy to see her best friend. Tears were already filling her eyes by the time she got her arms around Julie. "I've missed you so much."

"Me too, how are you holding up?"

"I'm getting there." She sobbed for a few seconds, before pulling herself together. "Aww, Lucas, come here." Poly grabbed Lucas into a hug as he held Will in his right arm. "And this must be Will." She pulled on his little baby hand and shook it. "He's so cute." *And normal*, she wanted to add. "Oh, this is Evelyn."

Julie stepped closer and Evelyn got up from the bench and extended a hand. "Oh no you don't," Julie said and pulled her in for a hug. "You've gotten so big."

"I'm growing more every day."

"You remember Lucas?" Julie asked.

"Of course," Evelyn said with a furrowed brow, looking from the baby to Lucas and back again. "Where's Will?"

Julie went wide-eyed and stood straight. "What do you mean? He's right there."

"This isn't him. This is some normal baby. Did you really think I wouldn't know the difference?"

Lucas adjusted the baby in his arms and looked at Julie. Poly's mouth hung open as questions assaulted her mind. At the top was, why would they have a different baby? Were they that scared of Evelyn?

"Why do you think this isn't him? It's him. This is Will." Lucas said, bouncing the boy on his hip.

Evelyn let out a long huff, then disappeared.

"Holy smokes, where'd she go?" he asked.

"Evelyn!" Poly yelled, wondering why she'd gone slo-mo.

Evelyn reappeared right in front of them with company—a small boy standing next to her, looking confused.

"Did you do that?" the boy asked Evelyn.

She nodded. "*This* is Will."

"How did—"

"And," Evelyn added, "I don't think keeping him in a house with that woman, his mom I take it," she pointed at the baby, "is the right thing to do. Will is special, like me, I knew it the second he was born." She put her hand on Will's shoulder.

"Is this true?" Poly asked.

Julie shook and stepped toward Will and Evelyn. "What are you going to do to him?"

"I'm going to change his fate. Since the untimely death of Marcus, it's become clear I'm going to need all the help I can get if we are going to save the world. Plus, I've figured out things about them, things that could help solve many of our great problems." She glanced at Poly. "I need them to come here, and I need Will's help."

"What?" Julie asked.

"I've led them to us. We don't have much time," Evelyn said.

"What are you talking about? Will, come to me."

"Come on over, Will," Lucas said.

"I'm fine, she's not going to hurt me," he answered.

Poly couldn't close her mouth from her astonishment. Will was a special just like Evelyn. In a way, she felt a great weight lifted, and in another way, she felt the burden of caring for a special child being passed on to Lucas and Julie. They even kept a woman's baby as a decoy? What the hell?

"Evelyn, what are you talking about? Who did you lead here?" Julie looked around, stopping at each suspicious looking person and moving on.

"You know who. They tried to take me and you all saved me, I'll forever be grateful, but as long as they are out there, they will eventually find us. If I'm not around at that precise moment, no one will stand a chance. So, I visited their planet and learned a great deal about who these people are and what they want. They don't see us as anything more than a crop that needs harvesting. They are collecting our quintessence, as they call it, and they should be here soon."

"You're talking about the purge people, aren't you?" Julie blurted out.

"Yes."

"You led them to us? Are you crazy?"

"Quite the opposite."

CHAPTER 30

"I'M SORRY, BUT WE DON'T have this kind of equipment."

"Well, you're going to have to make it then." Gladius crossed her arms and glared at the man holding her request and wearing a hard hat.

He glanced at the paper again and then back to her. "It's not going to be cheap. And you really should be wearing a hard hat, miss."

Gladius stepped forward, disregarding the idea of wearing a stupid plastic hat on her finely done hair. "Name your price."

"She really wants these made," Hank said.

The man rubbed the stubble on his chin and looked back at the factory behind him. Before the Cough had nearly destroyed Earth, they'd made bread there, and a few other bakery items.

"Think of the jobs," Gladius said.

"Miss, there is nothing I'd like more than to take your

money and give a go at this, but these cooking methods are new to me. I'm not even sure what some of this even does. Who made these plans for you again?"

Gladius took deep breath and thought of the factory meeting she had in Vanar with the Snackie Cakes corporation. She'd signed an agreement stating they would never make a Snackie Cake on Vanar. But they weren't on Vanar, and she had every intention of making her damned treat if it killed her. This was the one and only thing she remembered sharing with her mom.

"I had them made," Gladius said. "So, are we in agreement?"

He stared at the plans, turning them sideways.

"Hello?" Gladius said.

"Yes, I can do this. But it's going—"

"I don't ever want to hear a 'but' from you again. All I want to hear is 'yes I can.'"

"Yes . . . yes, I can."

"Good. You have three months to do it."

"But that's—"

"No buts. I don't care if you have to bring in a city of people, employ everyone!" She pulled out her Panavice and completed the awaiting task on the screen. "I just sent the first ten million to your company's account."

The man shuffled his feet and looked back at the factory. "We'll get it done."

"I want a twenty-four hour shift, around the clock. Pay everyone double."

"You're going to be one popular little lady." The man had the widest grin on his face.

"Thank you," Hank said and shook the man's hand. "We'll be in touch."

"Just get it done." Gladius said and walked away with Hank. When they got in their car and left the factory, Gladius wasn't as happy as she thought she would be. The fear simmering in her stomach wasn't diminished. It was then she knew, that the thing that kept her awake at night, needed to be addressed.

She gazed at Hank as he drove down the road and he looked back, giving her a questioning smile. "What?"

"Nothing."

"You seem to have a lot of nothing lately. You know, I'll make sure this factory deal goes your way, okay?"

"It's not the factory, or even Snackie Cakes."

"Then what is it?"

Gladius didn't want to say anything. The remaining Six were his family and he'd die for them. Gladius thought of Poly and Julie as sisters as well, even Lucas had an appeal to him, but she hadn't spent her whole life with them. She didn't have the history and she thought she saw the truth better than Hank on the matter.

"I don't think I want to live in Preston."

"What? I thought you were totally on board."

"I am, I am with you. It's just, I think as long as we live here, the rest of the Six are going to keep dragging us into whatever weird crap seems to revolve around them. And I think those kids of theirs are going to double their trouble."

"But they are my family. What about my dad?"

"He can come too. I just can't see another person die, Hank. I don't want to see you . . . ." She couldn't even bring herself to utter the words but she knew, if they kept on the current path, it'd only be a matter of time.

"Nothing is going to happen to me. I think that guy back

there just got you going. You aren't thinking this through."

"No, I've been thinking of this for a long time. I'm not saying we lose their number or anything, maybe just take them off speed dial."

Hank gripped the wheel and Gladius stared at the side of his head. The car's engine shut off and slowed down. Hank took his hand off the wheel, trying to restart it, but the ignition wouldn't work.

"Out of gas?" Gladius asked.

"I don't know, it just died." He pulled on the steering wheel and coasted to the shoulder. He turned the key but nothing, no click or even a turn of the engine.

"Bet it's electrical, the battery probably became disconnected. My dad taught me about some of these ancient motors. You want to pop the hood?" Gladius said with her hand on the door.

"Look at that plane." Hank leaned forward and looked out the windshield.

Gladius searched and spotted the plane flying low and at a steep angle. She cringed at the inevitable crash, and her heart jumped into her throat as the plane smacked into the field. It rolled and crumbled before igniting into a massive fire ball.

"What the hell is going on?" She opened the door and looked to the sky. A series of beeps blasted through the speakers of the car at maximum volume. She covered her ears as each tone blasted. "Turn it down."

Hank fumbled with the buttons and dials. "It won't stop."

The radio crackled and then a clear voice came across.

Gladius stumbled out of the car and with the raging inferno of the plane crash behind her and the woman's voice speaking out of all their devices, she knew . . . she'd have to wait a while